CRUSHING DAISY

KELLIE STORM

Crushing DAISY

KELLIE STORM

Published by Kellie Storm

Edits by Elaine York | Allusion Publishing LLC

Cover Design and Internal Formatting by Devin | Studio 5 Twenty-Five

To the ones who would rather risk it all to feel everything....

CONTENT WARNING

This book contains heavy elements, such as: Physical Fighting, Drug Use, Mental Abuse, Love-Bombing, Narcissism, Lewd Language, Attempted Murder, Anxiety, Depression, Panic Disorder, Kidnapping, Knife Play, Talk of Self-Harm, Cheating, Attempted Sexual Assault.

Crushing Daisy Playlist

What happens when you fall for the one person you're not allowed to have?
Exchanging secret touches...
Stealing seductive glances...

Trying everything you can to feel closer to them when they're not around...

When a force greater than both of you would prefer to see yourselves dead rather than happy.

Would you do anything to be together?
Or will you let your fate be chosen for you?
What if the forbidden is worth every ounce of pain you endure...
...and you finally give in no matter the consequences?

Do you think you'll survive?

CHAPTER
ONE

DAISY

"I DON'T KNOW what to do with these." Jeremy palms my double Ds, flicking his thumbs over the metal bars that run through my nipples. "Your mom still doesn't know about them?"

Normally, my nips are sensitive in the best of ways, but not when he mentions my family members while fondling them. We're not Hutterites. Incest is *not* our jam. "Oh, Jeremy! I love when you talk about my mom when you're grabbing my boobs," I sarcastically moan as I push against his hands. Finally, I'm starting to get aroused. If I let myself slip into a detached state of bliss, maybe—just this once—I can come on or around my boyfriend.

Jeremy Smith is lovely. He is the type of man who never pushes back. Never rolls his eyes. Never argues. He bends over backward to make me happy. Happy everywhere except the bedroom, and it shows…on my face. I'm still young, but I'm starting to get 'elevens' between my brows and I'm dead set on believing it's from being in a permanent state of sexual frustration.

I've worn a thong for two years straight hoping he would maybe slide a finger down the waist of my pants. And just *maybe*

the idea of a permanent string of floss between my ass cheeks would turn him on enough to have his way with me in one way or another.

This is officially the farthest we've gone in our two years of dating. We've kissed. A lot. And that's where our mothers have drawn the imaginary line. Unlike me, he wants to follow the "rules" and tries to bring me down with him. Jeremy's sweet, loyal, attractive as hell, my best friend for years, and here we are sitting in my 1997 Honda Civic. Straddling my boyfriend in the passenger seat makes me think this might be the day he untucks his balls from his mom's purse and finally uses them.

Jeremy would visit me at UCLA, where I *barely* studied Communications, but always insisted he stay at a hotel. Alone. And as much as we didn't fornicate, long distance worked for us. I was focused on learning to surf off the coast of California—not my schooling—and he was focused on his pre-med degree at Florida Atlantic University.

"Use your imagination, Jer." I try hyping him up before dipping my lips to his neck, and kissing him hard—but not too hard to leave a hickey. *God forbid.* I try not to lose focus. Try to stay in the moment, but let's be real, there must be something more entertaining outside of this car than the nothingness that's going on now. My eyes bounce to our new house I have yet to step foot in. I take in the quantity of windows and eye a blacked-out one above the front porch. *Interesting. Must explore later.*

I refocus on the man in front of me trying to pull a Hail Mary to save this relationship. Whatever that may be. "*We need to keep things innocent and respectful.*" His words, not mine. I pull back so he has free rein of what I'm offering. "Lick, suck…bite. Choose your own adventure here, babe." I stick my tongue between my teeth, trying to pull something—anything sexual—from this guy. If he wasn't phenomenally good at always avoiding eye contact in a normal conversation, I'd say right now, his lack of eye contact, means that he's uncomfortable.

Two almost twenty-year-olds who don't see each other often, you'd think we could yank off his chastity belt by now. His tongue darts out of his pinched lips like he's trying to squeeze out shit from his mouth. *Swoon!* He leans forward slowly, eyes crossed, tongue to nipple. It's like that scene from that Christmas movie when the boy sticks his tongue to the frozen pole. Jeremy doesn't move. He freezes, just like that kid.

"Okay. This is a start. Now move it back and forth. Or better yet, use your teeth." I move my body up and down a little, but his tongue is as stiff as a board and starting to dry out like one, too.

"How do you know how to do this stuff?" he asks, pulling away and leaving my semi-wettened nipple ice cold.

"I read romance, Jeremy." Those guys always know how to please their ladies. I don't give him too much more information on where my sources are from, and he doesn't care. Not. At. All. I can tell.

He keeps trying to look past me out the window as the warmth of his breath causes a puff of smoke between us. The car isn't running because if it was, we'd be drawing attention from passersby from the deep rumbling of the exhaust. It's the dead of winter here in South Florida, and it's finally dipped to thirty-four degrees Fahrenheit. This weather was not the selling point for me moving back from Southern California, but my mother insisted if my grades didn't improve, I had to come back. So, here I am; where possibly getting caught fornicating in a car is a slap on the wrist. And although we would be asked to get dressed and move on by authorities, our mothers would be sure to keep us in our own personal prisons—our homes.

Both my and Jeremy's dads were killed on police duty when we were fifteen. They were like two peas in a pod, patrolling the streets of the safest small town in the area. Each of them was taken down by a tourist who had turned psycho and dressed like a clown to go after his victims. Since then, helicopter parenting by our mothers has personally victimized both me and my well-behaved boyfriend.

There was a time when we were fourteen, I thought he'd be the one to rock my world. Be my first kiss. My first everything. He was my first kiss, but he has *not* been my everything since I'm obviously still a virgin.

"I should go home. My mom said she made me dinner. First day of winter break and all." Jeremy's hands are clammy against my arms, and that's where the romance ends and the ick begins. He's starting to give me a complex. He's nervous and I get it. I won't push him. After all, there's nothing a little one-on-one time with a toy from my special drawer can't solve.

I pull myself from his lap, falling to the driver's seat. "I'll drive you." Oh, did I mention Jeremy doesn't have his license? Mainly because he finds it a nuisance since South Florida drivers are insane. He isn't wrong, but he also hasn't been to California where the drivers there are a million times worse.

"It's okay. I can walk. It's only a block and a half." I glance over at my boyfriend and his shoulders are less tense, and despite the temperature of the car, the sweat on his forehead has dissipated. His sandy blonde hair is mussed just enough to give him that sexy surfer look, and if I mentioned it to him, he'd whip out a comb to fix it. But nothing compares to his hazel eyes. They are pretty dreamy. His eyes are what sold me when he first asked me out. He's handsome. His body is perfect. The typical dreamy dream house with a white picket fence type of man. Something my dad always wanted for me.

I lean over and kiss him. Like, really kiss him—hoping he'll say "screw it" and rip my clothes off. No such luck. He opens the door, shoots me a smile and a wave like I'm an unknown Uber driver, gets out, and closes the door before I can say anything.

After opening my door, I shout after him, "Don't forget to give me a five-star rating, sir. Pleasure meeting you!"

Okay, so my sarcasm is all I really have. That and my forever looming V-card.

Closing my door again, I take a few deep breaths. Considering I chose to see Jeremy for a mediocre kissing session before I chose to see my mother shreds another string of my dignity. *Who have I become?*

I'm a virgin by proxy. After Dad died, I locked myself in my room, fiddled with acrylic paints, and spent my time with my long list of red-flag book boyfriends. It wasn't until my mom suggested I go out with Jeremy that I finally decided to give the real-life opposite sex a chance. Since he's been my childhood friend since we were in diapers, he was the guy my mom never had to vet. It made sense, though. We had a great time. I felt comfortable with him. *Safe.* He knew what I was going through because he was going through it, too. Now we are together. Still virgins. Together.

Amazing.

DAISY

UNABLE TO SEE out of the steamed windows, I open my door and stare up at our oversized house that's planted across the street from the beach. This isn't my childhood home. We used to live a few neighborhoods inland. Still beautiful, but…this is flashy. Something straight out of a *Southern Living* magazine, sought out by elites near and far.

I reach down into the center console and pull out a ring pop I picked up at the gynecologist's office last week before I moved. They hand out candy like we are being rewarded with sugar for being good girls. After taking the plastic off, I slide it over my finger—the Red40 calling out to me.

No sooner does my boot hit the pavement than I hear a familiar squeal. "Daisy, you're home! I thought you wouldn't be home until later." That's right, the woman who's running down the steps like her world just arrived on a silver platter—my mom—named me Daisy. Like the duck. Not that I mind. Daisy—the duck—is strong-willed and sassy. At least I'm not a pushover like Minnie.

I wrap my arms around her, and she squeezes me tighter. "Hi, Mom. Ugh. Too tight."

She loosens her grip and holds me at arm's length. Her light blue eyes light up as her gaze brushes over my face. "Always so beautiful, my baby girl."

I don't know about beautiful. I feel mediocre, at best. My tan feels like it's gone already. Despite it being winter, the Florida humidity has already clung to my hair like a fish on fresh bait. Not to mention, my week-long drive here has bloated me. Gas station food and hole-in-the-wall diners have lined my intestines, and there is no release in sight. I haven't shit in five days. BUT! At least I'm not batting away mosquitoes yet.

"Let Tony grab your stuff when he gets back. Us ladies have a lot to catch up on." Since my mom started dating Tony this past spring, their marriage announcement came as a bit of a shock. I want my mom happy, and she needs a companion so she doesn't call me every five minutes telling me what she's doing during her day. *"I'm making bread…I'm dying my hair…Have you tried that new razor?…You should see Karen's hair! It's orange."* I have no idea who Karen is and don't particularly care to know, but it's constant calls like this when there isn't a love interest in the picture.

Tony is fine. He lets Mom and me have our own relationship. She completed her job and raised me, even after the tragedy of losing her husband, my father. I am who I am at this age. The only change I'm going to be doing is changing my location when I figure out what other surf town I want to move to. Although my mother seems obsessed with me in a loving mother-daughter way, I'm reminded at least weekly that my tattoos and piercings are that of white trash. Again, her words, not mine.

It's safe to say I privately harbor a love-hate relationship with the woman who gave birth to me, and she has no idea.

We walk up the steps and into the new house that still smells like fresh paint.

"I like what you did with the place." I look around the massive foyer. There's shiplap everywhere. It looks like Joanna Gaines herself decorated it. *Love her.* Real metal anchors hang on the hall and look heavy as hell. "Are those real?" I run my fingers along the crown to the tip of the fluke.

Note to self: Anchor could be used as a weapon if someone were to break in.

Navy blue and green accents adorn the walls, making it feel somewhat like a home.

Mom beams, looking around like she's seeing it for the first time. "Thank you! I watched HGTV for weeks trying to nail down a…vibe?"

I give her a small laugh. Mostly because I don't find too much funny anymore unless it's said with obvious sarcasm. Now that's my jam.

"Plus, we wanted to finish all the painting and decorating before Rocco gets here," she says quietly, searching my face—narrowed eyes, pursed lips, and all.

I raise a brow. "Should I be reacting to this news? Why are you looking at me like that?"

"Well, you've never met your new stepbrother before. In fact, I don't even think you've seen a picture of him. He's twenty-one. Keeps to himself. He's a little…different. And you, well…" Her face is pinched like she's worried I'm going to corrupt him. I've been known to get into some minor trouble. Mostly because I hate living by rules that so many other people don't follow. Tony's son is twenty-one and living at home. Maybe he needs to have his soul crushed a bit by me.

A loud exhaust rumbles down the street. Not the obnoxious kind that backfires and you think you've been shot. No. This is just loud enough—and expensive. My mom's eyes widen and she hesitates to smile. "That's him." She fixes her red and white floral dress and moves my wavy, long blonde hair from my chest to behind my shoulder.

"Relax, Mom, I won't corrupt him. I'll be a good girl."

"Oh yeah?" A deep voice mumbles from the doorway and my eyes follow the noise. This must be my stepbrother dressed all in black. Black sweats, black hoodie, topped off with a black beanie he pulls off his head. *No helmet. Noted.* His skin is dark like he's been in the sun. Eyes a beautiful brown. Hair? That's dark too, and unruly, falling all over the place. The hair on the back of my neck stands and my nerves tingle.

I now understand the look my mom gave me when he pulled up. She isn't afraid I'll corrupt him. She's obviously petrified of him corrupting me.

She clears her throat and moves awkwardly between us. "Rocco, this is my daughter Daisy. Daisy, this is—well, will soon be—your stepbrother, Rocco." I push my ring pop into my mouth, taking him in and his eyes fall to my mouth. Pushing out my lips a little more, I pull the ring pop out slowly as I gauge his reaction. It slides out with a satisfying pop and my mom clears her throat.

"Daisy? Like the duck?" he asks, almost seeming bored with the interaction.

My mom giggles like a nervous schoolgirl at his words. "Exactly! Daisy Duck Reynolds," she jokes.

She's not making any of this better. Something he meant with a facetious undertone, she took as an innocent question. Herein lies the problem with her. If she had just gotten out of this small town, she'd have been cultured in different interactions with all types of people. The good, bad, and the ugly. She'd know how to read people. How to read the interaction that just happened between her daughter and soon-to-be stepson. Pure, unadulterated lust.

Rocco raises one scarred brow and his deep brown eyes narrow on me. And that's it. He picks up his duffle and walks up the steps like he's been here a million times. My mom calls up the steps after him, "Rocco, yours is the third room on the right. You have your own bathroom!" Her voice is an octave higher. It's the same one she uses to talk on the phone to strangers, not the one that she uses when she's comfortable. I bet he hasn't heard about Karen's orange hair.

The smile she gives me is naïve—unknowing. I know his type. I *am* that type. The type that sneaks around, bends the rules as far as they can go right before they snap.

"He'll warm up to you," she whispers, laying her hand on my arm. Like I'm worried about someone like him accepting me. He's met his match because I don't take shit lying down. I'll give it right back. So if he thinks I'm a doormat, he's wrong because whether he knows it or not, I'm the main character of his story.

"Right. I'll just take my stuff up since Tony isn't here yet. Where's my room?" I start out the front door before she steps beside me, taking up the doorway.

"I promise, Daisy. This will be good for us. Them…our new family." The look in her blue eyes is begging and almost sad, but there's something inside them that I haven't seen in years. Hope.

"I know, Mom." I give her a tight smile, trying to predict how this situation is going to go. Maybe Rocco's bad behavior will overshadow mine and I can finally convince Jeremy to sleep over because Mom won't be helicoptering in the hallway wondering if her daughter is up to no good.

"In answer to your question, your room is next to Rocco's—the second room on the right. Your bathroom is across the hall."

I release a puff of air because, of course, the spoiled prince gets the bathroom in his room. I gaze out to the driveway and next to my vintage beauty sits his blacked-out Audi RS7. "He gets a bathroom in his room, but I'm forced to trot half-naked in public to get to my room. That's fair," I mumble under my breath, not that it matters as I'm pretty sure that it would fall on my mom's deaf ears anyway.

CHAPTER
THREE

DAISY

CUTTING my way through the steam, I find my towel on the hook. I'm not sure it was Tony's plan to *not* have a working ventilation system in here, but the idea of my own personal sauna is certainly brightening up the idea of having my very un-private bathroom across the hall. And I think the new guy needs a lesson on how *not* to use all the hot water.

I twist a towel over my hair and tuck another one around my body. It's been a full week, and I haven't ran into my new stepsibling in the hall while I'm half-naked, so I foolishly decide that fate is on my side. I twist the doorknob and open the door, letting the steam billow out with me like I'm in some seductive 90's music video. With slow steps, one foot in front of the other, I peek into the hallway. *All clear.* I turn to grab my phone from the sink and peel out of the bathroom like my ass is on fire.

Three steps—or maybe five, depending how big of strides I'm taking—but it's all I needed to get to my room. A task I have failed miserably. I run right into a brick wall that is tall, dark, and broody.

"Jesus. Watch where you're going." His voice is deep and raspy, and my eyes find his.

I back away, putting space between us with my body on fire. We freeze in front of each other for what feels like a bit too long, then both move to the right. Then to the left.

"Would you just pick a side?"

Oh. We have an attitude.

As a power move, or what little I have of that standing here in only a towel, I level my eyes with his eyes as much as possible before I pull the knot of my makeshift cover loose. The sound of it hitting the floor steals his focus. His eyes move down my body as best as they can with less than a foot between us, and his lips twitch when he notices my pierced nipples. *I win.*

My nerves start to tingle under his stare and heat pools in my lower belly. I'm pretty sure that I have blue ovaries from making out with Jeremy for so long and getting nowhere. I'm clearly not thinking straight that I thought *this* was my only power move; that showing off the goods to my almost stepbrother was the only play I could make.

Rocco leans down and picks up my towel. Then he tilts his body toward me as he rests his lips next to the shell of my ear. "Next time you're in the hall, hold on to your towel a little tighter. Girls with prepubescent bodies don't do it for me," he growls.

"Where did you come from? An all boys school? Majoring misogyny and a bad attitude?" This man has me seeing red and oddly turned on at the same time. It's the most confusing feeling I've even dealt with.

"I came from Wellington. About fifteen miles northwest of here." A smirk forms on his beautiful as he gives me another once-over. "It's cute you're trying to get to know me, sis."

He slips by me as I grab the towel out of his hands and wrap it back around me, and I can feel the heat radiating from my damp skin. And it's not the good kind of heat. The kind that makes you beg for a touch. No, it's all-out rage.

Steps later, I reach my bedroom door like I'm the only person living in this *wing* of the house. I open it with more force than necessary and slam it with an equal amount of frustration. "I know one person who likes my body...kinda," I grumble to myself, peeling the towel from my body as I stand in my room. Picking up my phone to text Jeremy, I start thinking about how differently an impromptu, post-shower meeting in the hallway naked would have turned out if Jeremy was here instead of Rocco. But I decide against texting him. I'm kidding myself; my boyfriend is an obvious prude who is apparently saving himself for marriage. Instead, I grab my hot pink dildo—the one I named Mr. Jones—from the nightstand drawer and get to work because it's very obvious that the only way I'll get anything accomplished is to do it myself.

IT'S ONLY BEEN days since I moved home. Jeremy still hasn't fucked me despite us being inseparable. He also hasn't stayed over. Snuck in. Given me the fingering. Nada, zip, zilch. Hell, he hasn't stayed out past the sun setting. But with plenty of free time at night, all alone, I've learned three things about Rocco—and they were so prophetic that I even wrote them down.

That's right. I have a list of topics of conversations that NEED to happen next time we're face to face—fully dressed, or not.

One:

Having the "save the hot water" discussion has yet to happen. I don't know what time he gets home from whatever the hell he does, but I wake up before the birds, go for a jog, come back, and the warmest water temperature is fifty-three degrees. I even measured it with my mom's meat thermometer. I'm not saying that unit of measurement is an accurate reading of liquid temps, but I'm guessing it's pretty damn close.

Two:

He comes back late and wakes up late. We've been bedroom

neighbors for a week, and he's either a recluse, or disappears for days at a time. Which I can only assume means that he's out of town on a bender, or he's running a super-sketchy operation out of his bedroom. Passing each other in the hall is about as exciting as passing a friendly ghost. After my towel-drop event, he avoids any and all eye contact. So, just like stepbrother dearest, I say nothing, remain fully clothed, and go about my day uninterrupted.

Three:

His taste in music—which has been blaring through the wall for days—is as strange as his taste in women. I've seen three different nameless females so far. They all have one thing in common: The amount of makeup on their faces is alarming. I'm speaking from an acne point of view, of course. Let your pores breathe, girls. Fortunately, I've heard nothing through the wall, but that's not to say they haven't been going at it like rabbits. Between the fan I have going as fast as a plane's propeller and my noise machine, I hear nothing and sleep like the dead. Not even the demons I hide in my soul that threaten to make surprise appearances can wake me from my almost slumber. His music, on the other hand, plays whether he's in his room or not. When does the guy sleep? At one point there was a song on repeat, so like anyone, I Shazam'd it. Now I, too, am obsessed with a song named "Feral" by a band called Escape the Fate. Seems pretty fitting to me.

"Daisy!" My mom shouts through the door. "Breakfast is ready."

"I'm not hungry," I shout back, pulling the covers up to my neck. The best thing I could have asked for in my new room was room-darkening curtains. My mom called for a list of my necessities for when I came home, and my only requests were Ho Hos stocked in the freezer, and long, opaque curtains that can hide the light of day. Sleeping has never felt so good.

"Daisy…I need to talk about the wedding! My wedding," she clarifies, like I forgot. "It's in two days." Instead of coming in, she's still shouting. "Please."

"Can it wait for an hour? I didn't sleep well last night." *Lie.*

"I'm coming back in five minutes if you don't come downstairs." I hear her footsteps fall farther and farther away. One point for Mom taking a hint.

As soon as I start to drift into a peaceful sleep, my door opens and I pop up, hair in disarray on top of my head and one boob partially hanging out of my tank top.

"Go down and talk about the damn wedding so I can fucking sleep." This is the first thing Rocco's said to me since Hallway Gate. If I remember correctly, he's only said twenty-nine words to me. I've replayed our interactions like a movie reel in my head repeatedly. Not like anyone can blame me. I'm starved for interaction thanks to Jeremy and his inattention.

Rocco knocks on the door, bringing back my attention to him. His dark eyes drop to my thin white tank that I stole from Jeremy. He is obviously slimmer in the chest department than I am considering Jer is a hundred-fifty pounds soaking wet. I look down and my nipples are pointing directly at a set of dark eyes. I pull my sheet over my chest a few seconds too late before he chuckles and says, "A lot of good covering does now. I already saw your tits in the hall, in case you forgot." He turns before I can say anything and pulls the door shut, leaving my heart pounding in my chest.

I take an empty cup from my nightstand and toss it at the door. "You could have knocked! *Asshole.*" *Misplaced anger. Projection.*

My therapist on the West Coast was constantly preaching phrases like this; about how not being in the present moment would lead to outbursts that were rendered unnecessary.

I don't know, I felt sublimely present in this moment and the anger didn't feel completely misplaced. *Excuse versus reason.*

"Ugh! Whatever!" I slam my body back onto the mattress like an infuriated toddler and stew in my own hangry-ness. *Is that bacon?*

"Fine," I mumble. I toss the blankets to the side and throw on a hoodie and sweats. After sliding on my knock-off UGG slippers,

I make my way downstairs. It's taken a couple days to get acclimated to the layout of this house. I pride myself on being smart. Knowledgeable. High in the common-sense department of life, but standing outside of our new family home and understanding the interior layout, it makes absolutely no fucking sense. There's a window on the outside that I noticed and I have no idea which room it belongs to. It's been irking me since I was straddling Jeremy that first day. I suppose now isn't the time to figure it out.

I can hear my mom's voice coming from the kitchen along with Tony's. "You go. I'll buy."

"Where are we going?" I interrupt. Both of them turn to me.

"I was telling your mother how she can run to the grocery store to pick up some food for tonight, and I'll give her my card. Isn't that right, Maribel?" Spoken like a true, soon-to-be husband as he rubs my mom's back. Tony has been nice to me the few times we've spoken. He is also the total opposite of Mom. She is part hippie, I swear, and Tony's…well, I'm pretty sure he's in the mafia. I mean, he's not, but he's always put together, well dressed, and like his son, I don't think he sleeps either.

Speak of the Devil and he shall appear…in all black; Black COMFORT hoodie, black sweats, and a black beanie, causing his dark hair to poke out of the sides. He doesn't say good morning. Doesn't make eye contact with his dad or me, but gives my mom a small nod. Most likely because she's standing in front of the coffee machine and he wants her to move. And she does. She goes and sits at the table where magazines and business cards are scattered around next to her open laptop.

Tony lowers his voice and mumbles to Rocco, "You're spending the day with us today."

And he nods. Again.

That was it. No pleasantries, no words at all. What I've seen of their dynamic is strange. Not that I'm one to judge. My mother thinks everything's okay between her and I and I'm pretending it is to avoid an argument with one of the only humans, other than Jeremy, who can stand my presence.

"Please dress nicely for dinner, Daisy. It's fancy." My mom sing-songs like that will make the tension in this room stop crackling with the consistency of burning wood.

I sip my coffee and shoot her narrowed eyes. "I always dress nicely." But my subpar comeback is ignored. The idea of putting any more thought into my outfits than I do my schooling triggers a sour taste in my mouth.

I recognize a zing flowing through me, and just as I thought, Rocco stands there with pouty lips and brown eyes staring into my soul. I could do without the zings. Well, it would suit me better if they came from Jeremy, but the only zinging that guy is giving me is to my continuously bruised ego and the long-lasting charge on Mr. Jones.

My mom and Tony start a conversation among themselves, and I walk toward him to put my half-empty 'Cunt' mug in the sink. I'm shocked my mother didn't throw this away before the big move. When I brought it home senior year of high school, she just about sent me to boarding school.

"Problem?" I ask with a cocked brow. What is his malfunction? His lids are low as if he's exhausted. Or high. If he's giving me bedroom eyes, he's failing. Not that I *want* his bedroom eyes.

My stomach brushes against his hip as I reach around him, ignoring the goosebumps that spread down my legs. After dropping my mug a little harder than I should have, I stand straight, scowling up at him. He has to be at least six-feet tall. I'm five-four and my eyesight aligns with the hollow of his neck.

"Daisy? I know it's only breakfast, but will you be inviting Jeremy over for dinner? I'd love for him to meet Tony and Rocco." She looks at her fiancé like the sun shines out of his ass, and then to his offspring, obviously hoping for some type of mother-son interaction. Rocco's either oblivious or doesn't give a shit. Maybe both.

He's still staring at me, but the scar follows his eyebrow upward, challenging me to answer. And I never back down from a challenge. Not that I understand his silent agenda, but why not invite Jeremy? He's smart. Maybe he'll see there's nothing to worry about when it comes to staying over, or coming over, period. Or maybe he'll get jealous and *want* to stake his claim on me. "Yep. I'll ask him."

"Great!" Mom cheers. Too much energy for this early in the morning. "We'll have your favorite." Now she's grinning at me. "Veggies, steak, and mashed potatoes."

"Great," I parrot. I start down the hall out of the kitchen and Rocco pushes past me and runs up the stairs. He's so strange. It's not like I have to shower. I already took all the hot water. "Ha," I laugh to myself as I imagine devil horns growing from my head.

"You have ten minutes to get your ass back down here, kid!" my mom yells from the table. I get reprimanded like I'm twelve. It's as if time stood still once I got my period and I'm not currently a stone's throw from turning twenty.

As I near the top of the stairs, I hear Rocco's shower start to run. "Oh hell no, frosty Satan! Not today!" I make a quick right into my bathroom and slam the door, stripping out of my clothes as fast as possible. Stepping into the shower, I bend to turn the handle on, but it's gone!

"Argh!" I yank the door open and throw my arms across my boobs and cover my pussy with my hand. Stomping through the hallway, I kick open Rocco's partially open bedroom door.

"Hey, fuckface!" I beeline to the bathroom and kick that door open, too. "Don't fuck with my shower!"

A guttural laugh echoes through the bathroom, and the hooks from the curtain slide across the metal. He peeks his head around, and although I can only see his face and shoulder, my breath hitches. I forget why I'm here. Oh yeah.

"You mess with my shit, I mess with yours!" I scream as his eyes fall to my barely covered areas.

He shakes his head and closes the curtain. "What did I tell you about covering up around me, kiddo?"

"I'm not a kid! I'm nineteen and I do NOT have a prepubescent body! They're double Ds, for Christ's sake, you fucktard!" After I write "fuck you" on his steamed-up mirror, I slam the door behind me and slam the bedroom door for good measure.

———

"DAISY, we need to talk about the wedding. We have two days. It's not going to plan itself." *No shit.* I twirl my hair into a clip as she pulls a chair out and taps the table beside her. The glass table sits over a mess of driftwood underneath. It's pretty on point for living in a coastal town. My mind drifts to a dangerous place. Sitting around the table. Maybe tonight Jeremy will surprise me and place his hand on my thigh. Maybe he'll slide it up my skirt, finally make me come. I'm not sure I even care if it's in front of everyone. I might like that, but I wouldn't know. The thought of not getting caught…I release an audible moan.

"Are you okay, sweetie? You look flushed. Mom's high-pitched voice could pull anyone out of a daydream. My eyes pop open and Rocco's sitting right across from me and I jump. "Jesus. Where did you come from?" Again, his eyes are unyielding, watching me. No smile. No emotions. Drenched hair that's illuminated from the window behind him. Like a goddamn halo even though he's the furthest thing from an angel.

But so am I.

"Daisy?" My mom nudges my arm with her elbow.

"I…yes." I'm speaking to my mom, but my eyes are on him. "Don't you have somewhere to be?" I aggressively grab a strip of now room temperature bacon from the center of the table, bend it, and shove it in my mouth. I may or may not moan at the juicy fat melting in my mouth, and Rocco's jaw tics before he shakes his head slowly.

"It's a shame." I grab another piece of bacon. "You seem to make yourself scarce any other time. What makes today any different." This guy waltzes into my life and stares at me like I'm a caged animal at the zoo. I'm not doing tricks for him. Maybe if I'm boring enough he'll get bored and go away. "You're twenty-one. There must be some bar or somewhere you can disappear to." And to add on an extra cherry on top, I say, "Not that I know what twenty-one-year-olds who live with their parents do, anyway." I wince like I'm disgusted. But I'm not one to talk. I'll be twenty in mere days.

"That's enough, Daisy," my mom snaps from beside me as Tony walks back into the room. I didn't even know he left.

"Rocco, why don't you go to your room and leave the ladies to the wedding talk?" Tony's voice says one thing, but his face says another. Rocco grunts and storms out the back door toward the patio. My mom starts talking, but my eyes are drawn to the twenty-one-year-old mystery man who is Rocco Mancini. He lights up a cigarette—*ew*—and Tony busts out the back door, startling both me and my mom.

She tsks her tongue against the roof of her mouth—a noise I despise—and whispers, "Tony hates it when he smokes. He's trying to get him to stop."

I hate gossip. But this information is useful. Maybe. I mean, I have nothing going on for the next three weeks of my life. Something needs to pass the time and bring me some joy because I know one thing that's not, and that's my almost-perfect prude of a boyfriend. If I can get to the bottom of why my stepbrother is seemingly as fucked up as I am, maybe we can find some common ground. The whole keep your enemies close thing isn't really working out for us currently because if I take one more cold shower, I'm initiating war.

DAISY

MY MOM GAVE me a quick run-down about the wedding that's taking longer than the actual event will be. The speed of the ceremony she's planning will put a Vegas chapel wedding to shame.

Wake up. Breakfast. Hair and makeup. Pictures. Ceremony with *maybe* thirty words exchanged, and the reception. That's where the load of her planning went to. Why she needed me to hear this is beyond me. There will also be food and drinks for the whole town of Briny Breeze, not to mention the snobs from the tri-county area coming to rub elbows with Tony.

I still don't know what he does.

An obnoxious noise—like a boat's horn—comes from the foyer, and I look around. Unless we are getting ready to set sail on a cruise, I'm not sure why anything has to make *that* sound.

"Aren't you going to answer the door? It's probably Jeremy," my mom says, looking at me like I've never heard a doorbell before.

"Does it need to sound like a boat horn? You'll confuse the yachts and sailboats going by every time someone comes over." I roll my eyes.

She pinches her brows. "It's a lovely sound, Daisy. Now, would you answer the door?"

I shake my head and walk to the foyer, covering my ears in case the horn sounds again. And it does! "This is a liability!" I shout back before I open the door to find Jeremy standing in front of me in his pink polo, khaki shorts, and Sperry shoes. Well, he's obviously dressed for a day on a boat.

He gives me a smile that's quite adorable. "What's a liability?" Jeremy walks through the door, trying to join the conversation, and I take this perfect chance to flirt. "You can't be talking about the boat horn doorbell." He flashes me his perfectly straight teeth and I melt.

"You're the liability, you stud. You have all my attention. It's dangerous." I rub my hand down his chest and his entire body tenses as he looks at my hand, then my mom.

"Dangerous? Ha." A deep laugh comes from the stairs behind us, and the butterflies in my stomach take flight. The same butterflies that were still in their cocoons seconds ago when Jeremy showed up. Every last one of them must've shed their chrysalis at once. A phenomenon I've never felt before. Jeremy's eyes bounce from my mom to the voice. I pull away from my boyfriend and look at the noise of heavy steps clomping down the steps.

His dark hair lays unruly on his head. He's wearing a long-sleeve cotton shirt with the fabric pushed up, showing off his inked and corded forearm muscles. This is the first time I've seen him in anything but a hoodie. Even walking around the house today, he was a silent ball of tension wrapped in a black leather jacket. Because of course, he was. My eyes drop to the dark denim wrapped around his thick thighs and I squeeze my own thighs together in reaction.

What the hell is happening?

I'm not proud of my body for reacting the way it does since we're about to be related. Rocco screams sex. The pheromones are strong with this one. My eyes graze back up his Adonis body, only to meet his deep brown gaze. I've been caught, and for the first time, he gives a crooked grin, exposing his stupid sexy smile. *I'm fucked.*

"Have something to say, Mancini?" I narrow my eyes at him, and he looks Jeremy up and down. His grin falls into a deep frown. "Nope."

Fuck. I'm turned on. It's not because I'm being touched, either. It's just my body's sexual reaction to this man I despise. But not to Jeremy. Because that reaction with him would be natural. Would be expected. But this…it's visceral. Unexplained. Jeremy clears his throat from behind me and I try to blink myself out of the trance as Rocco descends the last two steps. I turn back to my boyfriend. Poor Jeremy is wearing a frown and a wrinkled nose. Being someone who never gets shaken up, my soon-to-be stepbrother seems to have rattled him.

Rocco stops partially behind me, pressing his shoulder against mine. The heat of his body is that of a day at the beach mid-summer. A light sweat forms on the back of my neck. I'm contemplating running outside and saying fuck it. Fuck this dinner. Fuck this house. Fuck my life.

"Aren't you going to introduce me?" Jeremy gives me a wide smile.

Why is he smiling? *Read the room, my guy.*

"Right. Jer, this is Rocco. My…" My throat is dry. The poke of a thousand needles penetrates it as I try to swallow past the sting. "Rocco's my soon-to-be stepbrother."

Rocco tilts his head to Jeremy, and instead of greeting him, he nods and grumbles to me, "We'll never be related, *Angel.*"

He takes a sharp turn, disappearing into the house, leaving me and Jeremy in the foyer. I look for my mom to save me because I could have sworn she was still in the room. She must have wandered off after I opened the door.

"Asshole," I mumble under my breath. "Well, come in, Jer." I push the door closed behind him with Rocco's new nickname gnawing at my vagina. For me, having a nickname from a man is equivalent to being called a *good girl.*

Jeremy smiles and follows me into the house, quietly. "That's him, huh? He's intense," he whispers and nervously looks at me, down at his outfit, and then ahead, tucking his hands in his front pockets. I have a deep need to protect Jeremy from the bad in the world. And if that means warding off the intense, dark and broody Italian vibe of Rocco Mancini, then that's what I'll do.

"You look…" *Like a preppy guy, we always used to make fun of.* "…great, Jeremy. Is that a new polo?" We slowly make our way to the dining room, hand-in-hand. He used to wear Quiksilver tees, boardshorts, and Vans. But things changed last summer. This past June, the night I got home from the West Coast, I opened the door and he was there. Dressed like a frat boy who's ready to rub some girl's left labia for four seconds before asking her if she came. We mourned the loss of his surfer clothes and hesitantly welcomed his new attire. And by 'we' I mean 'I'.

"Yes. I'm really digging this style. Very *Florida Golfer.*" His cheeks turn as pink as his shirt like he's embarrassed, but I choose to ignore it. If he wants to dress like he's going golfing every day, who am I to stop him?

I've had less than a handful of interactions with Rocco that have made me batshit crazy. That's to be expected. He is broody and difficult and pops up out of nowhere. But now I'm starting to notice there are small things with Jeremy that have started getting under my skin. The pink polo is just the tip of the iceberg.

Everyone is already sitting around the table when we walk to the dining room. Tony looks like he's going to 'off' someone tonight dressed in all black. These Mancini men must only own black. Their wardrobe color palette is that of a gothic person. But I stand by my former assessment, that he is not in the mafia. He's simply a rich and powerful man who owns half of South Florida's largest entities. Or so I tell myself.

Jeremy pulls out the seat next to mine and instead of waiting until I'm seated and pushing my chair in, we sit at the same time. I never claimed he was a gentleman. "This is wonderful," my mom chimes from my right. She grabs my hand that's holding my fork and shakes with excitement.

"What's the holdup?" I ask, my eyes darting to everyone else.

"Tony, this is Jeremy," my mom starts. Oh yeah. Where are my manners? Must have been left in the foyer with that less-than-stellar interaction with Rocco.

My mom drops my hand, and I smile at Jeremy. "Tony, this is my boyfriend Jeremy. Jer, this is my soon-to-be stepfather."

Tony, sitting to Jeremy's left, extends his hand for a shake. I watch their clasped hands, and Jer has a dead-fish handshake happening. Nothing firm or manly about his grip. Tony notices. I know he does. I can see it on his face. But he never says anything. "Nice to meet you. I've heard a lot about you, Jeremy." Has he? Because he certainly hasn't heard anything from me.

I don't spare a glance at Rocco, who's sitting across from me. I don't need to deal with more testosterone than I already am. Or maybe there's less of that hormone circulating than I want to admit. I love Jeremy, but he seems to be less…testosterone-y than the Mancini men.

Jeremy is talking to Tony and my mom, and although I'd much rather be anywhere other than here, seeing him getting along with our new people means a lot. Jeremy's foot starts to rub my ankle, and I shift in my seat, shocked at the action. This is unlike him. Maybe the plant-based dinner my mom made triggered his inner sexual being to finally wake up. A little weird, but different strokes for different folks and all that. I won't yuck his yum. Maybe he has a foot fetish I didn't know about. A kink. I can work with this.

I turn to him and give him a knowing smile and he smiles back. I glance back down at the leftover potatoes on my plate and zone out as I start moving my foot against his. Slow. Methodical. I'm seconds away from kicking my shoes off when I look up. Rocco's jaw tics and his full lips are on display for the world to see. Except the world isn't here to see it. Nobody is. Falling under his trance, one side of his lips tilts up. Discreetly, I glance next to me and see Jeremy's leg moving a mile a minute with his other foot tucked under his chair. Christ on a cracker, it's not Jeremy who's playing footsy with me, it's Rocco. *Shit.* If the table wasn't covered with food, anyone would be able to see his Nike banging into my Converse.

I sit straight, pulling my legs under my chair as far as they can go. Tony and my mother grab the plates and start retreating to the kitchen. "Nobody moves! We have dessert!"

Ignoring Rocco's presence, I turn to Jeremy and try to keep my voice down. "Mom and Tony go to bed early, if you want to sneak in later." A nineteen-year-old trying to encourage her boyfriend to sneak in. I've reached the rock bottom of this relationship. I mean, this is my first and only relationship. I have nothing to go off of.

"I…they'd hear." His face scrunches while his hazel eyes dart from Rocco, who isn't even pretending not to listen, back to me. But he didn't say no. This is progress.

"No." I tilt my head in my stepbrother's direction and continue, "This guy is never home, and besides, we have our own wing in the house."

That seems to get Jeremy's attention. "You share a wing?" His eyes get big for a split second. It happens so quickly; I have to convince myself that what I saw really happened. Jealousy. I can use this.

"Yes. Our rooms are right next to each other," I add, fishing for a hint of emotion. I mean, I don't think it's him not being into me, necessarily. Maybe complacency?

He blinks a couple of times and lets out a breath. "I shouldn't, Daisy. No—"

I don't let him finish. Instead, I push away from the table, causing the chair legs to scrape against the wooden floor, making a beeline for my bathroom because I need to get out of here. "Excuse me." There is no reason he can't come up. I wouldn't push him to do anything. The fact that I have to beg for his attention is outrageous. I'm not the type of girl who demands her man spend every waking minute with her. I hate that. We can still be together and independent. Those two things can exist simultaneously.

I find myself in my bathroom, examining my reflection in the mirror. "Is it me?" I say quietly to myself.

I splash handfuls of cold water on my face, not caring if it's washing off what's left of my makeup. It's not like I wear a lot anyway. I turn off the light before I open the door. It's already almost twilight outside, which means our hallway is dimly lit by what's left of the sunset.

A hard body stops me, and a grunt flies from his mouth. The scent of cigarettes and juniper slaps me in the face. "Jesus, Rocco. Watch where you're going." I try to adjust my eyes to the twilight-lit hallway. "Maybe you should get some gum while you're at it. Cigarettes are disgusting. Nobody likes kissing an ashtray. Or maybe your *girlfriends* don't really mind that smell."

"They don't matter, though. So, it's a good thing I'm not going to kiss you then." His voice is low before I see the shadow of his hand move to his face. Neither of us move. I'm not sure what's going through his head, but it's like something has rooted my feet on the ground. Nothing can be heard except for the meshing of our breaths. Not even the ticking of the grandfather clock at the end of the hallway.

The air between is charged. It's sizzling like a supernatural phenomenon. Seconds pass, or maybe minutes before he takes a step toward me.

One step. Then another before he backs me into the wall next to the door—well, one of the doors. My vision tunnels as his scent swirls around me. Our bodies aren't touching, but if I leaned forward, my breasts would be flush against his body. My nipples harden at the thought of being up against a man's skin, and the metal pierced through them sends a zing right between my legs.

I'm sure this isn't something I should be feeling. He is about to be in my life permanently. As family. And I must remember my boyfriend. I have one of those, and I think he's still downstairs doing exactly as my mother told us. Not to move. Dessert was on the way.

My mind is choppy. Aimlessly jumping from incoherent to full thoughts.

The shiplap wall is cold against my back, taking away some of the heat from my body. "It's not you," he finally says, his eyes moving between mine. "You were asking yourself if it was you in the mirror. It's definitely not you."

My heart's pounding against my ribcage and there's no way he can't hear it. *Or feel it.* I suck on the inside of my cheeks, keeping myself from doing anything I won't be able to take back. Instead of falling into this rabbit hole of longing and lust, I bite back.

"What do you know?" I grit through my teeth.

"I do know you liked me rubbing up against you under the table." He leans in and his lips brush the outer shell of my ear before he pulls my earlobe between his teeth. "Your face flushed like you were about to come. And the way you were shifting in your chair, you were turned on- thinking it was Jeremy." The stubble on his cheek brushes mine as he backs up enough to look at me. "Or maybe subconsciously, you knew it was me." My body shutters as his knuckles graze my thigh and he offers a sinister smile. "Time for some dessert." And he walks away, stomping down the steps leaving me in my own puddle of shame.

ROCCO

DAISY, Daisy, Daisy. I expected her to be a good girl, worried about fixing her tiara made of precious metal and gems, perfect hair, pastel-colored sundresses by a top designer, and a smile so bright it hurts your eyes. But instead, she's an angel with dark wings and a crooked halo. I haven't seen her smile. Not once. She wears a different variation of black clothes usually covered in some type of flannel left unbuttoned. I have to say, her sneaker collection is impressive. Many of which are custom painted. Color me impressed.

But my favorite outfit of hers is the one she's wearing now—her short black shorts, a tied-up black tank with Doc Martens combat boots sans a flannel. Her sun-kissed legs I imagine squeezing my head as she straddles my face, all while I run my hands over her smooth skin.

Here we are. At a standoff in the hallway. Both of us refusing to move first. I lean closer, her body telling me a different story than her words. Something I'm good at picking up on. Reading people. Staying quiet. Looking past what they say and reading their actions.

I saw her pierced nipples this morning in her bedroom, and again when she charged into my bathroom. I tried to look away. My father warned me off of her. Threatened me was more like it. Having a live-in toy is bad for my psyche and will take away from the stamina I need to keep in check for my night gig. Daisy and I are a year and a half apart, and her body is far from pre-pubescent. I know her twentieth is coming up in a couple of days. I've done my homework.

Telling me I don't know her…it's laughable. The dude she calls her boyfriend downstairs is either gay or not into sex with her at all. I'm going with the latter. But it really isn't her.

"What? Cat got your tongue?" She pushes my chest with her finger, her face dark—covered in a mask. Something I know about all too well. Her body is heating at a rapid pace, and her breath is quick and messy, but her face owns a scowl like she was the one who invented it.

I fight back a grin. "I don't waste my breath on good girls."

Her eyes narrow at my words. "That's right, you'd rather pick up the nearest woman wearing the most makeup."

My stomach lurches at her words. I don't pick those girls up. My father does. That's his sick and twisted way of getting me to expend my pent-up energy on my days off. This girl in front of me wouldn't be able to handle any of it. She's high school grade emo at best. And even though I see a push-pull playfulness bouncing in her eyes, there is no time for me to play with this broken angel in front of me. There's no time off for me.

"Oh, Angel. You don't want a man like me. You wouldn't have the first idea of how to please me."

Before she can voice a rebuttal, which I was really looking forward to, we get interrupted. "Rocco! Daisy! Dessert is served. Come down before it melts," Maribel shouts from the bottom of the stairs. Little does Daisy's dear mother know, I have her daughter's body overheating and pinned to the wall. She has the chance to get out of my hold, but her pink cheeks, glassy eyes, and short breaths say otherwise. She needs a little excitement in her life. That deadbeat boyfriend of hers is probably committed to missionary fucking for life. I wonder when the last time she's been adequately fucked. I was going to ask her before she threw out that comment about the girls I've had over. So, for now, I'll wait.

I use Daisy's own words against her, but this time I lean closer, tangling her erratic breath with mine. "You know nothing about me." It's true. If I told her what I have to do, what *he* forces me to do, she'd want nothing to do with me anyway.

Just when I go to push away, she pushes her hard nipples into my chest before her body leans in just enough that her eyes close and her head falls back to the wall.

No.

I pull away, leaving her in my wake. Too far. I can't get involved with her. Fuck being stepsiblings. I don't give a shit about that pointless title. We're adults, and that means nothing to me. But I won't get her involved in my shit. Even if I only want to fuck her.

I leave instead of going back to the dining room and head straight for my car. The engine to my RS7 purrs to life. "Such a good girl," I breathe out, rubbing the dashboard like she's my emotional support animal. My car is the only girl I can afford to get attached to. That is, until it breaks down like the rest of them.

I reverse out of the driveway and hit the gas. Getting the hell out of that house is the only way I feel free. It's not the house. It's him. He has me stuck. I'm his puppet and I have no way of cutting the strings. I'm like my own version of Britney Spears in a conservatorship, except I'm not a risk to myself. I'm a risk to him. I know too much, and this is his way of keeping me close. He sells me...he treats me like a pit bull in a dog fight. Makes me do things I'm against. But it doesn't matter. I could get killed in the ring, but he wants more and more out of me. His money maker. I don't want to die, so I train day in and day out to be the best. Maybe one day I can finally get out of this hell I'm living in.

He suffocates me even though he's nowhere near me. He's in

my head and lives there, and the only way to drown out that noise is to numb myself. Tapping my phone screen, I fight for a breath, waiting for a response. Sweat trickles down my forehead as I drive.

Breathe.

Unknown:Meet me in 10

A few minutes later, I pull into a dark parking lot. My heart slams against my ribs with each measured step toward the door with a single light above it. A desolate area that even the locals are ignorant of. Two semi-trucks are reversed into loading dock areas. It's a disguise—all of it. Nothing's been loaded or unloaded from this warehouse in years.

I pull out a book I took from Daisy's bookshelf. She has at least a hundred books set up, so I know she won't miss this one. Must be nice to have had 'mommy' to set up her stuff for her before she arrived. Not sure with which I grabbed as I read the title. "'Howl and Other Poems' by Allen Ginsberg." Huh. Poems are never my go-to, but if it helps me breathe a little better, I'll take whatever I can get.

Pulling a pen from the center console, I start drawing in the margin. It's more like doodling. Reading and drawing—something that's always brought me down from being up too high for too long. After a few minutes, a set of headlights appear and disappear over on the other side of the building. *He's here.*

I step out of my car, lock it, and head toward the only door on this side of the warehouse. I pound twice with the side of my fist, and seconds later it opens, and I walk in. It's dark, and the only man who has my best interest at heart trails behind me, dragging his feet like I forced him out of bed. He switches on the lights behind me, electricity sizzling through the old wires, lighting up the ring. A bloodied floor with hundreds, maybe thousands of different individual's DNA lies there, unable to be scrubbed up with soap and water. Where some became paralyzed, dismembered…even died. The very spot where my nightmare started almost six years ago.

"You killed our dreams!" he screamed in my face. The nurses stood outside of the room in horror as my father got in my face. My body in a cast. "You killed your mother! She's dead. You'll pay. I will figure out your punishment."

And he did. Like everything, he skimps on nothing. He said I need to get my ass beat and pay for killing my mother, and he threw me into an underground fighting ring, where I have gotten my ass beat, but he's the only one who gets paid.

I would lose. Got beaten and bloodied every time until Santiago Cruz came along. He pulled me aside from a fight, barely coherent, and handed me his card. A few days of healing passed, and I called him. I trained and it felt good—hitting a bag without it hitting me back. After that, I started winning. Every time I won, my father would tell me how well I did and give me a slap on the back. Maybe that was the elation of him counting his winnings. But it was the validation I'd been craving for so long. I found it hard to quit. He still takes all of my winnings. Gives me a little every month to feed myself and fill my car with gas, but that's it.

"What's going on, kid?" Santi rubs his eyes with the heels of his hands. He was here for my first fight. A fight that brought me to my knees and almost killed me. I'm not sure why he was here that night, but he's been my personal guardian angel. I've asked him a few times why he was at the ring, but his answer was always vague. *"I was where I needed to be."* It came to a point where I didn't push it anymore. Why mess up something that isn't broken? I never understood why my father let Santi be such a big part of my life. I'm assuming it was because once I started to win, I made him money. Santi became and asset to have around. He's more than an asset to me. He saved my damn life and I'm forever in debt to him.

I take off my shirt and toss it on the metal folding chair in the corner. "I need to hit something. Or be hit." *Because physical pain always numbs the emotional pain.*

He shuffles over to the hanging bag, taps it, and gives it to me. "Jab, cross, jab, right hook, left roundhouse kick, jab, cross, uppercut."

And that's what I do. I do about forty rounds. My muscles are on fire and weakening as I give it my all. I give this my all because if I don't, I'm as good as dead. And if I don't fight, I'm dead anyway.

"You'll stop fighting when I tell you to. Remember, Rocco, I own this city…the state…the police. You have nowhere to run." My father lifted my face to look at him, hurting my neck in the process. "If you do, just know that I will find you and I will kill you myself."

Dramatic? I wish. He doesn't love me anymore. Because I took his wife from him, and this was my punishment…and I was his moneymaker.

DAISY

TODAY'S THE BIG DAY, and Mom is chatting away in the living room getting her makeup done. I've watched the woman dab a shit-ton of powdered concealer over my mother's pale skin. Almost as if she'd fit right in with the women traipsing in and out of Rocco's room all hours of the night. *Ew.*

The amount of people I've never seen before rushing through this house makes me think that this is a lot less than a "quick" wedding and more of a televised event. Which it's not.

I pull my burnt bagel out of the toaster oven, tsking in pain with every grab. You'd think I would have learned by now to use some tongs. But no. I subconsciously enjoy the pain not only on the tips of my fingers, but on the roof of my mouth when I try to bite through this brick of bread.

"Daisy, I need to run to the office. Can you make sure Rocco is out of bed and getting ready? He's my best man. I need him to be 'on' today." Tony stops a few feet from me, buttoning the cuffs of his dark gray button-down.

On. What a strange word to use.

"Office on your wedding day? No rest for the wicked, am I right?" I joke as I slather cream cheese all over my bagel. The charred bread makes the knife sound like it's grating against Velcro as it spreads the cream cheese, the sound making me inwardly cringe, but I'm starving. Out of nowhere, a hand grabs my wrist, turning me around while the knife is still gripped in my hand.

My wrist is free before Tony's voice rumbles in my face like rocks under a heavy tire. "You needn't question my daily whereabouts. You're a child," Tony spits. I feel the blood drain from my face, and I drop the knife. But nobody makes me feel like less than what I am. I don't deal with being small very well, so I fix my posture and raise my chin.

I swallow hard at the dark brown beady eyes that are staring down at me. "I wasn't questioning you, Tony. It was a joke. Lighten up." I shouldn't talk to him like that, but he has no right to touch me. No right to speak to me like that when I've done nothing to deserve it. He is not, and never will be, my father.

"Dad." Tony's head snaps in the direction of his son's voice before he puts more space between us. But me? Like always, I look away. I easily push people's buttons like an elevator operator, but right now, I don't need there to be any more drama. I've already endured enough for a lifetime at the ripe age of *almost* twenty.

Tony looks back at me and gives me a tight smile, still his eyes are narrowed. "Have a good morning, Daisy. Son." Watching Tony leave the room is like watching Ursula from *The Little Mermaid* being devoured by the ocean after Prince Eric hits her with a sharp board from the ship. It's refreshing. Needed to be done to clear the intense energy that shadowed the room.

Another set of brown eyes are stuck on me. What is with these Mancini men? I turn, ignoring him, to pick up my now cold and burned bagel. The cream cheese has melted into the bagel. Anyone who eats cream cheese bagels knows there is a small window that you can eat this specific meal before it becomes soggy and weird.

"Did he hurt you?" The question was quiet. But genuine.

I spin in my clog slippers to slam dunk my bagel into the trash. The meal is wasted, as is my appetite, and so is my almost-decent mood. "No. He would never."

A short huff comes from Rocco who's still standing next to the kitchen table. "You need to be a good boy and be *on* for the wedding. Whatever that means. But I'm not your babysitter."

I start to storm by him with my pride intact, but he grabs my arm and spins me so I'm against the refrigerator. His inked hand grips my neck, and against my mind's better judgment, my pussy declares that she's in charge right now. And she's telling me to smile against the pressure. His eyes go from a brilliant brown to almost black. The hustle and bustle of the makeup and hair crew fall by the wayside. Right now, it's me and this mystery man as we silently allow our egos to duke it out. Although it may seem to a passerby that I'm in a dire situation, I'm not. Not at all. My eyes fall to his lips while I still wear a reactive smirk. I pull my bottom lip between my teeth before he pulls it out with his thumb.

"Don't fucking do that," he growls, sight frozen on my lips.

"Don't tell me what to do." I lick them slowly for good measure.

His eyes snap back to mine. "Don't talk to me like you're better than I am."

"Then maybe you should act your age." His grip tightens around my neck, and I choke out the next words. "I'm starting to think you like me, *stepbrother.* You keep pinning me against walls like you want to fuck me." I'm almost cross-eyed staring at him because of how close we are. His breath doesn't smell of cigarettes, but mint and mouthwash, which is now making me self-conscious. I didn't eat my bagel or have my coffee. I'm his personal fire-breathing dragon, bellowing my morning breath all over his face.

But he obviously doesn't notice—or care. He leans closer, touching his lips to the shell of my ear. "If I wanted to fuck you, you'd know it. But judging by the way your boyfriend doesn't let you touch anything but his hand at the dinner table, I'd feel safe to place a bet on you being a virgin."

My mind spins. Part of me wants to grind on his leg, and the other part of me wants to knee him in the balls. So I do.

I bring my knee up to hit him right in the grundle, but he stops me like a cat who has been through all his lives except the last one, not willing to reach the ninth. Rocco backs away, taking his tattooed hand necklace with him. "Nice try, Angel."

I narrow my eyes at him and he's smiling. Holy shit, he's fucking handsome. No. Not handsome. Jeremy's handsome. This guy… he's dangerous. He has scars in all the right places. Scars that itch to be traced with my fingers. And day-old scruff that he wears very well covering his chiseled jaw. His lashes are longer than mine on a good day. But his smile. It's crooked, showing his perfect teeth. He definitely had braces.

I muster up what's left of my dignity. "Don't ever touch me again," I grind through gritted teeth. His mouth moves into a closed grin, and his jaw clenches. Something he catches me watching.

"Daisy. It's your turn for hair and makeup." My mom comes from around the corner, stopping short. "What's going on? Everything okay?" Her tone is unsure. I take us in from her perspective. We either look like we are ready to kill each other, or jump each other's bones. And from my experience reading dark romance, that line is pretty damn fine.

Rocco offers her a nod and doesn't move.

"Everything's fine. I burnt my bagel." Offering some sort of topic change has always worked with her. She's like a child…or a monkey.

Mom's brows crease and she frowns while patting my back and pulling me away from the refrigerator that I was still plastered against. "I'll make you a new one while you're getting your hair done. How's that?"

I nod, like a distraught toddler, and disappear out of the

kitchen, but a part of me wants to go back. If not to be choked against something, to have Rocco in my personal space looking at me like he just had been. There's something about the way he looks at me that does all the right things.

Not even an hour later, I've eaten my bagel, my hair is nestled on top of my head like I'm coming out as a debutant, and my face —like Rocco's playthings—is piled on thick, the makeup making it hard for me to open my mouth the whole way.

Sucks for Jeremy. Kidding. We don't have that type of fun.

"Are you ready, Daisy? It's time for us to walk down the aisle." The aisle being a pastel green liner laid on the sand in the backyard. This entire ceremony is unconventional in a way that Rocco is already next to the bower made of driftwood and covered in plumeria flowers. I wonder if my mother knows she used an invasive plant to get married under.

Rocco and his dad stand there looking like two apples that fell from the same section of the tree. I walk down the aisle toward the shoreline, embarrassingly looking past the pastor and into the oceanic abyss. After that run-in with Tony today—and the one with Rocco—both Mancini men can kiss my ass.

After I turn away from my wave-crashing solitude, my mom follows me as a steel drum version of *Canon in D* plays from the side. She takes her place in front of me on the sand. I should be taking in the coral color of my dress and the perfect contrast against the blue of the ocean and sky behind me, or the way her ivory dress makes her look like she isn't a day over forty, yet I'm fixated on counting chairs.

There are a total of eight chairs—four on the groom's side, and four on the bride's side. And only two of those eight chairs are filled.

One with Jeremy, who's dressed to the nines. I'm about eighty…okay, ninety percent sure he's wearing a cummerbund and bowtie. I was hoping it was just a waiter from the reception, but that ass and that sandy blonde hair I'd know anywhere from far away. I had asked him to be my plus one last night over text. He was hesitant at first, not wanting to because "weddings are too romantic" like he was turned off by that or something. But like always, I insisted he gets out of the house and accompanies me to an event full of rich strangers. The other person occupying the chair is a young woman. Of course, her makeup is done like she's Harley Quinn at a ComicCon event. No. She doesn't get to be Harley. I'm Harley. Completely unhinged and slowly falling under the spell of someone who is more than off limits.

She's cross-legged in a gown that has a slit that's cut up to her hip. Easy access for her date, I'm sure. Her bright green eyes beam in front of her toward my new stepbrother. Calling him that feels so wrong, but I have to remind myself that that is who he is. I glance at Rocco. He's complacent like he's just going through the motions. Standing next to his father. Wearing a suit that, I must admit, fits him well.

His eyes snap to mine as if he felt the heat of my gaze on him. This is a contest I refuse to lose, but ultimately, he wins. His brown eyes move to the girl in the chair. And so do mine. She knows he's watching her, so like any natural seductress who lacks conservativeness, she scrapes her middle, blood-red fingernail up her thigh through the slit of her dress. And with that turn of events, the pastor's words are lost in the sea breeze, and so is my patience.

I clear my throat, and all six people look at me. It got Jessica Rabbit to stop cutting herself with her pointy nails, so I consider this a full-on W. "Sorry. Bug." I cough again, this time a little less obvious before I give my mom a faint smile. But like a moth to a flame, I look at Jessica again. Except now she's looking at me and her lips twist into a cynical smile. "Holy shit," I mumble under my breath.

That's not some random girl. That's my mom's best friend.

**CHAPTER
SEVEN**

ROCCO

THIS WEDDING IS COSTING me valuable moments of my life I'll never be able to get back. I'd rather be in the ring than standing next to *him*, having to stare at *her*, while *that one* is trying to seduce me.

He insisted that I have a woman on my arm at the wedding today. Since it's not a fight night, I need to fuck to keep my adrenaline going. Or as he likes to call it, "habitual adrenaline feed." When what's-her-name got here, she introduced herself, but not before hugging her *best friend*, Maribel. If I knew my screw for the night was going to be basically an old family friend, I would have faked an injury. It's easy to gauge myself in the eye and pretend like it happened in the ring.

My dad almost showed his true self to Daisy this morning. We all hide behind masks and we're all damn good at it, but he almost dropped his. I heard the whole thing, and the way she dealt with it. It was commendable, at best. She had an easy out. It may have been a butter knife she was holding, but if she shoved it in his chest just right and finished it with a twist, all of my worries would have vanished. But she now has an invisible target on her back. One that he'll stop at nothing to eliminate. I'm just not sure how far he'll go with her since he's marrying her mother.

Daisy's blonde hair is piled high and falling over her forehead like she's a beached beluga. Why hair and makeup people have to go to extremes for weddings baffles the shit out of me. Should you not want to enter into a marriage exactly how you see each other daily? That's who you've "fallen in love with"…not a TikTok-filtered version of the person.

The only nice thing about today is that winter in Florida is as unpredictable as my father's moods. Last week it was freezing, and now it's eighty-five and sunny. Her light blue eyes blink away the sunlight, which is now scorching my back. And since she's most likely blinded by the light, I'm able to take in her dress without getting caught. It's a mix of orange and pink—and my favorite feature, it's tight against her tits. She must be wearing a padded bra, or some of those sticky things, because her piercings are nowhere in sight, which makes me wonder if her mom even knows about them. Jeremy doesn't seem to be looking at her at all. Watching them greet each other earlier was awkward as fuck. She leaned in and kissed him, his lips were closed, and his eyes were pinched shut. Greeting the girl you're fucking—or not fucking but want to —his hands should be roaming. She should be moaning in his mouth wanting more. His hands should be fisted in her hair, keeping her right where he wants her. And she would probably fight him on it because she's feisty as hell.

Having her pinned against the fridge earlier, my hands tight around her neck, I expected her to scream for her mom, or something equally as childish. But she didn't. She fucking smiled. *Smiled.* And arched her tits against me. Again. She's right. I have a new favorite thing to do, and that's pinning her against a flat surface. I'm almost positive she's a virgin, dying to be defiled by her boyfriend who wants nothing to do with that part of her—for some unknown reason.

I watch her crinkle her nose at my date. Daisy isn't one to hide her emotions. She fascinates me. She's like a caged animal, dying to escape from her own hell, and that intrigues me. I guess we have that in common.

"You may now kiss your bride." The pastor looks as uncomfortable as I feel at our parents' tangled tongues. I turn to look anywhere but at the back of my father's head that's coincidently blocking Daisy, and my eyes drift to Jeremy. That poor fucker. I haven't figured him out yet. I know he's nineteen, like Daisy, and one of her longtime friends. Maribel likes talking about her life pre-Mancini. So much so that she mentioned Daisy's old friend, Crew Gallagher, and how he was her best friend, even though Jeremy and she were together. Does Daisy not have any female friends? There has to be a reason why she sticks with the male species. But my current fixation comes from Jeremy and why he is adamant on not fucking his girlfriend.

Maribel smiles and waves to the chairs like there are more than two people in the crowd. I step forward at the same time Daisy does. Her sight drops to my exposed chest where I'd left a few buttons undone. It's what Maribel wanted. "It gives it a beachy vibe." That's what she said, and what the bride wants, the bride gets. I was just happy I didn't have to wear a fucking suit.

Her glossed lips start to open, but I don't wait to hear what she has to say as I start down the aisle. "Asshole," she mumbles to me, grabbing the attention of Jeremy and the old lady I'm supposed to have sex with. I stop, my feet sinking into the dry sand, and turn slowly to face her.

"Have something to say?"

The small bouquet of yellow flowers in her hands gets slammed onto the ground, petals scattering, and Jeremy stands in a panic. I hold up my hand to stop him from whatever he's thinking of doing, which is probably nothing more than shitting his pants. The old lady just sits with a smirk on her face, obviously thinking she's going to get a hate fuck at some point tonight.

Daisy stomps a few steps forward, her larger-than-life personality now in my face. Her scowl is directed right at me. Eyes no longer bright like the sky, but dark like the depths of the Mariana Trench. "You're my problem. You have a stick up your ass. Hot and cold. First, you're knee deep against my cunt, and then you're banging…" Her gaze moves over to my date. "That." Oh. So this is about what's-her-name. I smirk. Games. I play them in the ring. I play them in the bedroom. I love games. Because I win so much more than I ever lose.

I poke a finger into the ball of hair on her head and she slaps my hand away. Hard hit for a girl. She'd still get eaten alive in a fight. "And stop touching me! You're always touching me!" A light shade of pink covers her face and sweat sheens her forehead.

Jeremy's lanky body comes into my peripheral vision. *Always know your opponent's next move.*

Daisy's voice lowers yet still packs a punch. "Why are you always touching me?" This time she's the one to storm away before I can even formulate a response, but not before yanking Jeremy by the sleeve. She stops briefly to scoff at my "date" and mumbles something under her breath. Pulling my cheeks between my molars to stifle a laugh has become a habit around her.

Showing vulnerability is not a practice of mine. When I left the hospital six years ago, I had to learn to show no weakness. To my father, or anyone else in my life, except for Santi. He knows what a crazy fucker my father is. He's offered me a place to stay, to get out of the ring, out from under his thumb. That will only put Santi in the hot seat, though. Another target. Another death.

The only reason I haven't moved out is because of my father and his ongoing threat that he'd kill me as final payment for my mother's death.

"Ready, handsome?" I light up a cigarette and nod to Leanne. "You know, I'd appreciate it if we could keep this between you and me."

"What are you talking about?" I don't bother looking at her

because she's not worth my respect if my father talked her into a one-night stand. Trudging through the sand and back to the house, I hear her huffing behind me, trying to keep up.

She finally does and pulls on the back of my shirt, but pulling on me is a hard no. I spin around fast enough for my cigarette to fall through the panels on the deck. Her lips crash into mine, and stale cigarettes and cheap perfume invades my senses.

She doesn't let go, but wraps her arms around my tighter. *Trapped.*

I grab her wrists behind me and forcefully unlock her locked fingers and push her away. Leanne gasps as I strengthen my grip on her wrists. "Don't touch me. I hate being touched!" I want to yell. To scream. To run. But I can't. I was caught off guard, and now I can't catch my breath as I let go of her to clutch my chest.

"Fuck you, kid!" she grits through her teeth before storming into the house.

She fucking wishes.

I try hard to catch my breath. Head between my legs. In and out but nothing is helping. Being caught off guard is my kryptonite.

I start falling to the ground, grabbing at anything that can keep me upright. A dysregulated nervous system is one of the prices I have paid since my mother's death.

Pinching my eyes shut, I try to picture happy things. Nothing comes to mind. A puppy. Feeding a giraffe lettuce when I was a kid. Going out with my friends to restaurants...well, when I had friends. Nothing seems to be pulling me from this spiral.

"It's all in my head. You're safe. *I am safe.*" *Breathe. Breathe.* Except I can't because suddenly my clothes feel too tight, like they're suffocating me. I need—I don't know what the fuck I need anymore.

A door closes behind me. "Rocco?"

I don't have to look to know who it is, but it still startles me.

"Go...away..." I'm vulnerable. She can't see me like this.

Something hits the deck and her footsteps fall closer. A hand lays on my back moving in circles. "Breathe," she whispers in my ear.

I can't because my lungs feel tight and heavy.

A pink and orange blur crosses my line of sight as she moves me into a chair. Kneeling in front of me, her hands rest on my thighs. "Rocco. Look at me."

My eyes are jumpy and dark. "Follow my breath." Her hand grabs mine and she rests it on her chest. "Feel my breath. Breathe with me." Her skin is soft under my calloused hands. My lungs feel a little less tight as I focus on her inhalations and take a breath of my own.

"Good. Another."

And I do.

I breathe.

Again.

And again.

I finally allow my eyes to open, and they find hers. Filled with familiarity. Her hand rests over mine, still laying on her chest. Still kneeling between my legs, still holding eye contact, my breaths even out. "Does this happen a lot?"

I nod.

"I get them, too. You just have to calm your mind down and breathe. It's hard, but you get used to it." I feel her voice in her chest, and I pull away. Her eyes narrow.

Being anything other than a dick never crosses my mind. I push myself out of the chair and Daisy falls back on her ass. "I don't need your pity."

I descend the steps and head back to the beach, leaving Daisy to cuss me out as I never give her a second glance.

CHAPTER
EIGHT

DAISY

WHAT THE ACTUAL fuck is that dude's malfunction? If I wasn't so appalled at him knocking me on my ass and storming off after I helped him…oh I don't know, not die, I would have gone after him and pummeled his ass to the ground. I would have shown him how I'm just as capable of setting off a panic episode inside of him as much, if not more than what initially had set him off.

I wonder what triggers him?

But instead, I take the high road by posing for the stupid pictures of the wedding party—also known as the new fam sans Rocco—and get on with the show. Jeremy has been tailing me ever since the little kerfuffle with Rocco by the wedding arch. For a split second, I was taken by how he makes me feel. For half a minute, I thought he is exactly the type of man I need in my life. But after his stand-up performance on the deck, I think it's back to square one and the realization that Jeremy checks all of my boxes. Next time I see Rocco, I will be applauding him for his theatrical dramatics that allowed me to realize what an ass he is.

"Hey." I loop my hands through my boyfriend's arms from

behind as he stares off into the darkening sky. Clasping him around the waist, I peek my head around his arm. He's a good seven inches taller than I am, so I feel like I'm playing hide and seek, hiding behind a tree.

"Hi," he answers back. "What did you mean, Daisy?"

Oh. We aren't wasting any time here.

"What are you talking about?" I let go of his waist and wait for him to turn to me.

And he does, but now he's wearing a scowl. This man never wears anything other than a panicked face or a look of complacency. "Damnit, Daisy. Don't play. I hate games. You told Rocco not to touch you."

Internally, I'm screaming. Jeremy is jealous! Or mad that another man is touching *his* woman. I'm biting my lip so hard, I taste blood. If he sees me smiling, he'll think I'm legitimately crazy.

Breathe, Daisy.

By the time I can think of an answer that comes off as more than a question, he speaks first. "Does he hurt you? Hit you?"

Of course. Because God forbid a man wants to touch me because he's attracted to me. My body deflates at his words like a balloon losing all of its helium. My ego is now left to scrape the floor like a mylar gasbag that is left over after a birthday party. "Nope. If he hit me, Jer, I'd cut his dick off."

A smile finds his lips, quick to believe and let go. "That's what I thought." His hands slide into his pockets, and he looks back at the house behind us. "What do you say we head to the party?"

I nod with a tight smile. I don't know what I expect from Jeremy. I mean, I know what I expect, and I think after all of this wedding stuff is over, it's time we have a talk. All I know is that if I were a man, and I had doubts in my head about my woman receiving unwanted attention from another man, I'd lose my absolute shit. But Jeremy isn't a normal man. Jeremy is... Well, I'm still trying to figure that out.

After a few minutes of walking, we make it to the massive

reception tent set up in the sand. I'm sure the neighbors love this. Tony probably paid them off, or maybe he grabbed them while they were spreading cream cheese on their bagels and threatened them. *"Let me use your private beach, or else!"*

I'm still salty about my breakfast.

Fairy lights and lanterns light up about fifty tables filled with faces I've never seen before. Why these people weren't at the actual wedding is beyond me.

Not one person do I recognize, but I do see my award-winning, Hollywood-bound stepbrother. He seems to be filling his lungs just fine with that nasty cigarette hanging from his perfect lips. "These can't be all Mom's friends. The only friend she has is Leanne," I whisper to Jeremy.

He offers me a weak laugh and I ignore it as I peruse the guests. *Speaking of the Devil, where is she?*

Who am I kidding? Leanne's probably sucking off some random guy at the house, or in the car, or deep in some sawgrass that separates the beach from the houses. I never did get a good vibe from her growing up, but I was too interested in being a recluse than being concerned with anyone other than myself.

An over-exaggerated laugh sounds like an alarm as my eyes dart to the criminal. Leanne has my mom in a tight hug close to the bridal table. I eye the number of chairs at said table and thank my lucky stars there are only two. Rocco and I will not be sitting awkwardly next to our unfortunate assigned progenitors.

"Daisy! Come here." My mom's hand flaps in the wind like she's a seal, waving me to her. Except still in the grips of Leanne, they are moving toward me like conjoined twins from a horror movie. I lean toward Jeremy, who was to my left just seconds ago, but it's empty space. His recluse tendencies should probably scare me, but maybe that's the red flag type of behavior I crave from a potential lover that keeps me attached on him.

The conjoined ladies, who are the same damn age might I add, stop in front of me. My mom somehow escaped Leanne's grip before I'm brought into the cougar's embrace. I hate this for me. She smells like a cheap bottle of stripper's perfume, and it's making my nostrils sting and my eyes water. Although, I could only hope that this makeup gets ruined. It's horrendous. I look like Avril Lavigne. While she can pull off the racoon eyeliner from the early 2000s, I cannot. I look like I'm a manic depressed woman who wants to anchor myself to a few bricks and jump off Key Biscayne Bridge.

"Mmmm," Leanne moans in my ear, releasing her fire breath in my direction. That shit lingers like a burning puff of flatulence that escaped in a hot-boxed car. Before she lets go, she rasps in my ear. "You won't tell your mother about my little rendezvous with your brother, will you?" After her rhetorical question, I'm finally let go, and now I smell like a stripper myself. Not the famous ones from that fancy-looking sex store, Hustler Hollywood. The type that's in a sketchy building that used to be a Pizza Hut where the pole is where the kitchen used to be. I've seen a thing or two.

"Where is he?" Her icy blue eyes scan the room, quite similarly like mine did only minutes ago. "Ah!" Her hands touch the sky in excitement and her wings flap in the gentle coastal breeze. I'm going to stand here and pretend my body is perfect, because if there is one thing I've inherited from my mother's side of the family, it is the ability to gain weight in my upper arms before anywhere else. Funny enough, that same weight is the last to drop when I lose some pounds. It's a curse.

Leanne doesn't bother saying anything else to me before wandering over to Rocco, who somehow gets oddly more attractive every time I see him. Her arms wrap around his neck, and I wait for a wince. Or for him to pull her tentacles off of him, yet his face stays stone cold, and she stays suctioned to him.

"Take a seat, hun. The DJ is going to announce the new couple." My mom says it like she isn't half of the couple.

"Right." I scan the tables for Jeremy, hoping we'd be far away from Rocco and Leanne. Alas, we aren't at the same table, but he's facing me from one table over.

"There you are," Jeremy pats the seat next to him. *Chivalry isn't dead, folks.* I sit and Jeremy leans over to me. I think he's reaching for a kiss, and my heart jumps. I pucker my lips and close my eyes before he whispers, "Is that Leanne with your stepbrother?"

Oh, hell. I give up.

Like mom said, the DJ then announced the *happy couple,* and under God's good graces, he didn't call me or Rocco up for a bridal party dance. That would have been awkward as hell. Dinner was served to me and three-hundred-ninety-four strangers next, and Rocco managed to avoid eye contact the entire time, giving me a bit of a complex.

Wanting attention from him versus the attention that I'm getting from Jeremy, which is scarce, is starting to affect my psyche. Is it me? Do I smell? Am I really here? Or did my life just take a terrible turn?

My eyes, however, have been unwavering from him and his date. She tries talking to him, but he ignores her. She talks a lot, but he stays silent.

"Dance with me?" Jeremy's hand lands in front of me, waiting for mine. I glance down at it. Before I put my hand in his, I let my mind wander for just a moment.

What if, for one night, I laid my hand in his, but it wasn't his. It was another man. Dark and broody like me. Eyes so dark with a soul to match. Like mine. Someone who understands the level of hell I go through every day.

To some I may have the perfect life. School's paid for. Car's paid for. I live at home rent free. What more can I ask for? But I do need more. I'm lost and I haven't a clue how to figure out what I want out of life. But I do know living with a helicopter parent is its own special type of hell. I can't be myself to find myself. I have to constantly filter everything that comes out of my mouth. I can't get tattoos, or piercings unless they are my ears; two holes maximum. Broke that rule. Oops. *I can't speak freely about sex around my mother or my boyfriend. It's too taboo. It's as if they are both committed to misunderstanding me. Trying to constantly dim my light. Not that I have much light going for me right now. I was made to return home because of poor grades.*

Every day I wonder if life would be like this if my dad were still around. Would I have chosen the same path. Would I have still ventured off to the other side of the country? Would I have stayed there? Would Jeremy and I even be together? I doubt it since I'm almost one-hundred percent sure we are a couple because of our shared trauma bonding. It's the shit we've been through that holds us together. But maybe that's the only thing that we need. Maybe that is what love is supposed to be.

So, I lay my hand in his as I offer a smile that's so utterly empty and dry, like it's cracking in the Sahara sun. He pulls me onto the dance floor and wraps his hand around my waist. The party is all around us, laughing, drinking, smiling, throwing their hands up like they're dancing to a Bon Jovi song, but in my head, I'm dancing to my own depressing music.

"This one is for all the couples out there." The beat changes and couples pair off. Out of curiosity, and curiosity only, I look over Jeremy's shoulder and find dark brown eyes staring at me. I narrow mine, hoping he can pick up on my telepathy.

Hey, butt munch, nice try pulling the victim card. Next time I'm going to let you suffocate.

The corner of his mouth quirks like he heard my thoughts. For a split second I believe it. I watch as his hand moves slowly down Leanne's back to the top of her ass where he taps twice and whispers in her ear. He pulls her closer by the hand now splayed on her back, and her head tilts to the side like she's inviting him to kiss her neck.

Jealousy courses through me. Not because of those two dimwits, but more so because I'm with my boyfriend of *years,* and we have left enough space between us for Jesus *and* his parents to join in. There's no whispering of how he can't wait to get me out of this dress. No soft kisses planted on my neck or my lips. I feel a single tear slide down my cheek. I wipe it away quickly before I watch Rocco grab Leanne's hand, beeline for the bar, grab a bottle of some adult beverage, and leave the tent with her head thrown back in laughter.

I can't imagine what it's like, someone needing me so badly they can't wait until after a party. Out of nowhere, I feel *my* lungs getting tight. Restricted. I back away from Jeremy.

His eyes bounce between mine and I smile another empty smile. One that will buy me time. "I have to use the restroom. Excuse me."

He simply nods before I run out of the tent. I peel my shoes off and run through the sand, ripping these damn hairpins out while I'm at it.

Running won't help the breathlessness, but it will help the pain.

A sick and twisted game.

With a vengeance, I burst through the back patio door and run upstairs to my bathroom, my dress half off, exposing my strapless bra that's doing a piss-poor job of holding my boobs up. I will be writing a review.

No sooner do I slam the wooden door shut, than I fall to the cold white tile and lie in the fetal position. It's like my mom knew I'd be spending time down here. She knows black grout with white subway tiles is one of my favorite aesthetics.

"Alexa. Play 'Choices' by Kris Bowers." Alexa in my bathroom gives me life. Whether I'm doing my hair, or relaxing in a bath, she's a necessity to feel a little less alone.

I straighten out and lie so my back is against the cold floor. Somehow this helps me feel better. My eyes drift closed, and I start focusing more on my breath. It's not until I feel something touch my leg that I open my eyes. At first they're a little fuzzy, but then a familiar face comes into focus.

I try to sit up, but I can't. I feel stuck.

"Get off!"

His head turns slightly. "I tried, but you're in here panting like a dog." His dark hair is messy, and his shirt is completely unbuttoned.

"Get off of my dress or else!" I spit. His massive shoe is holding the back of my dress down.

He leans closer to me, and my breath hitches. "As much as your 'or else' might scare your perfect little boyfriend, it doesn't scare me." I lift my chin trying to hold my ground, but he's still like a tree next to me. Taking the only air that's left in the bathroom. Trying to be serious, half naked on the bathroom floor, isn't working for me. "Just because our parents are married now doesn't mean I'll treat you like family.

"Right. Because you'd rather choose the town whore to be nice to because she'll suck your dick. Is that it?" I can't help it. I'm not one to slut-shame. If I could be a slut, I would be, but with Jeremy that won't be an option. "You're just another notch on her bed post, but hey—" I raise my arms and let them fall dramatically on my lap. "Maybe she is on yours already."

Rocco's eyes go dark and his eyebrows furrow. I was mistaken before. Now he's taken the rest of the air from the room. I hold his gaze for what feels like eternity with my favorite song still looping in the background. Eventually I allow my eyes to fall down his chest that's lightly dusted with a line of dark hair that trickles down through the valley of his abs leading below the waistline of his dress pants. Of course he has abs. But he is also a canvas of scars; newer red ones and healed white ones.

My eyes move to his again. He doesn't shy away from my gaze or make me feel bad for looking. Instead, his browns hold my blues almost in a dare. Daring me to ask what happened. Daring me to ask him to open his personal Pandora's Box that I can surmise is filled with demons. Lots of them based on the number of scars that riddle his body.

Who are you, Rocco Mancini?

ROCCO

LEANNE IS WASTED and fully naked, waiting for me on my bed right now. I've never been into older women, though, and certainly never invited them to my bed. No offense, but I'm a young stud and I prefer my mare's young too.

When I heard the bathroom door slam and Daisy shout at her Alexa, I knew something was off. Although she is a lunatic, she doesn't loudly flaunt her demons. She pretty much keeps to herself. Or so it seems over these few short days I've been around her.

I needed to make sure she wasn't dying, because if she was, my father would hold that against me. It would no longer be me in a ring. He'd most likely sell me on the black market to wealthy sadists who enjoy torturing and killing their victims.

That shit that they show in movies is child's play compared to the real thing, I'm sure.

Seeing her in a deep sleep on the floor, tits barely contained by the strapless bra she's wearing, it was all I could do not to drag her to her room and take her virginity. The idea of her waking up with my dick inside of her stirs a bunch of fucked-up shit inside me. My dick is rock hard. It hasn't gotten hard without drugs since I was seventeen. After so many blows to the head and bring forced to have sex with women I didn't know, it's been pretty difficult to keep it up.

"Why are you staring at me like that?" She's a spitfire. A spitfire who's afraid to be seen by her mother, yet dresses in all black and runs her mouth enough to stand out.

"If I remember correctly, you were just ogling me." She was looking at my scars. The question was right there on the tip of her tongue. But unlike the other women who give me a look of pity, Daisy's was pure curiosity. I finally give in. Something I'm not used to, but I'm just so damn tired tonight. "Just making sure you're alive. If you end up dead, it will be on me."

She adjusts her bra like it's going to help the overflow. "I'm a big girl. Get back to Leanne. Wouldn't want Mom to figure out what you're up to." She knows, I heard her and *him* talking about how Leanne was my date. Although he left out the fucking part, he sold her on the idea. *"Leanne is lonely. A widow. It may light something inside of her if she was chaperoned by a handsome young man to the wedding."*

I find myself staring at Daisy's lips again before I get up.

"Wait!" A small hand wraps around my wrist, and my searing gaze is so intense that it would make a hole through my skin. I don't bother looking at her in case she asks me something heartfelt. She is a woman after all. "If it's not me, then why won't he touch me?"

I snicker at her naivete. I don't have time for this. There's something more important than dealing with the half-naked woman on the floor. It's now crucial I get Leanne clothed and out of my bed. It's going to take an eternity to remove the stench of her cheap perfume from my mattress.

"Don't ask me. You're not my type. But you know who you can ask? Your boyfriend."

She gasps, now clutching my hand. "Please," she begs, gazing up at me with puppy-dog eyes. Crazy Daisy isn't crazy right now. She's…almost pathetic.

"I didn't know you'd be begging me so soon." I want to say more, but instead I leave, closing the door a little harder than I mean to. I don't need her drama, or for her to look at me like I'm her knight in shining armor.

My footsteps weigh heavy as I move mere feet down the hall. Already I can smell the off-brand perfume from the lady who is starfished across my bed. Dreading the next five to fifteen minutes, I push the door to my bedroom open and it smells like cat piss. Only I don't have a cat.

"Great. Now I have to burn the mattress."

There's no way I'm sleeping in there. And hell will freeze over if *he* finds me sleeping anywhere other than next to her. But opening my door is never a line he crosses.

Maybe…just maybe…

Like a teenager sneaking out of the house, I tread lightly back to Daisy's bathroom. My ear rests gently on the wood as I listen for sounds of life. That same damn song is on loop, and I'm pretty sure I just heard snoring. Great. If she sleeps in there, I can leave her bed before she wakes up and Tony will be none the wiser.

I grin to myself for my own little win. Any win outside of the ring is few and far between when it comes to that man. I'll take what I can get.

CHAPTER
TEN

DAISY

LAST NIGHT I was so exhausted from my panic attack, I barely made it to my room. After Rocco left me in the bathroom with his oh-so-soothing words (insert loud eye roll here), I sat with my back against the wall, willing myself to continue with this life.

I'm not suicidal. At least I don't think I am. Have I had thoughts of swimming face first into a shark's mouth? Yes. Have I imagined what would happen if I tried flying off the roof of this four-story house that is surrounded by a marble driveway? Also, yes. But those intrusive thoughts are no different than a mom of four seeing a corn field on her right wondering what would happen if she cut a sharp turn into said corn field. I think those are normal feelings. At least that's what I assume.

I wouldn't know. I need therapy—I know this, but can't afford it. My two fleeting sessions where I complained most of the time about how I felt abandoned by my default parent took every extra penny I had earned over my lifetime. There were no lasting effects. I asked my mother if she could foot the bill for the appointments at one point, and she refused. This was before my dad's death. Her answer was always, "Why do you need therapy? We give you everything you need."

One time…that's right, just the one time I answered, "Because of dealing with you." She could probably afford it now being married to Tony, but I won't ask her for anything except for this temporary roof over my head.

Of course, I was gaslit in the typical narcissistic mother kind of way, and I'll never forget her answer as long as I live. "I know! I'm a terrible mother. I was never here for you, right? Tell me how awful I was a little more." It lives rent free in my head every time I think about having a conversation about how well and good she fucked me all the way up. But now that I'm grown and I have no issues standing up to her, it seems as if she's tucked away those tendencies. Or maybe, just maybe, she healed.

That phase of my life did some damage. I'm aware of the slightest mood shifts in the people around me. Reading the energy of a room comes like it's second nature. After that little narcissist spotlight she shone herself in, I refuse to speak about anything of substance with her. No deep conversations. Nothing. But that's beside the point here.

After I contemplated the importance of living another day on the bathroom floor and the value I bring to those around me while resting on the tile, which said value is equivalent to the horse shit used to grow mushrooms, I traipse back to my bedroom. It was dark, thank God.

The only thing that could top this night is seeing Leanne stumbling through the hallway post-sex. *Ew.* Or maybe it's the idea of her post-sex with Rocco that makes it feel like there's a dull knife being twisted in my stomach. I'll chalk it up to being a concerned citizen…for his health, that is.

I stripped naked and laid on my usual side of the bed—the side closest to the door. Anyone who says they sleep on the side farthest away from the door is a psychopath. My phone landed somewhere between the door and the bed, and didn't move until the morning…and neither did I.

———

HERE I AM. The bright Florida sun shining in through the blinds, threatening to raise my vitamin D levels because I was careless enough not to close the curtains.

A semi-familiar scent wafts across my face, and I pinch my brows trying to place it. *Is that Rocco?*

I fly up, tits bouncing side to side, and look around. Even if he's hiding somewhere in my room, I'd be able to see him. And I doubt he'd hide in the walk-in closet like a stalker. He would certainly get an eye-full, though.

"Hello?" I say quietly. I wait. Listen for a noise. Breathing. Anything.

"What the hell is wrong with me." Another eye roll.

I lie back down and shift to the center of the bed on my stomach and that's when it hits. Shoving my nose in the other pillow, I inhale like a police dog sniffing out a criminal.

Was he in my bed?

I sniff a little harder, like a legitimate Belgian Malinois. Rolling out of bed has never been less strenuous than when I'm seeing red. The only other time I've been this mad in the morning is when Jeremy and I first got together, and I had a dream he cheated on me with Melissa Winters. My enemy from fifth grade. She moved away the year after, but that trauma never died. She pantsed me during our chorus concert, and my crush, Tanner Lee, never spoke to me again.

I rolled out of bed, threw on clothes and stomped all the way to Jeremy's house demanding answers. And that's what's about to go down. Except I'm not demanding answers from my boyfriend. I'm demanding answers from the man who has my brain turned into a dumpster fire. I grabbed a bobby pin in case I have to pick his lock.

Not bothering to close my door, I tip-toe less than fifteen steps down the hall, and what do you know, his door is locked.

"I was born for this," I say to myself as I stick the small pin into the knob to pick his lock. "You want to break in my room? Well, I'll break into yours right back!" I mumble to myself. The metal's in the hole, but it keeps slipping from where it needs to twist.

Just when I think I have it, the door flies open and he's standing in front of me completely naked, cupping his dick with his hand. I swallow hard.

"What the fuck do you think you're doing?" His face is hard. Well, so is his dick, but I look away. "Are you trying to break into my room?"

"More like spy," I admit. What's the use in hiding it? I drop my eyes down to his crotch and bring them hesitantly back to his. "Not like it's *hard* or anything." I smirk and he scowls.

Families tease each other like this all the time, right?

"Spy with a hair pin?" His mouth falls even more before his jaw tics under the overgrown scruff on his face. The scars on his body are on full display. Almost illuminated one by one from the light in the hallway.

Fighting for every inch of my dignity, I hold up the bobby pin. "Call me Inspector Gadget." Still no smile…from either of us.

I take a whiff of his room, and just as I thought, it smells of Leanne Dobbs and Jenna Jameson's perfume I bought at a sex store once. The stench makes me want to vomit. I cover my nose and mouth with the sleeve of a hoodie I threw on and gag. "Smells fucking foul in here."

"No shit. Now get out."

"Aw. Don't be like that, *big brother.*" I push into his room. This wasn't my intention, but he makes me want to punch him in the stomach. Something about the energy Rocco gives off is both unforgiving and border-line depressing.

I stop to look around his room. He has a black accent wall and has hung paintings. One is black and white that looks like an abstract open wound with dark red blood leaking from the side. It's actually quite beautiful.

The wind is knocked out of me before I can register what has just happened. His inked hand that was covering his dick seconds ago is around my neck, and once again, I'm pushed against the wall next to the door.

"You aren't an angel. You're batshit crazy. Crazy Daisy suits you better," he snarls in my face. I almost expect some foul morning breath, but this man breathes out fucking cookies and butterflies. He probably shits unicorns. But he will not get away with calling me 'crazy'.

I shove him with every ounce of strength I have, and he laughs in my face. His stupid crooked smile and straight teeth. Why can't he have a snaggle tooth and cigarette-stained teeth? Because God has a messed-up sense of humor. That's why.

"Don't call me crazy!" I try to push him once more, but he doesn't budge. He's like a rock—no, a boulder—and pushing him hurt my wrist.

My eyes fall to his mouth where his tongue is slowly moving over each upper tooth as if he's contemplating his next move. "Oh. Does *crazy* hit a nerve?" He lets out a deep laugh before he pushes into me. His hard length is pushed against my lower belly. "You know what would be crazy? If I fucked you, *little sister.*"

I swallow hard, but don't let him see me falter.

"This escalated quickly, *brother.* What's wrong? Couldn't finish the deal with Leanne, so you trap me in your room to use me instead?" I grit out. I'm pissed, but I'm so fucking turned on. Both of us stare at each other. Maybe we're measuring the fragility of the situation if we did cross some type of line. Or maybe we hate each other so much, it's more of a war of the minds—who will be the one to crack first.

The pressure around my neck gets a little tighter before his other hand grazes up my thigh.

"I don't know, Crazy Daisy. I think the idea of me using you turns you on." His knuckles move at a snail's pace. So slow yet my brain is trying to catch up.

Do we want this, Daisy?

I try shoving him one more time, but his hand finds me drenched through my cotton shorts and he tries to stifle a moan. His forehead falls to the wall next to my head.

"You'll never fuck me, Rocco. That would be sick!"

His wide gaze finds mine once he pushes away from me, leaving me planted to the wall. "I said get the hell out of here! Now!" he roars, and for a second I think he's going to lunge at me, but he doesn't. He spins like a cat falling from a building and punches the floor.

The crack of his knuckles is enough to make my stomach weak, but not him. His fingers stretch wide before he storms off into his bathroom, slamming the door behind him.

My breath is ragged. "What the hell just happened?"

I tuck my tail between my soaked thighs and run back to my room. Not because I'm scared, but because I've never been so turned on in my entire life, and I'm not sure if I should masturbate to thoughts of him or cry.

———

TWO WEEKS HAVE PASSED by slowly and holy shit, it has been b-o-r-i-n-g. Rocco has been MIA, and Tony and Mom have been aimlessly buying new wardrobes for their month-long honeymoon in Barbados. One month, day in, day out on vacation with the same person. It sounds wretched, but whatever floats their boats. Tony and I haven't had any other run-ins mostly because when I see his car out front, I avoid common areas…like the entire downstairs of the house. Not once has my mother asked why she's seeing less of me. It's not like I'm taking online classes for the spring semester. Or working. Or selling my body on the streets.

Jeremy has been around, but he's been…off. Part of me is

saying cut him free, but the other part of me is holding on to him like he's my only lifeline.

What I really need to do is make some friends, which has been an ongoing issue since middle school. I had one good friend all through high school aside from Jeremy.

Crew Gallagher. And while Crew—or Galley, as I would call him—was my best friend, we lost contact after I left for UCLA. I didn't have girlfriends. I always found them to be either fake or annoying. This leaves me here in this small surf town of Briny Breeze, friendless, and some would say lonely with only my boyfriend who acts more like a gay friend. And no, in my heart I know that he is not gay.

"Jer, will you pass me the pepper?"

I grab the pepper he's handing me with a napkin. I'm not sure why, but it's almost gospel for diners to have sticky condiment bottles. As if they let children douse their hands in maple syrup and have a run of the place before they open at six in the morning.

I've held the conversation to this point. I even told Jeremy about getting a job at the public library. I mean, I won't be a librarian, but I will be selling coffee at the store connected to it, and that's close enough.

"So…I think we should talk." Jeremy's pretty eyes find mine and I can't help but get nervous. Does he know I had a dick that wasn't his on my clothed belly the morning after the wedding? Does he know I masturbate almost daily—okay, sometimes twice a day—to that moment in Rocco's bedroom when he rubbed my clit briefly through my shorts?

I shove a fork full of egg in my mouth because what makes someone appear less guilty and more 'I don't give a shit' than talking with a mouth full of food? "Oh yeah? What's up?"

Jeremy holds eye contact with me as he takes a slow sip of his water with lemon.

"I think you know." His Adam's apple bobs up and down as he swallows over and over.

I shake my head. "Huh-uh." More food into the mouth, except this time it's a whole strip of bacon.

"You want more from me," he starts, then pauses before looking around. "You know s-e-x." A flutter ignites in my stomach like butterflies are flapping, ready for takeoff.

"This is what we've been waiting for," I think to myself, like my other seven personalities care that horny me gets laid.

I finish chewing and give him my full mouth. No pun intended.

"I've been meaning to talk to you about this, but I didn't want to scare you away." I lean as close as I can. I wish we weren't across the table from each other; otherwise, I could teach him a lesson in public play. Something that gets my lady parts heated and ready.

Instead of leaning closer, though, he backs up so he's leaning against the padding of the booth. "You won't scare me away, but I think we need to have this talk." Before I can say anything, he grabs my hand that's practically next to his plate. If I were leaning any farther over the table, my boobs would be laying in my over-easy eggs. "I love you, Daisy. And I've been so afraid to take it to the next step. We've been so good up to this point."

He takes a deep breath like he's waiting for me to save him. "I love you too, Jer. And yes, it's frustrating being a virgin at my age, but I guess at least we're in this together?" It comes out as more of a question, and I'm not sure why. Talking to other people annoys me, and usually I'm dubbed as a sarcastic bitch, but I can't be that way to Jeremy. He's seen every part of me. Well, almost. More than anyone else.

Jeremy still doesn't say anything, but he takes a big bite of his breakfast sandwich.

"So..." At this point, he has me nervous as I imagine all the ways he could shoot me down. Not that I'm not used to it. I've been denied about three dozen times. Yes, I'm keeping a rough tally sheet in my head. I roll the straw paper around between my fingers. "Would you, like, *want* to have sex?" Keeping my voice down is a challenge considering how blood is bolting through my veins. Usain Bolt, that Jamaican Olympic track star, has nothing on my pulse right now.

His eyes narrow at my question and he swallows. Not sure if it's the half-masticated bite in his mouth or because he's nervous, but he nods.

Wait. He nodded. A nod is as good as a 'yes'!

"Really?!" I squeal, but hurry and lower my voice after offering a few sets of eyes an apologetic smile. "I mean, I'd love that, Jeremy. My mom is leaving with Tony in a couple of days, and like I mentioned before, Rocco is never home."

Jeremy smiles his beautiful, perfect smile and I can't help but smile back. Everything with him is finally about to be right. And bringing up my mishap in Rocco's bedroom a couple of weeks ago would be a major setback. But I'm having an internal existential issue. It's not the fact of whatever is going on between me and Rocco happened, but why isn't it eating me alive? Why do I not feel guilty? Am I the narcissist? Have I been emotionally neglected so much in my life, I don't know what a healthy relationship looks like? My life is full of unanswered questions.

"Good. Then it's settled." He takes another bite of a sandwich after his declaration, and I make a vow to myself.

What's happened with Rocco up to this point will never happen again. He's family now. And that's where anything between us ends.

CHAPTER
ELEVEN

DAISY

TO BE BORN into a generation when MTV actually played music videos would have been ideal. I've heard all about them from my mom—an almost forty-year-old woman who used to be cool, wore all the latest fashion trends, and had the hottest skater boyfriend. Her words, not mine. And although she wasn't a brainless cheerleader like the girls in my school, she was popular.

She had me at nineteen, so it's almost like we've grown up together. "Never in my life did she make me feel like I ruined her life by being born," I mumble over my mouth full of popcorn watching reruns of *Teen Mom*. "Until I learned what the three personality traits of the dark triad was, then I questioned everything."

"Well, we're leaving." I jump at my mom's voice as I turned to her. She's decked out in a floor-length sundress, which she has never owned, and a hat that could be worn at the Kentucky Derby, smiling like she's about to get railed for a month straight.

I check the clock on the wall that sometimes ticks louder than the TV, which should be investigated. If it's from an antique shop, beach house style be damned, it might be haunted. And that's not the type of story I'm looking to be a part of.

"I thought you said your flight was at six? It's not even noon." Her smile falls. Oh no. I hope she didn't take that as I wanted her around longer. What's that saying—curiosity killed the cat? Although she exudes confidence, that's not always the case. Anyone can make this woman second-guess her decisions despite her narcissistic tendencies. "Not that I'm concerned. Just thought I'd follow your flight online...make sure you made it there and all." *Lie.*

Another smile. "You're sweet. Will you be okay?" *Did she just ignore the question?*

Tony steps in the room, demanding all the attention. Seriously, if that man doesn't get stopped and searched by customs, I'll be surprised. "You'll barely know Rocco's here. It'll be like having a house to yourself for a month," Tony chimes in while his hands snake around my mom's waist. She beams up at him like he hung the moon. "All we ask is you don't throw any parties."

"No offense, guys, but since I've been home, have you seen me with anyone who isn't Jeremy?" I ask flatly. Are they that self-absorbed? Or am I just doing a fantastic job of hiding myself in the shadows?

Tony shrugs, grabs my mom's luggage, and exits stage left.

My mom walks closer to me like she's about to force us to have a moment and I side-eye her. "I wanted to talk to you about Jeremy. We never had *the* talk."

"Ahh!" I hold up my hand. "Trust me. There's *nothing* to worry about on that front." *Yet.*

Now it's her turn to side-eye me. A puff of air escapes her mouth and her shoulders fall, which makes me curious. Does she think Jer and I are banging on every surface like a bunch of hormone-sick teenagers? The audacity. "Thank goodness. Well, on that note, I left some money in your room for food. Just don't spend it all at once." After a tap on the shoulder, and a quick kiss on my cheek, she's gone.

I never told her I got a job at the local library. I don't want her to stop by the only place I enjoy going that isn't my house. It's somewhere that will be my sanctuary. Plus, she wouldn't care. She has Tony now, and I have many years worth of closeted narcissistic abuse to sort out. I plan on using this house as shelter, her money for food, and my money for therapy so I can get the hell out of here and heal. Or maybe I'll skip the therapy, buy a small shack in Jamaica, and become a local. That alone sounds healing.

Six hours later, give or take, the front door slams and heavy footsteps trudge through the foyer. I don't need to turn around. I'm assuming it's Rocco. If it's not, I can only hope whoever or whatever it is makes it quick. I'm not opposed to dying, but I am opposed to pain. I'm not saying I give off a heap full of positive energy, but when he walks in the room, the air shifts. It's heavy—almost sad. "What are you watching?" his voice rumbles from behind me.

I look around the living room, because I'm pretty sure this "non-grumpy" man standing here is not Rocco, and if it is, it's not me he's talking to.

"You talking to me?" I'm sure he can see the confusion written all over my face because his crooked smile deepens as he walks toward me. Toeing the heel of each boot, he kicks them to the side before sitting on the cushion next to me. He smells like cinnamon and mint. Strange combination tonight.

I decide to answer him because honestly, I'm not sure what else to talk to this man about. "*Teen Mom.*"

He hums, chewing on the pad of his thumb. "We should order some pizza." His gaze is fixed on the ocean outside of the window behind the television, but I'm not buying what he's selling. He's trying to kill me. He wants to poison me. It will be made to look like an accident and my mom will believe every lying, filthy word that comes out of his stupid, sexy mouth.

I don't get a chance to answer because an obnoxious ding comes from my phone. It's almost as loud and unpleasant as the horn doorbell we have bellowing through the house every time we get a package. And it's only when we get packages because everyone knows none of us have friends who come and visit. My mom only loves herself, Rocco is never here, I'm a recluse, and well, Tony… I'm still figuring that one out.

Another ding.

"You going to answer?" Rocco's dark eyes land on the lit screen between us and back at me.

"Whoever it is, it isn't important." The look on my face must still show the skepticism of why exactly he's here…with me…in this room…alone.

"So, pizza? Thought we could hang out over a pie. And I was looking forward to getting to know you without the 'rents being around." He taps my head, and I swear it echoes inside my brain. "What." *Tap.* "Makes." *Tap.* "Daisy." *Tap.* "Tick." *Tap.*

"Why are you in such a good mood?" Another ding reminder that I have a text waiting. Dammit. I don't want to break whatever this is between us, but this annoying phone won't let me concentrate. So, I tap the screen to read the text, which is equivalent to walking into the gyno's office. You hope it's just routine, but you never know what you're in for once you get in there.

"Don't get used to it. And definitely don't point it out. You'll ruin it," he says in a low, gravelly voice. It's almost like the cigarettes gave him the sexy voice and somehow, he dodged the bad breath and gross teeth part of being a smoker.

I allow my eyes to leave his to finally read over Jeremy's text.

> Jeremy: Want to hang out tonight? Or would you rather tomorrow?

Once again, nothing tingles inside of me when I imagine Jeremy seducing me. He'd never pin me to anything, would he? I guess I won't know until I find out. Perhaps I'm terrified to learn my boyfriend is vanilla and loves missionary. But I guess something's better than nothing.

"So…the pizza? What do you want on it?" Rocco swipes his phone, checking toppings.

Time to test this man's character. "Pineapple."

His long finger stills on the screen and his dark brown eyes move to me like he's ready to fuck me or kill me. We have had several of these moments, and I'll be damned if I don't point them out to myself. I should start keeping a tally sheet in my Notes app.

"'Kay." Moment over. *'Kay?* Like he's cool with pineapple on pizza? Maybe he really is as deranged as I am. "It will be here in forty minutes." He takes my phone from my hand and stacks it on top of his before laying them on the coffee table. "What ever shall we do for forty minutes?" His voice is suggestive, but I don't flinch. He has an obvious flirty side to him, and if I'm being honest with myself, I gave up on flirting with Jeremy because I subconsciously knew that it wouldn't get me anywhere. I don't know how to flirt. I think.

"I know what I'm going to do." I turn toward him, my knee bent between us, brushing his upper thigh. I tap his head like he did mine a minute ago. "I'm going to find out what makes Rocco tick." Mr. Silent is talking right now so I need to use this time wisely.

"Good luck, Angel." His face is unfair. He probably uses a stupidly delicious smelling 3-in-1. If a woman uses a shampoo, conditioner, body wash all in one, we have dry skin in places that are usually hydrated, and zits in places we don't want them. Not to mention how flat our hair gets. It's truly unfair.

Rocco chews the inside of his cheek that accentuates his lips even more than they already are. I wonder if they are strong when he kisses. *Mmmm.* Or maybe they're fluffy and limp. *Oof! That would suck.*

"Back to Angel, I see. What happened to 'Crazy Daisy'?" The

not-cute nickname brings my internal anger to a boil. It's zero to sixty real quick with that moniker.

"Don't act crazy, don't get called crazy. But nothing about you is…normal," he says as he kicks his feet up on the coffee table.

"I could say the same thing about you. So?" I lean forward like a dog waiting for a treat. "Tell me something."

Rocco doesn't bother backing away; in fact, he leans a little closer. To the naked eye it may seem like he stayed in his spot, but from where I am, even millimeters of movement toward me ignites some internal flame that seems to be reserved solely for him.

"I don't go to school. I used to play football. And now I don't."

I'm probably staring at him, but I refuse to move. I won't settle for a modicum of information when he has an entire twenty-one years of life I don't know about. "Although I appreciate the three-sentence debrief of your life, I was hoping for more of an evening tour of your psyche."

His bottom lip practically disappears between his teeth, causing his thin soul patch to come front and center. I heard some guys refer to that spot as "flavor savers" and I've never been able to erase that from my memory. The lip reappears as fast as it leaves. "Nope. That's all you get. But it's my turn."

I don't get nervous. I get excited, and not the giddy type, the dangerous type. I know the demons that each of us have stem from different places. To him I'm sure mine seem so much lighter than his, but he hasn't dug deep enough. Nobody has ever taken the time to break out the shovel and continue the job.

"Hit me with your best shot," I challenge him.

"I plan to." He gets closer, our mouths centimeters apart. I think he's going to kiss me until I feel him reach behind me for the remote and returns to his original spot. Space is welcomed between us when he mutes the volume and tosses the remote over his shoulder.

"Does your precious boyfriend get you off?" The room is only lit by the TV screen and a dull lamp on the other side of the room, but just like his very intimate question, his eyes are lethal. Dark. Feral.

"Why? Are you going to do the job for me?" I won't back down.

His lips quirk at the ends briefly. "I hear you…all alone in your room, moaning. It's almost like you want me to hear you."

"It's my room. I can *come* and go as much as I want." I raise a brow.

You're playing with fire, Rocco. I have years' worth of pent-up sexual frustration. I'm going to take a wild guess and say the orgasms I give myself are nothing like the real thing.

The ticking of the clock gets louder as we sit there showered in tense silence. "You never answered my question," his voice comes out deep, an almost whisper.

"Ask me the question again." I know the question, but I need to bide my time.

"Does your boyfriend…" My gaze falls to his mouth as he enunciates each word, slowly. "Get you off? Does he fuck you well enough that your legs shake, and you beg him to stop because it feels like you might die if he doesn't?"

And of course, he already knows the answer. He heard Jeremy at dinner the night I moved in. In the short time since I've been back, Jeremy won't step foot past the first step that leads to my bedroom. In fact, if my mom or Tony isn't home, he won't come over at all.

But the proverbial tide is turning. If our conversation at breakfast was any indication of what's to come, it's going to be me and him in my bed within the next few days.

"No. He doesn't. But that's all about to change." I swallow, unable to read Rocco's facial expression.

"Good to know. I'll invest in some earplugs. The last thing I want to hear is the clanking of chains that are binding you to our adjoined wall." He stands abruptly and heads toward the back door that leads to the beach. "On second thought… Jeremy seems like the type who enjoys missionary. Or maybe dudes."

"Wait… Where are you going?" I shout after him. Who have I become? Shouting after a man? *That* will never happen again.

"I changed my mind. I'm not hungry." The door slams behind me, leaving me alone with his words echoing in my head. *Does your boyfriend get you off?...*

It's official. I hate him.

———

NOT EVEN TWO HOURS LATER, Jeremy is here in my foyer. I aggressively texted him back after I ate a shit ton of pineapple-topped pizza *alone.*

I'll be sure to be extra loud just for Rocco.

"Should we…" I gesture to the stairs, and he nods. He slips off his Sperry boat shoes, leaving him in his no-show socks.

"Uh. Yeah." The nervousness in his voice is that of a child walking into the principal's office. His voice is shaky and quiet while his steps are light behind me. If he thinks we are keeping those socks on, he's got another thing comin'.

"Here it is! My humble abode." I wave my arm into my room, inviting him in. He barely takes a step inside. Yep. His feet are positioned with one on the carpet in my room and the other on the wooden planks in the hallway.

I step into the center of my room, allowing the new puppy to get used to his surroundings. Seriously, is this how it's supposed to be the first time? Awkward? Unsure? Is the guy supposed to be this skittish?

I scroll through my phone finding my "Sex Playlist" on Spotify and press play. "Sugar" by Sleep Token starts playing, and Jeremy finally steps in the room.

"I don't really like Sleep Token," Jeremy practically mumbles, playing with his fingers. I swear I hear a scoff coming from the hallway, but I ignore it because Rocco isn't home.

Jeremy starts unbuttoning his short-sleeve dress shirt and winces as he stares at the speakers like the actual band is in the corner of my room, serenading us during our first time fornicating. It's obvious that he's disgusted at my taste in music as much as I'm disgusted with his choice of apparel.

I would lay my hand on the Bible when I say this…if I owned a Bible…if Sleep Token's lead singer, Vessel, was in my room, I'd kick Jer right the fuck out. He's my hall pass.

That aside, what the fuck? Who doesn't like Sleep Token?

"Okay? What about…" I swipe…and swipe… "Oh! Here's a good one!"

I turn on one of my favorite songs by Cheyanne called "One Night." It's the slower version. Perfect to put this guy into the mood—or at least put his mouth to better use than hating on my music choices.

"I guess." He folds his shirt in half and lays it on the back of my desk chair.

"How about before we start undressing, we kiss a little bit?" I pull my bottom lip between my teeth, trying to flirt, yet offer some guidance to make this entire encounter a little more natural. I'm giving him options, but instead of feeling sexual, it's feeling more like I'm coercing a toddler to tell me what he wants to eat for breakfast.

Another nod. This is painful. I walk over to him, using my foot to kick the door shut.

Jeremy's taken his shirt off despite my request and lies back on my bed, propping himself up on his elbows. His body is perfect. He works hard on it. In high school, we used to work out together at the gym before I stopped going. What's the use of having a tight little body if Jeremy's not gawking at it like he wants to devour me?

I know. *Do it for me. Blah, blah, blah.*

"Jer. You're so sexy, babe," I say as I pull my shirt over my head.

He frowns at the name 'babe'. Over the years I've refrained from calling him anything but his name because he hates it. He always says 'babe' reminds him of the pig movie.

I'm also trying not to read into the fact that I exposed my chest and he frowned. It was just the name that caused that reaction. Just the word "babe."

I crawl over him and straddle his hips. Leaning forward, I run my tongue along his lips and he grows hard under me. *Yesss!* The feel of him pushing against me shoots through my loins like a bullet. I take notice that the blankets are in disarray around us, and if he sees those, I'll be thrown from him so fast in order that he can straighten them. So, like anybody in a panic, I stretch to the side of the bed and turn off the lamp.

His hands grab onto my hips as I position myself back on him and I start grinding as our kisses get more intense.

"Jer. This is…oh. This feels so good." He must need encouragement! Maybe that's all he's needed this whole time. Perhaps praise is his love language!

My body is flung to the mattress in record speed. Being manhandled in bed is a surefire way to get in my pants, but he knows that. We've talked about it. Well, I've talked about it, and he awkwardly listened while petting his dog Pumbaa.

The gyration of his hips is that of a hippopotamus swirling a hula hoop around her waist…fully clothed.

Yes. We're still wearing clothes on our bottom halves. I'm not sure if he knows to take his pants off at this point, or if he thinks he's pushing his khaki cargos inside of me.

I tap his shoulder, trying not to ruin the moment too much. "Jeremy, let's take these off." My hands move to the button of his shorts, and he jumps.

"I can't! I'm sorry, Daisy!" Jeremy rubs his hands up and down his face aggressively. "I don't want you to break up with me because I can't have sex with you." He rolls to the side, falling onto the bed dramatically. If I didn't know any better, I would think he's crying.

"I was close. What you were doing was working…I mean, if you want, I can get on top? It's not unheard of." I'm not sure how I can convince him that sex is normal. And that I fucking need it before my insides explode. Okay, I'm being dramatic now, but I do. I need it. I'm in a constant state of horniness. I just need a quick fix. One hit. Then I can deal with the fallout.

"No. I don't think it's going to happen at all."

The air gets sucked out of me. "Wha—So you *can't* have sex with me. Why can't you? Just help me understand!" I feel mentally fucked right now. He won't have sex with me, but he wants me to stay with him. I can't imagine losing him, but personally, I find that intimacy is an important part of a relationship.

I turn to look at him, but he's turned away. I lay my hand on his shoulder, and I fight a battle on whether I want to scream at him out of anger or cry because of how insecure and confused I feel. So I whisper, "Jeremy…"

I nudge him lightly. "I can't do this anymore. Us," I say into his back, staring into the dark of night. I want to ask why he's against exploring more intimacy with me. But every time we had a conversation in the past, he would shut down. Now is not the time to have this talk. No good comes from having serious conversations past nine at night—or at least that's what my grandmother used to tell me.

"I can't either. I can't have sex with you. Ever," he mutters. There it is. I wait for it. For the pounding of my heart. The tears. *Nothing.* He rolls over to face me and grabs my hand. Even though it's dark, I can make out his eyes. They are wide open, staring at me. "We grieved our fathers together. We cried together for weeks, holding each other, being each other's rock." His voice cracks and I hear him swallow hard. "Out of respect, I can't have sex with you. They would have wanted me to protect you. Not defile you. I can't take advantage of your virtue, Daisy. I tried…" His voice breaks. "I tried and failed. I'm so sorry."

I don't push the conversation but pull him into a hug while he cries against me. His tears fall onto my arm and it brings me back to those nights where we comforted each other. Crying in each other's arms knowing we will never be able to hug our fathers again. Or him never being able to throw a baseball with his dad. Or how I'd never be able to walk in the door and him ask me how my day was at school. Or those nights I couldn't sleep; I'd find my dad in the kitchen warming up leftovers and he'd always save some for me. We'd stay up late, staying quiet so we didn't wake mom. He'd tuck me in, and I fell fast asleep.

Am I that broken that I don't feel anything about this sudden break-up? Am I damaged enough to be so selfish that I never thought about how he felt or what he wanted? My attachment must have been trauma related. Perhaps I never really love-loved him. Not like a girlfriend is supposed to love a boyfriend.

Jeremy pulls away and kisses the tip of my nose. "I should go," he whispers. And there it is. One tear. Then two. I wipe them quickly, ashamed of my weakness and vulnerability. *Pull yourself together, Daisy. This day was coming. He knew it. And deep down I knew it, too.*

Finding myself on my back again maybe an hour or two later, I debate whether or not to take care of the ache between my legs. The idea of finishing the job myself is spiraling me into a dark headspace. So, in an effort to skip the spiral, I flick on some Sleep Token and wait for it to lull me to sleep. It never comes. Instead, I toss and turn, and wonder if Jeremy was using our father's death to get out of this? Is it me? *It's not you.*

The smell of him has invaded my room and it's playing tricks on me. What was once the soft scent of pear is now invaded with Ralph Lauren's newest line.

I push the covers off, roll out of bed, and slowly make my way to the door. My brain is telling me "no," but the throb between my legs is begging for a release. What does being properly fucked mean? What does real pleasure from a man feel like?

As if I floated, I'm standing in a pitch-black room, only lit from the light sneaking in from the gap at the bottom of the door I just closed.

Rocco's room.

I kneel on his bed, trying not to shake it, both hoping he's in here and hoping he isn't.

I must be losing my mind. This is what it feels like, right? To want something so bad it hurts. That you would stop at nothing to get it no matter who you hurt along the way.

The Daisy who lurks in the shadows finally rears her ugly head. I've been wondering when she would take over. The girl who doesn't give a shit about repercussions, but just wants the hit of dopamine. Hours after breaking up with a man, warming another man's bed.

A rush of air moves past my face, and before I can blink, I'm pinned down to his bed. He straddles my hips and has my wrists in a one-hand vise grip by my stomach.

"What the fuck do you think you're doing in here?" Rocco growls, and I hear his sheets ruffle. "Are you naked?!"

Great. All I need right now is to disappoint another man.

His free hand moves from my stomach, up over my breast, before he pinches my nipple…hard.

"Oh, God." I try to not be affected. But the pain feels so fucking good. There is no holding back for me. This is it. I need this. I need to feel something and not anything at all.

The feel of his skin on mine has every sense heightened. When two dark entities collide, there is no light that's needed.

"You like not answering me, don't you?" His breath moves across my face. "What's wrong? Boyfriend couldn't get you off?" A few of his breaths skate over my skin. "Knew it. I could hear your disappointment from here." I squirm under him. "So you come over to my room, to what? What do you want me to do to you when your boyfriend's in the next room?" I smile knowing he can't see me. And I certainly don't bother telling him Jeremy left. Rocco's like me; we both find the thrill in indulging in something we can't have.

He sits up before slapping my lower belly with his hard dick. "You in the mood to play, Angel? Coming over here naked to find out what all the hype's about with your stepbrother."

"Don't flatter yourself." I try to keep my dignity intact, but him straddling me like this, it's hard to concentrate on anything other than the feel of him on every part of my body.

His weight on me feels so good. The weight of a man who is showing me something other than pity. "Mmm. You're not an angel. You're *dead* inside just like I am. But I'm about to bring you back to life."

The weight of him lifts from me as he shifts to the side, but I can't calculate his next move.

Without a warning, his finger slowly slides through my arousal, pushing over my clit, and my body arches into him. The feeling's foreign. Addictive. I've never been touched by anyone but me, and to say I want more is an understatement.

"Fuck," he grunts as he pushes a finger inside of me and I lose any sense of mental clarity that's been hanging on. My morals—that were hanging on by a thread—have flown out the window.

His thumb circles over my swollen bundle of nerves, causing my hips to buck underneath him. "Rocco, I'm going to—" Before I can say "come," he pulls away so abruptly, my head is spinning with more than arousal.

"You are absolutely not about to finish. I only use women for *my* pleasure. They don't use me." A rush of blood travels to my legs after he rolls away from me and storms toward his bathroom in the dark. "Now get the hell out of my room."

I allow myself a minute to come off of the first almost orgasm given to me by someone other than myself. It's pathetic. Lines were blurred in the last few minutes, and I don't give a shit anymore.

Is this what rock bottom feels like, or did I just break out the shovel myself and dig a little deeper?

DAISY

I WOULD RATHER DO the walk of shame through a college campus in my slutty Halloween costume than walk naked, vagina dripping, and morally distraught from one bedroom to another. Nothing screams potential existential meltdown like those vulnerable steps where everyone is looking at you. Not to mention the angel on your shoulder cussing you out, while the devil on the other one is patting you on the back.

Sleep was a solid miss last night. Instead, I focused on how my conversation with Jeremy would go. Every time my mind would drift to the boy next door, I got pissed and then turned on. This vessel is a traitor.

Fortunately, my room is filled with hues of gray and green, which tones down the harshness of the morning light, which I'm thankful for. Opening my eyes in a bright room after a night of semi-adultery will only make me hate myself even more. Swimming into that shark's mouth isn't an intrusive thought for much longer. It's time to make some plans.

———

A WEEK GOES by without any word from Rocco. I'm not sure if he's even staying at the house anymore. As for my mother, I've gotten one call letting me know what they're up to and that— lucky for them—they may extend their stay, or head to Turks and Caicos.

Rich people.

But I have my new day job keeping me busy. So far it's been just me and an old guy named Jim who spent his life as a librarian. Since I'm the only employee able to work daytime hours at the café, Jim and I have seen a lot of each other.

Many slow hours are passed listening to him talk about his late wife, Bertha, and how they used to live in a house that was part of the Underground Railroad.

"Hey, girlie. Are you sure you're okay closing for me this week?" Elle, my co-worker, has been planning an intense, one-week hiking trip with her boyfriend somewhere in the Appalachian Mountains

"I'm sure. Have fun." I smile, wiping down the counter. The most monotonous task I've been assigned, but getting paid close to twenty dollars an hour, it's worth it.

"I'll tell you all about our outdoor sexcapades in the woods," she jokes, grabbing her purse from the cubby.

I shiver out of pure hatred when sex is mentioned now. "Please don't." I toss the dirty rag in the bucket on the floor and watch my co-worker saunter out the door as happy as a lark.

Hanging mugs in patterns from hooks on the back wall has become my new favorite form of OCD. The café has such a hippie vibe. Coffee, tea, and books adds to the theme, and the place is overrun by plants—which I'm obsessed with—and is why it's so popular. Regulars say it's like being outside without the dreadful South Florida heat and pesky mosquitoes.

Almost my entire closing checklist is finished. Just a few more things and I can call this day productive. *I'm so fucking pathetic.*

"Should I hang the handles from the left or the right?" I prop my chin on my fist, deep in thought. If anyone would have told me when I was a kid that I would concentrate so hard on how to hang mugs, I would have laughed in their faces.

"I think it would look better from the left."

I jump at the low, unfamiliar voice, dropping a mug in the process. "Shit." Kneeling on the hard, gross tile, I start picking up the pieces. If this isn't a metaphor for my life, I don't know what is.

"Here. Let me help." The man whom I have yet to look at comes around the counter to help. He kneels in front of me, and I dare myself to look at him. His blonde hair is slicked back, almost like Draco Malfoy's, and his eyes are dark. Almost black. Not dark brown with a mix of red like Rocco's. This man's eyes are filled with danger. *Death.* Forget the Mancinis, this man will bring the worst of them to their knees, and not with good looks and money, but maybe a gun and a curb stomp.

"You shouldn't be back here." I've become even more of a recluse. Anything that involves having to deal with people other than taking orders and telling them to have a nice day has become torturous.

"I don't follow rules." He cups his hand under mine, taking the broken pieces I've picked up. His hands are calloused, and his knuckles are cut. Some old and some new.

"Oh great, a cliché bad boy." I stand, watching him on his knees before me, like he's beneath me. I'm so sick of men right now. "Please, do tell me how you love danger and how much you'll corrupt me. I beg of you."

I roll my eyes so deep in the back of my head, I have a quick flashback of when I was nine and my mother told me if I did it again, they'd stick like that.

His body lifts like he's a growing bean stalk in a fairytale. He towers over me. The sound of the broken mug clanks against the counter as he sets it down gently. He takes the same dirty hand and tilts my chin up to look at his steel-colored eyes as I pull away.

A smug smile forms on his bow-shaped lips. "You're feisty. I like it."

His boots scrape against the floor as he walks back to the other side of the counter. He rests his hand on the coffee display and looks like he just made himself at home, like a hen hovering over her eggs.

"What will it take for you to leave?" It's not like I can call Jim, even though he's not that far away. He'd probably have a heart attack if he saw this guy.

"Let me take you out."

"Try again. Can I interest you in a coffee? A book, perhaps?" I march over to the shelf and grab *The Hatchet* by Gary Paulsen and push it into his leather-jacketed chest. "Here. I read it in sixth grade. Let me know if you need something with smaller words and shorter sentences."

A deep chuckle erupts from him as he holds the book up to look at it. "Fine. I'll take the book, a coffee…and your number." I give myself a long second to look at him. Okay, maybe three. He has a scar down the center of his forehead, and one over his lip. His eyes. They're like shadows at midnight. They're beautiful—but fatal.

"Again. Not happening." I would love to say my mother warned me about these types of men. The dangerous vibes, playing the bad boy who will only do incredible things to you. But she never did. Maybe because she was never taught about them, and it shows. And guys like that, they aren't real life. They are fictitious beings written for women by women.

The bell on the café door chimes again, and in walks the death of me. The literal last nail in my coffin.

Leanne.

"For fuck's sake, can this night get any worse?" I mumble, and Malfoy stares at me with a quizzical grin.

"Daisy, babe, I didn't know you were working here," my mom's best friend chimes like we aren't standing in part of the library. Leanne never looks at me, though. Instead, she's eyeing up the blonde tree still standing in front of me. This is one of those days I had to tear myself out of bed to be here. My body told me to stay home, but after it's traitorous move with Rocco, I no longer listen to my body. I go against it.

"Damn. Who are you?" Her eyes rake from his feet to his hair. I have to give it to her, if she wants someone, no matter the legal age, she will go after it, tits first. She pushes out her exposed cleavage from her neon yellow shirt and his eyes follow.

And he looks!

Pervs. All of them!

They play the cat and mouse game with eyes and tits for about a minute before she *finally* turns to me. "Have you seen your brother? I have a bone to pick with him."

Oh yeah? Same, girl. "*Step*brother. And nope. He goes missing randomly. I'm sure he'll pop up at some point." I wave my hand haphazardly in the air. "Is that why you're here…" I check my watch. "Five minutes before I close?"

"Sure is, honey? Well, he left me naked, high, and dry on his bed that night. He left to check on your ass in the bathroom and never came back til early morning to kick my ass out." The bitch's voice raises a few octaves, so all the other dogs can hear her. "I'm not sure what he'd want with *you*."

Malfoy releases a puff of air and widens his eyes.

Ah, yes. Miss Leanne here can play nice in front of her bestie, making her seem like she's the perfect best friend. Meanwhile, she's screwing—or trying to screw—said best friend's new stepson, and speaking to her daughter with the utmost disrespect. But Leanne doesn't know about the me who hides in the shadows of my mind. The me who's unhinged and done putting others first in my life when I'm constantly just a placeholder in theirs.

"First off, he was checking on me, and it's not your damn business why. Second, who the hell do you think you're talking to? And we're closing, so you need to leave." I tilt my head to the side and smirk. Nothing says crazy like a stare comparable to the Joker.

Leanne wrinkles her nose and juts out her hip. "Why are you talking like that?"

"I have to enunciate every word and talk slowly so you understand what I'm saying." I walk to the other side of the counter trying to hold myself together. If Jim hears me raise my voice, he'll come out here, and with Bonnie and Clyde standing in front of me, he'll think I'm planning some elaborate library heist. "I have no control over what Rocco does. Nor do I care."

Leanne makes a choking sound, something she's good at I'm sure, and looks at Malfoy. "You're barking up the wrong tree with this one." She looks at me and adds, "You're not into the *fun* guys. You prefer penny loafer and polo-dressed virgins, am I right?"

Staring at the forty-year-old bully in front of me, I feel something in my psyche snap. It's unlike something I've ever felt. I see red, and the pop of her gum in my face is the last straw.

Before I can register what I'm doing, I'm pushing her. Step by step out the door, and she's squawking like a bird, flapping her hands at me, and stumbling backward. But I don't care. I keep pushing her until she's completely out the door.

Malfoy is now standing next to me watching it all go down like I'm his personal entertainment. His eyes rake over Leanne, like all men's do.

I yank my apron off, toss my hat on a table, pull the keys out from my pocket, and dangle them in his face.

"Are you fucking leaving, or staying overnight in the library?" I walk out the door and wait for him to follow so I can lock up. Jim usually stays late, and sometimes falls asleep on the couch in his office; otherwise, I would have to tell him I was leaving. But I don't need Tweedledee and Tweedledum attracting unwanted attention. You are who you are associated with.

"I'm telling your mother about this!" Leanne is still beefing from the other side of the sidewalk.

I look around for a car that this stranger rode in on, but all I find is a blacked-out motorcycle, because of course.

He straddles his bike and offers me his hand, and I hop on. "I hope you fucking do tell my mother, Leanne! Tell her I just met this guy, too! Go bother someone else."

The engine rumbles the bike, and the vibration jolts between my legs. I hold on to the stranger in front of me and we ride off into the proverbial sunset.

CHAPTER
THIRTEEN

DAISY

THIS ISN'T the brightest decision I've ever made. Currently holding on tight to a complete stranger whose name still remains a mystery, other than the one I gave him—a romanticized villain from *Harry Potter*.

It's right up there with drinking heavily before surfing—well, trying to surf. Not like I'll be doing that again. I sold my board before I left California

He stopped at a red light and asked me where I wanted to go, and I told him anywhere. It's easy to hear him since neither of us are wearing a helmet. My mother would be *so* proud.

The usual afternoon storms have started much later today. Something Florida is infamous for. Although it's not summer, it is the rainy season, and I feel it all over my face as the drops pelt my skin. It's both painful and refreshing.

We come to a stop outside of a bar in an area I vowed to avoid. Crime rates are a little higher in these parts.

"My name is Brad, by the way," he says while getting off the bike. "Nice to meet you, Daisy." Brad. Of course he has a super douchey name. *Brad* holds his hand out to help me off the bike. I think this is where gentlemanly gestures stop. It's just a vibe I'm getting.

I cock a brow while staring at a neon sign that says "Beehive." Clever name, but it's a hole in the wall if I ever saw one. I'm ninety-nine percent sure I never knew this street existed. "You know I'm not twenty-one, right?"

"Oh yeah?" He doesn't seem to care, but instead walks right in like he owns the place, and lets the door almost slam in my face until some other guy holds it open for me.

I look around and realize I know absolutely no one. Not that I expect to. All of my two friends are nineteen and twenty, and neither Crew nor Jeremy would hang out at a place like this. It smells of stale cigarette smoke and cheap beer. The jukebox in the corner has seen better days as Amy Winehouse's "Back to Black" plays over the blown speakers. *Random.*

The posters that adorn the walls are colored on and are barely staying upright. "You going to join me? Or are you scared?" Brad calls from the bar, tapping the worn stool next to him.

I roll my eyes again. Something I seem to be doing a lot lately. I wonder if they have an eye rolling support group. Like an app. That would be a way to make money. I'll figure out those logistics later when I'm not accumulating black lung disease. Although I'm not inhaling coal from a mine, the vibe here is dark and the smoke is thick.

I slide onto the stool next to Brad. My thighs stick to the leather, because of course they do. "Whatever happened to upgrading to those high wooden chairs? These are disgusting against the skin."

"Maybe you shouldn't be wearing those sexy little shorts then." His kohl-colored eyes drop to my thighs, and an evil grin spreads across his face before his tongue darts out as it sweeps over his bottom lip. "What can I get ya to drink?" he asks, moving his eyes to the bartender like she'll be put on the backburner for later if shit goes haywire with me.

I want to play it safe. And Brad is the archetype for "she was asking for it wearing x-y-z," but I'm sick of 'safe'. One drink won't hurt—famous last words. "I'll take a whiskey."

His head snaps back to me like I criticized his upbringing. "Whiskey girl, hmm? Trying to show off?" His large frame crowds my space, and he leans in, resting his lips close to my ear. "Unless you're just trying to loosen up for me."

"Neither. I like whiskey, and it seems my morals are already loose enough simply by being here with you." *Not to mention me trying to drown my thoughts from rehashing the night in Rocco's bed.* I hate that I wanted more from him.

Also, Brad's breath smells like old beer, weed, and a shit ton of bad decisions.

I offer him a pathetic excuse for a smile. One he knows is fake.

Nobody gives you a How-To handbook on how to navigate different stages of your life based on the path you're on. There is the obvious path pushed onto us by society. Grade school. Graduate. College. More college. Debt for some. Work. Die.

But what happens when one's life doesn't fall into that expected societal flow? What happens when the girl who lost her dad hates college and moves back home. What happens when that girl is unhappy with her perfect, yet unattainable boyfriend, but craves every possible bit of newness and thrill her boring town has to offer? I'm not saying I want to go skydiving or bungee jumping, but I want to sneak out to see my boyfriend because my mom doesn't approve. I want him to pick me up in a fast car. I want to smoke weed. I want to get trashed and make a bad decision or two. I crave a little danger in my life, because so far, it's been really fucking dull. It's as if life is passing me by, and all I'm doing is watching it happen.

The gorgeous bartender slides me my drink while making eyes at the man who is paying for it.

"Now tell me what you do besides working in that café, Daisy." Brad's hand wraps around the bottle, and he brings it to his lips. His onyx stones stare at me over the bottle. Watching me. "Mmm. Hit the spot."

"I…umm…" What *do* I do? "I read. Work. Live at home with my mom and her new husband. You know…nothing special."

His body swivels to mine, spinning on the stool. "What do you mean, nothing special, doll?" The pad of his thumb slides against my jaw, and I swear I can hear the leather of his jacket rubbing against itself over the Jason Aldean song that's playing. I'm hyperaware of everything. The man touching me. How it makes me feel. I don't feel the tingle. The heat. But that doesn't have to happen in order for things to progress. I'm young, after all.

His eyes fall to my lips and mine to his. "If you're going to kiss me, you better do it. I don't particularly like games."

And he does. I pinch my eyes closed and feel his fist grip the back of my hair. His mouth tastes like beer, and his tongue is thick and aggressive, dominating my mouth. Our teeth clash with his assaulting kiss and it makes me wince. My teeth. I love my teeth. And my oral hygiene as a whole—he could learn a thing or two from me.

I pull back, breathless. Not because I loved the kiss, but because he wouldn't let me breathe.

His tall frame moves from the barstool and towers over me. "Let's go. I want to take you somewhere."

"No. I'm tired. I think I should go home now." His eyes go dark for a split second, but like a thief in the night, the darkness disappears.

He slides a twenty across the bar, pounds the rest of his beer, picks up my whiskey, and pounds that too before heading to the door. Those drinks are only adding insult to injury on that breath of his.

"Oh. Okay. I guess we're leaving," I say to nobody in particular.

It's the strangest thing. My 'stranger danger' alarm isn't sounding, yet something about this man is off. But like red flags that are so obvious in books, sometimes we don't find out the true nature of the danger that we're in until it's too late.

DAISY

"I TOLD you I wanted to go home." I push my foot out to the side and cross my arms over my chest. It's the universal symbol for 'I'm pissed and I don't care who knows it'.

Brad's blond hair blows in the wind. The palm trees swaying causes a peaceful white noise despite us standing in a desolate parking lot outside of what looks like an abandoned warehouse. In every horror movie ever, this scenario will end up with me, the innocent female, dead in a body of water somewhere.

Not tonight, Satan.

"Don't be like that, Daisy." He holds his hand out to mine. It's not inked like the inked hand that touched me days ago. But I will take it. It's this exact moment when the siren sounds in my head.

Wee-Woo! Stop.

Wee-Woo! Go home.

But I can't do that. I've been waiting for something more. And here it is. Whatever *something* is must be inside of this warehouse.

"Are you going to kill me, Brad? Because I have to give you an F on originality."

His bowed lips quirk and his eyebrows dip. "Do you think I'm going to kill you?"

"When you do that with your face, I'm leaning toward a hard yes." I pull away playfully, still wearing a stone-cold face.

"I'm not. But you might see someone die tonight."

"Oh good," I mutter sarcastically.

He tugs me along, and the closer we get to the lone door with a flickering lamp above it, light muffled noises sound from the inside.

My feet crunch along the gravel and I look down. I'm ecstatic I wore my black combat boots. If I have to kick someone's ass tonight, at least I'm wearing a heavy pair of Doc Martens. A swift toe to the gooch will give me time to run.

Brad pounds three times and the door opens to a dark hallway. The noise no longer hushed, but screams and shouts are now coming from the inside.

"Thanks, brother," Brad says to the man in a ski mask who says nothing in return.

Well, this is how I die. I don't even bother screaming. I'm pretty sure I've finally let the intrusive thoughts win. No sharks. No jackknifing onto my marble driveway. I'm willingly entering into my own version of the movie *Hostel.*

Except I'm not. We reach the end of the dark hallway by following the dim light.

"Fighting? You brought me to a wrestling match?"

Brad snakes his arm around my waist and pulls me closer. I can't see much. All I can see are two people fighting and everyone is cheering "Death."

"This is anything but a wrestling match, babe," he shouts over the roaring crowd.

Now I can see why Jeremy hated being called 'babe'. I feel like a piece of dirty meat with that one-syllabled word coming from his lips. I'll have to make sure I apologize if we ever hang out again. I look up at the man who has his tentacles wrapped around me. This has to be a rebound ordeal, right? Or am I just so hard up to get a little bit of attention that my long-buried daddy-issues are screaming to get out?

"What do you mean it's 'anything but a wrestling match'?" I turn back to the two muscular men going at it, waiting for Brad to answer.

"This is underground fighting. There are only a few rules, like no red paint." Brad pulls me through the crowd so we're a little closer. There is a tall, muscular, one with his face painted like a skull and his hair covered in a black bandana. Like a sexy, badass grown version of Miguel from *Coco*. The shorter, paler man with dark hair has silver and white paint split down the center of his face.

No red paint. Hmm…that's random.

"Why can't they have red paint?" I look up to see Brad zeroed in on the tall man with the skull face. His eyes are narrowed, and his lips are snarling. I'm sensing some toxic, hostile masculinity type of thing happening, and I'm not into it.

"Death is going to kick his ass," he says, ignoring my question. Death must be the skull guy, because the other guy has blood coming from almost every orifice. This is all just too much.

"Yeah. I kinda want to go home," I try shouting over the screams. This dude is either ignoring me, or deaf in his left ear.

The repetitive sounds of fists meeting bare skin is making my stomach queasy, so like I do best, I disassociate. My eyes wander from the ceiling to the old, discolored cement wall back to the other until they land on a large board with rules written on them in dark red.

RULES

BARE KNUCKLES ONLY

3-MINUTE ROUND

NO WEAPONS

EYE GOUGING/BITING ENCOURAGED

DISMEMBERMENT ALLOWED

Crowd determines the winner

What the hell kind of place is this? I look back to the ring and see the short guy on the ground, his face paint's now red from the blood. The hair on the back of my neck stands up, like someone is watching me. Lucky for me, I'm as stealthy as a leopard. Like the jungle cat, I'm also both reclusive and adaptable to my environment. I turn to my left, then to my right, looking for something that I'm not sure of and find nothing. Everyone is watching Death. Cheering. Chanting. Declaring the night's winner.

Then I find the eyes. Death is staring right at me, and I at him. Something about the way he's holding himself. Confident. Proud. Yet out of place. I tilt my head, studying the man who knocked the other guy to the brink of death. Death's head follows as it tilts. My heart starts beating faster, and I'm starting to feel out of breath.

There's something familiar about him. Not that I frequent these types of places or associate with cold-blooded murderers, yet something in my chest is calling to me to get closer to him.

Brad lets out a growl, startling me, and tugs my hand. "Let's get out of here, yeah?"

I nod and blink.

When I turn back to the fighter, he's gone.

"I'm ready." I'm excruciatingly uncomfortable here. As dark as I feel some days, I hate physical violence, so it's long past time that I get out of here.

We walk out to the bike and I'm trailing behind him, trying to remember how we even got here. I've lived in this area my entire life, and I had no idea this place even existed. The roar that came from inside would have to be heard from the streets. Except it's not. It's old, but soundproof. Whoever built this place knew exactly what it was going to be used for. Underground fighting. I thought that shit was only in the movies.

"How did you know this was here?" I ask before I hop behind him.

"Did you see the guy who won?" Brad flips his blond hair out of his face and gestures to the building.

"Death?"

He nods. "He and I are both undefeated. They won't fight us together."

My mouth falls. I try to close it, but I can't. I don't know why his confession shocks me. This is dangerous. He has scars on his skin. He also has the 'I don't give a flying fuck' attitude.

"Wait! You fight?" A cocky grin sweeps across his face, and it's all I can do not to regurgitate the muffin I ate before this shit show all began.

"Yeah. Like I was saying before you opened your mouth to show me how well you're going to take this dick later, Death and I don't fight. We're the money makers. They know that if they put us in the ring together, one of us will die." Another grin. I refuse to ask him his ring name. He might mistake me for being genuinely interested.

I should run home instead of going anywhere with him, except I have no clue where I am, and honestly, I don't want to. I don't want to know in case I'm ever questioned by the police. I tap my pocket and come up short for what I'm looking for. My phone. In a hurry to leave the café, I left my phone. At least it's safe and close to my car. Something I don't think I am right now.

My dad would be disappointed in me. I'm disappointed in myself right now. But it's survival. I want to go home to my bed. Get a new job. A new name. Because no matter how much I try to convince myself that this night was a harmless, almost date, it's a lot more than that. My gut has been screaming at me for the past thirty minutes, and I know that it's time to get away from this guy.

CHAPTER
FIFTEEN

ROCCO

I CAN'T WASTE time talking to the bookies tonight. I know they were waiting for me after the fight; dodging them is a cinch, but it's not something I need to get in the habit of. I know *he* likes to check in on me after every match. Make sure I'm not running away with his money. But when I see Daisy here with one of the most dangerous men who jumps at the opportunity to step into the ring, I have no other choice than to follow her. What the hell is she thinking? And where the hell is her perfect little boyfriend?

I'm not supposed to know who Brad is outside of the warehouse, but since my father is the one running this shit show, I know all of the fighters both in and out of their painted faces. Who the soft ones are who will either dip out and run away, or eventually lose their lives, and who the ones who want to fight to the death are. And Brad's—I mean, Beast—the latter.

My feet feel heavy as I run to my bike I have hidden in the brush. I didn't get too many blows to my face tonight, but my body is still exhausted. The poor bastard they put me up against never stood a chance. He has a baby at home, and this is his only option for making money. I felt bad taking the win from him, but if I lose to him, my father will kill me himself.

I didn't want him to lose, but I can't *lose.*

Nobody knows I own a motorcycle. It's harder to track than my blacked-out Audi. I take seconds to secure my helmet and pull out onto the road. While I weave through cars to catch up to Brad, I make sure I don't see Daisy lying in the middle of the highway.

Neither of them is wearing helmets. They sped by me in the parking lot, and Daisy's blond hair was whipping everywhere. I don't trust that if something happened, he wouldn't leave her in his dust.

Brad only cares about Brad.

Twenty minutes of bobbing and weaving later, I watch them pull into my driveway so I decide to park my bike in an empty lot down the street. I hit the kill switch and make my way to the oversized abode. A place that has felt more like home than when it was just me and *him.* That doesn't mean I don't hate living there now. I just hate it a little less.

My boots crunch fallen palm fronds in the driveway. South Florida winds have a way of making afternoon storms seem worse than tropical storms sometimes. Trying to stay in the shadows, I slowly climb the steps, looking in the windows for movement until I see my reflection. I still have the paint on my face.

"Shit." I hurry back down the steps to the side of the house. There has to be a hose hookup somewhere here. Using the flashlight on my phone would make this a hell of a lot easier, but the last thing I need is for Brad to come out throwing hands and being "protective" because he's trying to get in Daisy's pants.

She won't give it up to him. She can't. But why the fuck would she bring him here? Unless she's trying to fill a void, which I understand that completely.

"There it is," I mutter to myself, turning the water on. I look around and try to find something to wash my face with but fall short, so I pull my shirt over my head and start scrubbing. My face is sore, and I'm sure I have a cut or two above my eyebrow.

I make one more pass over my face until the water runs smooth against my skin, and I dip my whole head underneath. A hoodie from my car will have to do to hide the bruises on my body. Reaching my arms over my head is the last thing I want to do. I took one fall tonight and it happened to be on my shoulder. My guess is it's dislocated, but I'm sure I can have Santi work his magic in the morning.

Using my fingers, I brush my hair forward to fall over my forehead and rush back up the steps.

Daisy must have turned the porch light on, unless it's on a timer. I spare myself one more glance in the reflection in the window, making sure I have no paint on my face and hope for the best.

"Rocco?" Noooo. Not right now.

"Leanne. What are you doing here?" I growl before I turn around to face her. Her makeup makes her look like she's doing a beauty pageant in the eighties. Blue eyeshadow? At least I think it's blue. The porch light isn't doing her any favors.

"I was told you were asking about me," she purrs as she climbs the stairs in her leopard mini skirt and knee-high boots.

Ahhh. Yes. Tony Mancini always has an agenda, even when he isn't around. "Go home, Leanne." I tuck my hand in the front pocket of my hoodie. She'll take anything you give her and run with it. I could raise my eyebrows, and she'd think I'd wife her. "I'm tired and going to bed."

Leanne ignores my request and walks up to me, instantly palming my dick through my pants. I don't react, and neither does she. I breathe through the panic since she's obviously forgotten the last time she touched me when I didn't ask her to, and I grab her by the wrist, twisting it up toward her chest. She winces. "Ouch! What are you—?

"No," I growl, trying not to cause a scene. "What are *you* doing?

You don't just walk up to men grabbing their dicks. I told you to go home. That wasn't an invitation to touch me." I squeeze her arm a little harder and tears start to well in her eyes. "You touch me again, you'll be lucky if I don't kill you."

Leanne's eyes narrow, trying to challenge me. "You wouldn't kill me." Her tongue licks the air before she half-ass moans, "Maybe I like it a little rough."

Still gripping her wrist, I guide her down the stairs. "Stop being so desperate and find a man your own age."

She pulls her wrist away and wraps her other hand around it like she's been burned. "I know what you're up to with *her.*" Leanne's eyes point toward the door.

"This has nothing to do with Daisy. But it has everything to do with you needing to be tested for STDs, and maybe stop being so fucking psycho." Her eyes widen and the silence is deafening before she smiles like a psycho "You have no idea, Rocco Mancini, what you've done."

"Okay. Bye." Deciding not to engage in this conversation, I walk up the steps once more. I'm too tired for this shit. The noise of her car door slams behind me before I hear her pull away. *Thank fuck.*

Wasting no time, I push through the door and hope to hell Brad isn't balls deep in Daisy; otherwise, this will be the night he dies. I look around the family room and it's only dimly lit by the light from the kitchen.

"Rocco. You're home?" Daisy calls from the other room, and the chair scrapes against the floor like she's getting up to greet me. My footsteps still heavy, I drag myself toward her voice. Except it wasn't her who stood, it's Brad. His stance is wide, and his one hand is cupped over the other that's balled in a fist.

"Who's this?" Brad asks Daisy, but never takes his black eyes away from mine. My jaw tics and I can't actively stop myself from grinding my teeth.

"Oh. This is Rocco, my…" She hesitates. Her eyes bounce to

mine quickly before turning back to a piece of apple pie in front of her. "My stepbrother."

I don't bother correcting her. I need this man to think I'm no threat. He doesn't know me without the paint. But sure as hell knows him. "The Beast." He kills opponents without giving them a second look. In other underground fighting rings, killing is illegal. But this one—the man who runs it—is the Devil himself. Stealing lives of the innocent who are trying to make money the only way they can.

"You good?" Brad's hand is on my shoulder as he pulls me from the shadows of my mind. I laser focus on his other hand in front of me. He wants to shake hands. So I do. Fucking hard. I need something to take the focus off of him grabbing my sore shoulder.

"Why the fuck are you touching me?" I growl. He backs up as I let go of his hand, walk around him and pull out the chair next to Daisy. Daisy's eyes move to my legs as I spin the chair around so I can straddle it, and Brad follows me like a cat following a mouse.

I know this game, Brad.

I offer him a fake smile before I take Daisy's hand and bite the piece of pie off of Daisy's fork that had been inches from her mouth.

Brad cocks a brow and sits down across from us. "So, you're close?"

"No," Daisy says at the same time as I say, "Extremely."

Our inquisitive friend watches us and chews on his cheek as I steal another piece of pie from Daisy before the fork makes it to her mouth.

"Jesus, you baboon! Get your own slice." She's mad. Feisty. On guard. As she should being around this guy. She doesn't know him, but judging by the side-eye she's been giving him, she just may be. Hell, she should have her guard up around me, too. I'm not any better than the man across from me, looking at the bigger picture.

"I don't want my own slice. I want *your* slice," I say slowly and low, and she swallows hard. The rest of the room fades as her blue eyes land on mine. Her face is starting to get freckles from her being back in sunny south Florida. She doesn't know I see her laying out on our private beach. The way she rubs sunscreen on her skin, slow and calculated, like she knows I'm watching.

Her eyes drop to my lips, and I snap my head to Brad. "You should go."

"Nope. I'm good here." He smiles at Daisy. For what? I have no fucking clue, but I turn to her, and she looks as lost as I am.

I stand and swing my leg around the chair in case he wants to start something. "Get the fuck out of my house."

Brad stands and the chair falls backward, drawing a gasp from Daisy who just dropped her fork.

"Damnit." She pounds her fist on the glass table. "Look what you've made me do! That was the last bite of pie, and now it's on the floor."

Daisy pushes her chair out so now we're all standing like a western duel is about to commence.

"Would you both tuck your ginormous egos back into your asses. You look like two toddlers who are fighting over whose toy truck is bigger." She turns her attention to Brad after she pushes my arm. My shoulder has never gotten this much attention when it's not throbbing. "I think it's time you go. I'm tired."

Daisy doesn't wait for him to follow, but I can hear her open the front door anyway. Brad says nothing and walks past me, and like the cool dude he is, shoulder bumps my bad one. Fuck. My. Life. He doesn't know who I am. He wasn't there to see the fall happen tonight. He's just that much of a dick.

I follow him to the front door to make sure he doesn't try anything.

He leans down and kisses Daisy on the cheek, and she gives him a little grin.

"Call me, kid," he says the phrase in a James Dean type of way. Then closes the door behind him and I can't help but scoff. That guy can't be serious. Even on a good day, he's the equivalent of the Temu James Dean.

Daisy locks the door and stops in front of me. "You obviously have to run your mouth, so say it. Get it out."

"Your bed isn't even cold from Jeremy leaving it yet, and you found the biggest fucking douchebag in South Florida to warm it? Real classy." Before I can say anything else, my cheek is burning. *Throbbing.* "Did you just *slap me*?"

"Yes, I did. And if you plan on slut shaming me one more time, I'll slap you again." She steps toward me, pushing her tits against my chest. I'm not stupid. She fucking wants me. Coming to my bed naked a couple of weeks ago. She knew what she was doing. I almost blurred the line. Almost crossed it. But the outcome of us getting entangled isn't worth fucking her.

"That's what you are though, right?" I have to push her away before I pull her up to my bed and fuck her senseless. "A slut. Trying to screw me when your ex-boyfriend's body isn't even cold yet. And now this guy." Even I'm internally wincing at my words.

Daisy winds her hand back like she wants to punch me, but it never comes. Instead, she gets in my face and grits her teeth. "Fuck you, Rocco. Fuck. You!" Her voice breaks before she runs up the steps and slams her door.

"You wish, Crazy Daisy!"

Actually, I wish for that too.

CHAPTER
SIXTEEN

ROCCO

FOR BEING SUCH A NEWER, well-built house, these walls are paper thin.

After Daisy ran to her room, I came to bed. I then listened to the phone call she had with her mom. Somehow my little stepsister convinced her mother she's doing well and looking at colleges that she can attend in the fall instead of telling her that she's been crying her eyes out and dating some asshole. And where the fuck is Jeremy?

When she hung up, a muffled scream really perked me up. Was she being suffocated? Suffocating herself? Or just letting out a primal scream into her pillow, and not out loud so the neighbors wouldn't think I was attacking her.

I see the way they look at me when I climb out of my car. Or when I leave to go anywhere. Like I'm on the wrong side of the tracks. The guy always dressed in dark colors, messy hair with his hood up. Too old to live at home, and whatever else people can judge others for.

But I don't give a shit about any of that. My father, on the other hand…we must maintain our conservative nature. Stay classy. Act poised. *Blah. Blah. Blah.* He makes me fucking sick.

Lying naked in my bed with the fan blasting in the corner helps me drown out the noise and affords me a chance to focus. I need to think about how to get Brad out of here. He's dangerous. And if he finds out who I am outside of the ring, that creates danger in real life. I don't trust him. For all I know, he's getting closer to Daisy to get to me. I wouldn't put it past him. But how would he know who I am unless he would follow me?

I finally have a break, and I have to figure this puzzle out.

A low moan comes through the wall followed by, "Yes. Oh… God. Oh…"

"Is she—" I roll out of bed and move across the room, only to press my ear against the wall.

"Mmmm…"

"My little slut. You want me to hear you," I say to myself, palming my growing dick. I haven't caved to my father's demands by screwing a woman when I don't have a fight. What he doesn't know won't hurt him. And for him to send Leanne over while on his honeymoon just proves what a sick fuck he is. I will not be dipping into her…ever.

The moans get a little louder and I stroke myself a little harder —a little faster.

Her moans become shorter and louder as I imagine her using her fingers to strum over her drenched clit. "Roccoooo. Mmmm, yes."

"What the—" I don't get a second to enjoy the buildup before I come all over the side of my oak bookshelf. "Shit!" I let my head hit the wall with a thud and her noises stop.

I have seconds to decide what my next move is. So here we go.

Swiping the towel from my hamper, I wipe myself as fast as I can before I pull on a hoodie and slide a pair of basketball shorts on. They're a little too big and hang low on my hips since I've been fighting so much. Before I can stop myself, I walk into her bedroom and flick the light switch on the wall.

"What the hell!? Were you spying on me?" Her hair is matted to her forehead and her chest is covered in sweat. Lucky for me, she's wearing a tank top. Not like that helps her case. It's practically see-through.

I lean against the doorframe with my arm above my head, pausing only long enough for the blood get to my head before I pass out. It's still below my waist, which isn't helping a damn thing.

"A double date." *What. The. Fuck.*

"What are you talking about?" She rubs her forehead with the back of her hand like she wasn't just coming to thoughts of me. I wonder what I was doing to her. Eating her out. Fucking her from behind. Pulling her hair. Was she fighting it? Or was she all-in? "Rocco! If you're going to stare at me like a creep, get the hell out. I've had enough for one night."

"A double date. You, Brad…" I almost choke at his douchey name. "Me and a girl."

Her brow raises, and I hate how fucking sexy she is without makeup. She barely wears any, but when her face is freshly washed…fuck. *Stop it!*

She leans against her headboard and her tits push against her tank top. "What do I get out of it?" I look around her room. It's bright. White walls, with one picture of her and who I'm assuming is her dad. They look exactly alike.

What will she get out of it? Hell if I know. But I'll get to show lover-boy that he can't fuck with her and leave her for dead. "We need to start getting along. And what better way to do that than to hang out and get to know each other in the company of others." I'll make Brad think we're close. Like she tells me everything. If he's going to be around, then so am I.

She pulls her full lip into her mouth and narrows her eyes, contemplating my suggestion.

"Fine. But I decide where. I can't be taking you two hoodlums and your hoe to a fancy restaurant. People will stare, and I hate unwanted attention."

I fight back a chuckle and clench my teeth instead.

"And you need to stop doing that," she demands, crinkling her nose.

Genuine confusion rarely ever happens for me. It's as if I'm in a constant state of fight or flight. Always aware. "Stop doing what?"

"Stop doing that thing with your jaw. It clenches the muscles, and your face is already chiseled enough, you don't need to keep rubbing in all of your perfections to people who aren't you."

Perfections. It's laughable. I'm far from perfect, and the scars all over my body and the burn marks on my back say so. I'll never have to explain those to her because she'll never see my back.

I half expect her to lie down, pull the covers over her head, and tell me to get the fuck out, but she doesn't. Instead, the magnetism between us is charged and she is my power supply. And I think I just might be hers, too.

Her chest rises and falls evenly—her breathing calm. So I mimic her slow and steady breaths, putting us in sync. I'm not sure what's happening right now. No words, only inhalations from across the room.

"Get some sleep. You look like shit." I tell her before I push off from the doorframe.

"I hate you," she whispers.

My eyes fall to my feet, and for the first time in a long time I genuinely smile. I feel it everywhere. "That's the thing… I don't think you do, Angel." I wink at her, switch off her light, and close the door behind me.

As I walk back to my room, I'm hard all over again, and I have a feeling there is no amount of cold showers that will take care of the feelings I have her my stepsister.

CHAPTER
SEVENTEEN

DAISY

I SLEPT like shit last night after Rocco left my room. That wink was a sin. I'm not sure what Rocco's mother looked like, but she had to be a knockout. In fact, I don't think I've seen any photos of her. I make a mental note to snoop for some the next time he goes out to wherever the hell he goes. I'm going to figure that out too while I'm at it.

"If this coffee brews any slower, I'm going to chuck the whole machine into the ocean," I mutter to myself, rubbing my eyes.

"Polluting the ocean is illegal." Rocco's voice is raspy in the morning. Not that we've shared pleasantries more than a handful of times, but this is one thing I've caught on to. Because why not get the man whose aura screams sex and also uses a bedroom voice while we're at it?

I turn to face him, barely, and eye his attire. "You look like you're going to kill someone."

"Maybe I am." He grabs a mug that says "And Tony? He's Italian," and pushes me out of the way with his hip. I'm too busy getting a whiff of his cologne—Deodorant? Pheromones? —to

109

realize he's taking the coffee I just brewed. It's only a small, single-serving pot.

I elbow him in the ribs when he goes to take a sip, and he barely flinches. "Dude! That was mine! And why are you dressed like that? Seriously. Where do you go all the time?"

Steam is billowing in front of his face from the scalding hot liquid as he chugs the coffee. "Jesus. Are you a robot? Who can drink coffee that piping hot and not flinch?" I pinch his forearm, and he backs away.

I know who he looks like! Almost like a young Josh Hartnett in that movie *Pearl Harbor*. No wonder my ovaries are bursting every time I'm around him.

After he drinks the coffee faster than I shoot a shot of whiskey, he drops the mug almost violently in the sink. If it's not broken, I'll be shocked.

"First off, Daisy…" He drags out my name like it's made for his mouth. "Don't call me 'dude'." He walks toward me but is sure to stop with a couple feet between us. "Secondly, it's none of your business about where I go and what I do. The less you know the better."

He throws his hood over his head and starts to leave the kitchen.

"It's going to be hot today. You should wear something cooler," I offer. I sound like my mother and I'm almost embarrassed.

"No thanks, Mom. I'll be fine. Double date tonight at seven."

He spares me one long, appraising stare. My body ignites in flames as his eyes rake down my body. That lip of his pulls between his teeth, which look stupid—stupidly sexy. "You talk too much in the morning."

And he's gone. Again. And now I have to schedule a double date with a man I couldn't wait to get rid of. I pull the phone out of my back pocket and pull up Brad's number that I put in my phone last night when we got to the house. I didn't want to give him mine, so I distracted him by cutting a piece of pie. But I guess he'll have my number now.

Me: Double date tonight at 7? Bowling.

Brad: I don't like bowling.

Cool, bro. This guy is already annoying me. I'm convinced I'm only doing this to see what Rocco has up his sleeve.

Me: I didn't ask what you liked.

Brad: I also don't like double dates.

Is this guy for real? Moments like this are what make me miss Jeremy.

Me: Cool, bro.

Consider it this way…you don't go on the double date, you don't see me at all.

Brad:I'll pick you up.

"Over my dead body, sir." I hope he at least sweeps some strong mint toothpaste with fluoride over his tongue tonight. If he wants even the slightest chance for our tongues to collide, Colgate will be his only savior.

Me: I have a ride. See you at 7

@ Cosmic Rays

Three dots never appear for a response. At least he knows better than to argue with me.

I don

I really don't want to have to do this, but it's my only option.

This further proves I need to make friends. But the idea alone gives me heart palpitations.

"I know she has a list somewhere." I pull open each cabinet door. Somewhere in this monstrosity of a kitchen, my mother has all of our phone numbers taped to the inside. It includes medical personnel, a handyman, an electrician, etcetera. I've got to give it to her. Smart idea.

"Ah! Gotcha." I tap viciously at the screen, hating myself for having to do this, but also hating myself for the unexplained butterflies that are flipping around in my stomach like Olympian gymnasts right now.

> Me: It's Daisy. I need a ride tonight
>
> I don't want to ride with Brad.

I save him in my phone and his name pops up. He's probably going to give me shit, like, "Why are you dating a guy you're uncomfortable with?" At least that's what I would say. But then I'd so kindly remind him that this was his idea.

> Rocco: Angel? Be ready at 6.

I hate how traitorous my reproductive organs are right now. It's noon now. Plenty of time to hit the beach and afterward rub one out. The last thing I need to do is go out tonight all aroused and ready to jump on the first male who gives me positive attention.

Recognizing I have daddy-issues is the first step to healing.

Not that my father intentionally abandoned me, but his death has left a significant void in my life. This double-date could end up catastrophic if I'm not actively trying to fill said void. Okay, that was dramatic. Maybe not catastrophic, but it could lead to self-enabling behavior. I can't be better if I keep making excuses.

I RUN a rose-pink plumping gloss over my lips and check my mascara again. I opted out of makeup tonight since the sun was kind enough to kiss me with a tan and some flushed cheeks.

"I'm feeling myself right now," I smirk into the mirror and admire the new tube top I got from the surf shop. I'm pairing it with my favorite denim shorts, and black Converse high tops. A look that can never go wrong. Once I pull on my flannel and leather jacket before doing a full turn in the mirror. "Chef's kiss, Daisy."

This would be a prime time to have a best friend so she can tell me if this confidence is all in my head or not.

"Daisy!" Rocco calls from the bottom of the stairs. I heard him get home an hour ago, but I was in the middle of primping. "I'm not waiting if you're late."

I grab what I'll need for the night, shove it in my mini-backpack, and head down the steps. Rocco is turned around looking at the heavy metal anchor hanging in the foyer. I wonder if he imagines using it as a weapon like I do.

I tread lightly down the steps so he doesn't hear me. I want to scare him, but the closer I get, the more the memory of his panic attack surfaces. I clang my bag against the railing and make sure to take the two last steps a little harder.

"You weren't going to scare me. I heard you at the top of the steps." He turns around and holy shit. I'm not sure if he's channeling some Adonis energy right now, but he's wearing a black, long-sleeve Henley and dark denim jeans. His thick thighs look like they're ready to Hulk through the seams, and I would be fortunate enough to have the front-row seat to the show. After I realize I'm staring, I rake my eyes up his torso to his face, only to find him admiring me like I had just done to him.

"You ready?" His Adam's apple bobs as he jingles keys in his hands and turns to go. "I have a favor to ask of you." Rocco doesn't bother looking at me. Instead, he focuses on the key ring in his hand that's lined with more keychains than keys.

"Uh-oh. Are we fake dating tonight?" I joke. Well, kind of. The whole town knows our parents are married, if we were fake dating, or dating, in general, Briny Breeze would have a lot to say. I don't see him as my stepbrother, though. He's just a guy who lives in the same house as I do, and our parents signed a contract to love each other.

"I have a motorcycle. We need to take it tonight." Unless my eyes are deceiving me, there is no motorcycle in the driveway. They bounce from one end to the other, and nothing. "My car is making a weird noise, and it's nothing I've heard before."

I shake my head to say I don't care, but it comes out more of an, "Oh, cool." I grab my jacket off the hook and walk outside, unfazed by this turn of events, and he follows. "How's your date getting there if I'm riding with you?"

"Do you really care?" he asks with a cocked brow.

My gaze to shoots to the sky and back at him as my bottom lip sticks out. "Not really."

I get a curt nod in response as we start our trek to the bike that's hidden in a lot down the road, neither one of us saying anything. If it wasn't for the frogs croaking and a dog barking from a few houses down, this walk would be even more awkward.

As much as I want to, I don't bother to ask why the bike's not in the driveway because I have a feeling he wouldn't tell me since he keeps so much to himself.

He hands me the helmet that was hanging on the back seat of his bike before he secures his.

The comparison between Rocco and Brad are night and day. It's almost obnoxious. I should have had a shot of something before I left the house to calm my nerves. I would have if the parental units hadn't decided it was better to hide the liquor as well.

The panic inside of me is starting to take over, causing my shoulders to tense, and Rocco pauses before getting on the bike.

"Daisy." He can only see my eyes yet can sense my jitters. Rocco is either greatly in tune with the look of oncoming anxiety, or he has telepathic powers. "Breathe." He taps my helmet twice before he straddles the bike. I swing my leg over, leveraging myself with his shoulders, and try hard to keep some distance between us.

"Hold on," Rocco shouts before the engine rumbles underneath us.

This feeling of foreboding nags in the pit of my stomach. Like somehow, without realizing it, this will be the night that's going to change the rest of my life.

And I'm just along for the ride.

CHAPTER
EIGHTEEN

ROCCO

EVER SINCE THAT blonde firecracker crept in my bedroom buck naked, I've kept my distance. I also started sleeping with my door locked and shorts on just in case. Being well behaved it not exactly my forté, but I promised myself I wouldn't touch her again. It's legitimately a matter of life or death. Even though her creamy, sun kissed skin is begging to be rubbed and kissed, I've been doing a damn good job. She makes it so damn hard.

But now? Not so much. Her warm body is flush with mine. Her slender hands are wrapped tightly around my stomach. I can tell she's trying to keep space between us, but the speed we're going is preventing it entirely. If she loosens her grip, she'll be roadkill.

If she thinks this is going to be a regular double date, she's in for a surprise.

Because there's nothing more enjoyable than 'the chase'.

No. *I lied.*

The need to touch something that's off limits.. It's the idea of wanting a person that is taboo—when everything and everyone is telling you that you can't have them. Craving the forbidden. That first kiss. The looming and all-consuming need to have a taste of them dripping from your tongue. Those stolen glances. The secret touches. We just have to decide how far we're willing to go and commit to it.

We slide into a spot at the bowling alley and Daisy hops off like her ass is on fire. Her black helmet is in her hands before I even get mine off my head.

I take it from her hands before she decides to drop kick it across the parking lot. She's working through something. Her puffy bottom lip is pushed out and her brows are tightly knitted together as she starts toward the entrance.

Oh, Angel, this isn't the last time that pretty little face will be scrunched up with contemplation tonight. I smirk and start walking in behind her, admiring her curvy ass.

The smell of fried food and feet greet us as we walk in. Daisy comes to a hard stop and looks around before we reach the cashier.

"Is this bowling alley not up to your pretentious standards, Angel?" I neglected to tell her it was Cosmic R&B night. All lights are off and we'll be bowling under black and neon lighting rocking out there are more couples making out than actually bowling.. Perfect for sliding her into a dark corner. Or better yet, perfect for pushing Brad into a dark corner and—

"Hey, you," my date swoons, wrapping her arms around my waist. No matter the distraction, Brad's ass is on the line. Daisy practically growls next to me, rolling her eyes.

I dip my head to look at Melissa and give her a wink. She's easy to please. If I'm around, she'll bend over backward to appease me. Even if that means bending over in front of me and giving me a show.

I need her to put on that show tonight, but not for me. I have a foolproof plan. Brad will admire Melissa in front of Daisy. And if I know anything about the little spitfire, she'll have a few choice words and take Brad out of the equation for the both of us. The less

I get my hands dirty with other fighters outside of the ring the better.

"Melissa. This is Daisy." Daisy eyes Melissa like she's just another sheep with a face full of makeup, fake lashes, fake nails, fake tits. She kind of is, but Melissa was paid tonight, and not for sex.

To my surprise, the young woman who was named after a delicate flower holds out her hand. "Nice to meet you, Melissa." Daisy offers a closed-mouth smile before her eyes dart around looking for Mr. Asshole.

"There she is." Like clockwork, Brad appears and spins Daisy around so she's facing him. His faux-leather jacket is tearing in random places all over the arms. Maybe Daisy doesn't notice, or maybe she doesn't care. His arms snake around her waist and her body arches into his. Not because she's turned on. Can't be. He has the hygiene of a pig in a sty, and the social etiquette of Mr. Bean.

The reason I'm undefeated in the ring is because I study body language. Her fine ass and massive boobs are smashed against him, causing her waist to hyper-extend. But I have to admit, her ass in that position, in those shorts, is perfection. The way I'd drag my hands down her body and violently grab each cheek, making her yelp and blush just for me.

Before my dick gets too hard, I notice her furrowed eyebrows completely negating the smile on her face before he dips his and kisses her.

I open and close my fists, trying to calm the fuck down before Melissa grabs my hand and tugs. "Let's pay and get to the lane." My jaw tics and I turn away, letting Daisy fend for herself. For now.

A few minutes and a shot of whiskey later, we're all sitting at a stupidly small plastic table that hasn't been upgraded since the mid-80s with snacks, shoes, and enough collective bad decisions we could write an anthology.

"So, Brad, where do you hail from?" Melissa sticks a fry in her mouth, wrapping her painted red lips around it. I know her schtick all too well, so my eyes find Brad's, and she's got him exactly where she wants him. His black eyes are zeroed in on her tongue twirling around the fry as she brings it into her mouth. I should pay her extra for that move.

I glance over at Daisy, and she's in deep thought, looking at Melissa like she's a gazelle. "Problem?" I ask so only Daisy can hear me as I nudge her foot with mine.

The amount of aggression she uses to pull her foot away from mine is astonishing. Daisy ignores me and leans diagonally toward Melissa, resting her tits on the table. "Didn't you used to go to Palm Beach Middle School? Your last name is Winters, isn't it?" Her blue eyes narrow waiting for her question to be answered.

I may be calculated, and prepared, but I fucked up. I told Melissa everything she needed to know about Brad, but I left out the part about Daisy—about how she needs to act around her. Daisy is feisty and takes no shit from anyone, not even me. This could all implode faster than a handmade submarine diving to see the Titanic.

I clear my throat at Melissa and her light eyes flash to mine as she subtly raises an eyebrow. By now we can read each other like a book. She doesn't like talking about the times my father used to pay her to screw my brains out, and I don't like to talk about anything.

Melissa's face changes and the tension eases. "I did. You're Daisy Reynolds."

Daisy sits back slowly in her chair and grabs a French fry. "You know her?" Brad asks while putting his hand over the back of Daisy's chair. His thumb starts tracing circles on her bare shoulder, and I feel the vein in my forehead start to throb. She's wearing a tube top. Here I thought she was wearing that flannel all night underneath her leather jacket. But she keeps taking off layer after layer, leaving nothing to the imagination. I'm not sure if Brad's noticed her piercings or not. He's either a real gentleman or fixated on my date a little more than his own.

"Hey." His fingers grip Daisy's shoulder, pushing into her soft tan skin. "I asked you a question."

"Of course I know her. She pantsed me in front of my crush in school. It's fine. All forgiven. Let's get this game started, shall we?" Her eyes move to mine before she stands up and walks over to the game console. I hate logging everyone's names. It takes forever and somehow at the end of the game, everyone is blaming poor Joe Schmo for winning only because he went first.

"I hate bowling," Brad says to both of us. Melissa appeases him, but I turn to look at his date.

"Then why did you come?" I'm finding myself not taking any type of pity on this guy. Maybe pity is a strong word. Supplying him with any benefit of the doubt would put me in a vulnerable position. Something I'm not keen on.

"I came because the girl I'm screwing wants to bowl and wasn't taking no for an answer." He leans back, stretching his legs under the table, his fake leather jacket making an awful noise while it rubs against the chair.

"Screwing. Really?" I can't help but smile. I'm not claiming to know Daisy *that* well, but I'd like to think she wouldn't have given her virginity to this ass-twat.

"Yeah." He pounds his hand with his fist. "Girl can fuck, if you know what I mean."

I stifle a laugh. "Yeah? She can fuck, huh?"

Melissa stands and rolls her eyes while Brad's creepily rake over her body. "I'm going to let you boys pee all over the place here and go help Daisy."

Ignoring her, I choose verbal violence. "Daisy seems like she's unhinged enough to have piercings."

Brad shakes his head. Unbeknownst to him, I know for a fact Daisy has her nipples pierced and not her pussy. "She's as clean as a whistle." Then he whistles, leaning forward. "She has a landing strip, bro." All lies.

I don't know if I'm more upset that he's talking about her like this without her knowing, or talking about her like he knows her and lying straight to my face.

"Hmmmm." I don't say anything else. I don't even blink.

He finally fucking leaves the table and walks over to the girls. I track his movements like there's a target on his head and I'm a sniper. His arms swing over both girls' shoulders, and he pulls them closer. Just then I find myself imagining picking up a ten-pound bowling bowl and swinging it. A nice uppercut to the chin should knock him out for the rest of the night. *No weapons.* A rule from the ring that rings in my head every time I think of picking up a gun and shooting my father. The thought alone makes me feel like I'm being deprived of oxygen.

"Are you going to join us? Or are you going to sit there and pout?" Daisy's voice snaps me out of the cusp of a whirlpool of emotions. Something I fall into frequently around her. Not right now, though. Not until I'm in the comfort of my own room with the door locked.

"Wouldn't be anywhere else, Angel." I smirk at her knowing this night is just beginning.

CHAPTER NINETEEN

DAISY

MELISSA WINTERS HAS BEEN STANDING NEXT to me pushing these sticky alphabet keys while we listen to the pissing match behind us. Wasn't this Rocco's idea? Was the point of all of this to get Brad in the same room to find out if we fucked? I would have told him we didn't if he'd only asked. Brad might look good, but it ends there. His personality is as exciting as burnt toast.

"Do you ever wonder why people say 'as exciting as a slice of bread'?" I don't turn to look at her as I ask my question, but instead tap on the screen annoyingly with my nails.

"People don't say that," she answers, concentrating on the screen. "I've literally never heard anyone say that."

They do. "I mean, a slice of bread is exciting. You can turn it into a sandwich, or slather it with butter, or you can dip it in egg and make French toast. So many possibilities...unlike burnt toast."

Finally, Melissa Winters turns to me and tilts one side of her mouth. "Do you have a bread fetish? I mean, do you go home and snuggle with a soft loaf of sourdough or something?"

I frown at her insinuation. Like I'm mentally unstable or something. "No. No. Nothing like that." I smile because making people feel uncomfortable is my favorite pastime. "I do, however, like lying in a ball on the kitchen floor."

Her eyebrows pinch and she frowns. It's not very becoming on her otherwise beautiful face. "Ew. Why would you do that?"

"To pretend I'm a crumb. Hoping someday somebody will eat me." I shake my head like it's completely normal, and she's the crazy one for asking. It's not like she doesn't deserve to be mind-fucked after what she did to me in grade school all those years ago.

I'm standing next to the girl who stole Tanner Lee in sixth grade. And my crush, Ryan, in fifth. And Joseph in seventh. I thought we were friends...I told her about the boys I liked, and she went after them. Of course, she's no longer a brunette, but now has bleach blonde hair that looks healthier than my natural dark blonde hair.

Luckily in middle school, Jeremy wanted nothing to do with her because I'm sure she would've stuck her perfectly straight teeth into him, too. Was it luck, though? Or has it stunted my ability to seduce the opposite sex properly? I'm not even sure I want it anymore. It seems as though I've officially become a nineteen-year-old curmudgeon.

Maybe it was because I finally grew into my head. I played tennis, had muscles. I could have easily curb-stomped her. Maybe for once I intimidated her.

"Are you twenty-one yet?" Melissa Winters finally breaks the silence, and I nod.

"Nope. I turn twenty tomorrow. Twelve sixteen in the morning." A heavy arm and a waft of bad breath billows past me, causing me to wince.

Fucking Brad. Standing between us, capturing both Melissa Winters and me with his talons, he growls in my hair. Not sure why. Brad has let me down as much as the beast's transformation into the prince in *Beauty and the Beast*. My brain was more into the idea of him than who he really turned out to be.

"This is just the place I want to be. Between two beautiful ladies." His head dips to Melissa Winters's, and I can't be jealous. If anything, it's karma. She gets to inhale fiery dragon breath for stealing my past potential boyfriend.

I'm not petty. And we're in the 21st century. I believe in equal opportunities.

"Are we playing or what? I'm getting bored." Rocco interrupts our little love fest and I'm forever grateful.

"People with low IQs get bored easily," Brad says, poking the Rocco bear. I hear Rocco hum—well, it sounds more like a growl, but I can't see his face.

I step out of Brad's unyielding grip and shoot Rocco a death glare, being sure to drive my finger in his chest enough for him to wince—but it never comes. "You're the one who wanted to come bowling, Rocco. Find a fucking ball and roll. You're first!"

With the absolute petulance of a bratty teenager, I start stomping past Rocco, but he grabs me by the neck, pulling me back to him.

"What the hell do you think you're doing?" I try to seethe and show him my uneven breath rising and falling in my chest fueled by anger. But I'd be lying to both of us. His possessive hand grips me tightly with his thumb pushing into the perfect spot on my neck, causing my vision to blur. And everything around us fades into the background, awakening a deep hunger inside of me for the pain he's willing to give me along with the pleasure of his lips so dangerously close to mine.

He rests his full lips on the shell of my ear, pulling me closer, and he rumbles, "That's right, Daisy. *I am first. In everything.*"

I exhale because I know that he doesn't mean bowling. Despite his best efforts at pushing me away, he's after my virginity.

"Look at me, Daisy." The warmth of his breath is gone, and a subtle squeeze on my neck forces my eyes to find his. "Don't forget that."

Melissa clears her throat from behind me, and Rocco's grip loosens as his hand falls to his side. I don't turn around to look at Brad as I heave in a breath. Not because I'm afraid of what he'll see in my eyes—which is some type of burning lust for my stepbrother—but because the idea of him sticking his tongue down my throat again will end up with his dick being cut off.

Somehow my feet drag me to a tower of colorful balls. I've officially become detached from this night as I pick up one by one, deciding on one that's more aesthetically pleasing rather than what weight would be best for me.

"Daisy?" A soothing voice I know all too well jolts a tiny hit of dopamine inside of me.

Without turning, I answer with a smile. "Jeremy."

He steps beside me looking like he just got off from a shift at Hollister. "How are you?" I sit the ball back in its home and hug him.

A huge part of me wants to lose my shit and sob in his arms. But I don't cry. I hate crying. I learned a long time ago that crying in front of my mother always became transactional. The one person who should unconditionally nurture you throughout life would take my tears and tell me how her life was that much worse.

I pull back and take a good look at him. "You look good, Jer."

His eyes quickly fall over my outfit and back to my eyes. "So do you." He rubs his chin nervously, looking past me. "Are you okay? You seem off." His head slowly swivels to find three people standing at the edge of a lane staring at our interaction.

"I will be. Just trying to find myself. What I'm supposed to be doing. All that stuff." I slap both hands on my thighs awkwardly as he gives me an unbelieving smile.

Jeremy's hand rests on my shoulder. "Just be careful with them. Okay?"

"Them?" I gesture to the three behind me and he nods.

"There are some rumors going around the station about Mancini's.," he says, nervously rubbing his chin again.

Feeling slightly defensive of Rocco, I try to bite back my aggressive tone. "Are you a cop now?" My hand lands on my hip and I stick up my chin.

Jeremy's eyes bounce around behind me and glances behind him. A cute little blonde girl waves at him and he gives her a tight closed-mouth smile. "Listen I should be getting back." It's one thing when you personally move on from a past relationship. But I don't hear many people talk about how hard it is watching the other party move on, too.

I nod. Because if I say anything, it will come off as a sob, and the last place I want to be is rolled up in the fetal position on this dark carpet that hasn't been switched out since this place opened in 1985.

"I'll see you around, Daisy."

Jeremy was my first boyfriend, and even though that version of him was mediocre, the best friend version of him blew the word friendship out of the water.

Being the gentleman that he is, Jeremy offers a friendly wave to Rocco and walks away.

Taking a small piece of my heart with him.

———

THREE ROUNDS OF BOWLING LATER, we're all sitting back at the table. The awkwardness has not subsided. Not one fucking bit. Brad is ogling over Melissa while she is pouring herself all over Rocco. And I'm here worried about why the pins didn't reset after my last strike. That's right. *I'm winning.*

"So, Brad. What do you do?" Rocco has a way of asking people questions that make you want to spill your guts out because if you don't, you'll die.

"Underground fighting." Blonde guy hotshot cracks his

knuckles next to me like it's about to turn into Thunderdome in the middle of a Jeremih song. It's actually quite fitting, this song. "Imma Star" is practically written about Brad's self-admiration. Too bad he can't put as much time into his oral hygiene as he does in inflating his ego.

"Oh yeah? Underground fighting, hmm? Around here?"

"Yeah."

"Where about?"

Brad's eyes narrow on Rocco while my and Melissa's heads bounce back and forth between the two like ping-pong balls.

"You wouldn't know it," Brad chides, shifting in his seat. *Is he nervous?*

Though Rocco doesn't move. "Try me."

I swear if these two man-children start to fight, I'm going to leave them alone in this place and Melissa can have her choice.

Brad turns to me, his dark eyes even darker. Which seems impossible, but his demeanor has deviated from what I assume was his happy self. "Daisy, I think the night is coming to an end. Let's go. I'll take you home."

I look at him, unamused by his demand. "Okay, no? Random as fuck. I still have my bowling shoes on. I have to turn them in." The sound of pins resetting down the lane echoes and I turn to watch. "Plus, I'm winning, and I really want to finish this round."

"Leave the shoes. I'm sure your *brother* will turn them in for you. And we all can agree you won, okay? Now let's go," he practically growls. I swear his dark eyes are overcome by rage, because a chill rolls through me—not the good kind—but I shake it off.

"He's not my brother." I glance at Rocco with a scowl. I'm not sure if I'm mad at Brad, Rocco, or the entire premise of this night. Or maybe that I'm actually starting to like Melissa as a person now that she's an adult. Given our brief interaction, it seems like she's matured. A real girl's girl.

Rocco folds his hands on the table in front of him. "I'll take her."

"Oh, Jesus Christ," I mumble under my breath and my head falls back.

I kick off my bowling shoes and push my Converses. "I'm riding back home with Rocco. I have a headache…I think." I turn to Brad. "Something hurts. And I'm not sure if it's my head or the fact that you gave me a complex."

He stands and towers over me. "How did I give you a complex?"

"You were too busy watching Melissa Winter's dick-sucking lips and her perfect ass the whole time to notice I was even here."

Melissa's beautiful lips fall open like she's Angelina Jolie before I turn to Rocco and try not to slump my shoulders. "I'm ready to go home." There is nothing about me that's remotely attracted to the egocentric Brad No-last-name, yet his words and attention—or lack thereof—somehow made me feel invisible. Something I felt for so long before Jeremy waltzed into my life. Even then, the novelty wore off, and those feelings resurfaced. Turns out, I do have to take my therapist's advice and have to work on myself and not use others to fill the void.

Easier said than done.

Rocco nods, but Brad grabs my arm. What is with people grabbing my arms?

"I'm your guy. I'll take you home," Brad rumbles like he's still in Thunderdome next to me.

I turn slowly, like I'm about to recite the famous skit about Niagara Falls by the Three Stooges. "Ha! My guy? You're kidding me." I try to pull away from his grip but fail. "We went out twice, this being one of them, and both times you aggressively held me against you until I kissed you back," I spit. "To be honest, you should schedule a trip to the dentist. You have some type of oral issue happening, and it may be past the point of a decent toothbrush-toothpaste cleansing."

His pupils blow and my eyes drop to the floor.

There is a rule with men. Be sure to have a backup plan if you're willingly taking a shot at their ego. They won't cry. They'll get verbally or physically aggressive. At least the men I know.

…Or maybe don't date an egotistical man to begin with.

I don't know this guy. We just met; I know nothing. I know it was stupid to get on the back of his bike the first time. It seems like getting involved with Brad has its own little Hotel California vibe —you can check out when you want, but can never actually leave. You can break up with Brad, but he'll never actually leave you alone.

I wait for what's about to come—whether it's words or a hand —but it never does. A gargle sound comes from Brad, and when I look up, a familiar, inked hand is around his throat.

"You fucking hit her, I'll end your life right here."

Brad doesn't put up a fight. His hands fall to his side while he wears a psychotic smile.

"You talk big shit, Rocco. Do you even know who I am?" Rocco doesn't budge. Brad's eyes drift to mine. "I wouldn't hit you. Not ever. I don't hit women."

Faster than I can blink, Brad uses his arms to push Rocco's hand away from his neck. "You don't want to mess with me, Rocco." Before Brad leaves, his black eyes sear into my soul. His arm extends with his finger pointed, almost touching me. "You. Me. Tomorrow after your shift, lovely. I won't take no for an answer." And he must think that this works because the man winks at me like the last three hours at this hell hole didn't just happen.

"Right." I shoot him with a double pair of finger guns and walk my shoes to the counter. I don't bother telling Melissa goodbye. My energy expenditure has reached its maximum tonight, and all I really want to do is get naked and take a scalding hot bath. Any physical pain in my body will end the emotional pain in my mind.

"You really have a way of picking them," Rocco growls from behind me. "You're fucking crazy. Crazy ass Daisy."

I whip my body around fully, ensuring he can see my face. "Crazy?! You're one to talk. You choose the town whore and my childhood nemesis to hook up with? Who next? You want the number to my old best friend, Crew? Would he suit your fancy?"

And to add insult to injury, I keep going because my projectile word vomit is coming out without a filter and with a vengeance. "Probably not. Crew doesn't have fake tits, or a loose pussy for you to throw your tiny dick into. It would be like throwing a mini hot dog down a hallway with your coquette."

His lips quirk before he clenches his teeth. "There's nothing small about my dick."

Ugh. This man is committed to pissing me off. "I'm over this conversation."

"Where are you going?" Rocco screams after me as I push out the exit. Hopefully, the door hits him in his perfect face. My shoes pound through the gravel lot toward his bike, the only noise around me is a running car and crickets.

"Daisy! For fuck's sake, wait!" I guess a door to the face was no such luck.

I spin. Again. Spinning and spinning. Spiraling, actually. I have a tight grip on losing my shit lately and realize that I've made a semi-comfy bed at rock bottom made up of lies and personal deceit.

"Yes, my dearest stepbrother. Looking to wrap your hand around my neck again?" He closes the space between us, pulling the air from my lungs. As much as my body craves his touch, it never comes.

"You'd like that, wouldn't you?" Rocco's knuckle grazes up my thigh to my shorts and his eyes fall to my lips, and mine to his. The air between us goes still. The crickets aren't any match to my heartbeat pounding in my ears. *Can he hear it?*

"We should go," he says, pulling away before he hands me my helmet from earlier.

A deep heat floods my lower tummy, and an ache starts

between my legs. The want for this untouchable man has lit an inferno inside of me.

The engine revs to life and I hop on. I grip my hands around his waist and push my chest to his back as his muscles tense at my touch.

And my mind is hyperfocused on one question…and one question only.

What if we pushed all the rules aside? *Just for one night.*

CHAPTER
TWENTY

ROCCO

THAT STUPID MUSIC from the bowling alley keeps playing in my head, and the only thing that's silencing the noise in my brain is the rumble of my bike underneath me and the slender hands resting on my torso, practically burning a hole through my shirt.

The way she looks at me. The need to kiss Daisy is creating an inappropriate number of unhinged thoughts about how I want to tie her up and take the one thing she hasn't given to anybody. Not even her pushover of an ex-boyfriend. I saw him talking to her. By the looks of it, as usual, he didn't pose a threat. I never asked what happened between them, and I'm not sure I want to know. There are a million things running through my mind daily, and why Jeremy didn't pan out as a boyfriend is not one of them.

I turn on the Bluetooth to our in-helmet speakers and "Movement" by Hozier comes on. I'd change it, but my phone is in my seat, and sitting here between her legs is driving my rock-hard dick against the zipper of my jeans. If I stand, I might just come.

I give her a tap on her knee to let her know we're ready to go, and she squeezes me subtly with her thighs. *Goddamnit.* I grip the clutch and shift faster than a rocket into space, which is also the equivalent of how fast I'd paint her face with my cum if she'd let me. Daisy's infuriating. She doesn't just lie down and take shit. She pushes every one of my buttons, and I've developed a taste for it.

Going against every siren ringing in my head, I reach back and put my hand on her knee again. The urge to touch her anywhere and everywhere is overwhelming as the feeling has stopped coming in waves because it's reached full-on tsunami.

Eventually, my body relaxes as her small caresses stop. But as we speed down I-95, her hands drop a little lower…and a little lower. My thumb rubs small circles on her leg—as far back as I can reach.

Her hand moves closer to my dick next, and my vision starts exploding with colors and my head falls forward. I need to be inside this woman as fast as possible, and I don't care how I get there.

Her little movements behind me hint that she's as turned on as I am. The small, subtle shifting as she pushes into me, or the rubbing of her legs against the outside of my own. It's all a recipe for disaster.

I cut the corner to the driveway and park behind the car. At this point, my father has seen Brad's bike on the camera. I'll just keep my helmet on until I get inside and move the bike in the morning.

I hit the kill switch and help her off before I dig out my phone from inside of the seat.

She shifts, standing in front of me, rubbing her thighs together in those short shorts. She's wet. But how wet?

She sets her helmet on the seat and we walk to the door silently. If she looks down, she'll see me hard as a rock for her. Part of me hopes she does if she didn't realize it on the ride here.

Daisy fiddles with the key in the dark. I'd shine a light, but I can't risk him knowing it's me. We finally enter the foyer, and I pull off the helmet. Her eyes find mine, and she's out of breath like she ran the whole way home. I swallow hard. Who will be the first to make a move?

Without looking, she tosses the keys on the slim table but misses. They hit the floor, clanking, but neither of us does a damn thing about it.

I take a step toward her. Then another, and I grab her fingers in mine. Her eyes fall to the connection. Tension crackles between us. I've been dick-deep in a hell of a lot of pussy, but never felt something this intense. Like I want to protect her? Or maybe I'm feral because she's talking to one of the two men I wouldn't hesitate to kill.

My eyes fall to hers, and blue eyes jolt directly at me through her mascaraed lashes, making them pop.

"We shouldn't do this," Daisy almost whispers.

I let out a sardonic chuckle. "You shifting behind me on the bike, and the squeezing of your legs says otherwise, Angel." She swallows hard as our fingers move through each other, as if it's securing a bond between us through our veins.

"Tell me not to kiss you." I dip my head, and our lips are centimeters apart. Like the daring bastard I am, I drop a hand to her denim waist band. Not even a flinch. *Good.* I pop open the button.

"Don't…" She pauses and her tongue sweeps across her bottom lip. "…Kiss me." Her hands rub up my forearms to my biceps before they drop to her zipper. It's not long before she shimmies her bottoms off, exposing her black silk thong.

"Is this what you want, Rocco? To see me naked and exposed?" Her eyes narrow on mine before she lets out a breathy laugh. "No longer tucked away in the darkness of your room."

I brush my lips across hers. "I'm not some knight in shining armor, Daisy. I'm nothing like your little preppy boating boyfriend."

"Ex-boyfriend."

I'm not sure if I say "fuck it" or audibly growl before I grab her bottom lip with my teeth. She releases a soft moan, and that alone makes it next to impossible to contain myself.

So I don't.

I hoist her up and she wraps her legs low around my hips as I carry her into the kitchen. The heat from her pussy heats my lower stomach as her lips fall to my neck, and I plop her ass on the glass table.

"You don't think I know you're different? You're a wannabe bad boy," she spits with a cocked eyebrow and an evil, closed-lip smile. Her light hair is draped across half of her face like she's already been properly fucked. "All mysterious with a secret motorcycle. A secret life."

I pull away and dig my phone out of my back pocket and she keeps running her mouth. "You're probably a pimp." Her tongue slowly glides over her lower lip before her eyes widen in mockery. "Or a drug dealer. What are you—"

Her pink pouty lips are silenced by my finger as I open the camera app. This black lace thong she's wearing leaves nothing to the imagination. I'd be a dumb fuck not to check the view.

"I'm not what you think I am. But what I want you to know is that I wouldn't hesitate to spit in your mouth so you can wet my dick with that pretty little mouth of yours."

Her mouth opens and snaps shut like an alligator. But my declaration shuts her up. For now.

"I can create my own saliva. Thanks." And there goes the silence before she rolls her eyes.

I reverse the camera and hold it under the table before I tap the white button, getting exactly the view that I want. "What a perfect new background for my phone." I admire my photography skills and look up to her. She's not blushing. Not embarrassed, but more inquisitive.

I flip my phone around and show the picture of her thighs squeezing the thin piece of cloth to death before it disappears between her ass cheeks. Not sure why I thought she'd cower at the view of herself, but instead she widens her legs.

Jesus fuck.

Being around this woman is like dancing with the Devil. Seductive. Entertaining. And fucking dangerous.

"You like taking pictures of me?" she dares, looking down at the black fabric that has a very obvious wet spot. "Take another, Rocco."

I've barely touched her and she's soaking through her panties for me. I go to hold up my phone, willing to take another like she wants—I mean, I never back down from a dare. Like a moth to a flame, Daisy is pulling me in one feisty remark at a time.

The table glass is smudged from her arousal, and I have this insatiable need to lick it clean and slurp up what's dripping out of her like a teenage boy tasting pussy for the first time.

Just then, my phone vibrates in my hand and a notification pops up.

No.

"Shit." Of course, one night off from a fight is just enough rest, but *two* nights off? It's unheard of to *him*. When Santi says a fight opens, that means I need to get my ass there ASAP. If I don't, my father will kick my ass. Literally. I have more than enough scars, physically and mentally, from him, all because I took a night off.

Not only do the cigar burns cover my back, but they covered my left arm to my wrist to my shoulder before I got my tattoo sleeve. He always said something along the lines of 'until I take responsibility for my actions, my punishments will be those he sees fit'. Those scars are covered with tattoos. Random ass tattoos that have a lot of shading. A lot of pain. The pain I allowed myself to have, not the kind he gave me. Covering up those small circles was the day I had my first panic attack.

The mind is a crazy thing. The muscle memory of my brain is

used to things being done to me, not for me, so I collapsed—felt like I was having a heart attack. Or what I would imagine a heart attack would feel like. After the seventh episode, I got a grip. Though, to this day, some panic attacks are worse than others.

"Who is it? Melissa?" Daisy's voice startles me out of my head, eyes darting to my phone briefly before searing into my soul. Her cheeks are pulled between her teeth, narrowing her already thin face.

My eyes find hers and travel back to my phone as I text Santi back. "I gotta go."

"Whatever." She shakes her head and slides off the table as I walk away, trying to find the keys to my bike. All I can do is imagine how sliding off the table caused her panties to soak up that wet spot.

We both look down at the puddle she left on the glass. She looks up at me like she's asking me what I'm going to do about it.

I walk back toward her, bend over, gripping the ends of the table like I would if I were licking her pussy. She gasps as I roll my tongue over the puddle and slurp it up like it's the last drop of water in the sweltering desert.

Once I straighten and my eyes find hers, I give her a sideways grin and wipe my mouth with the back of my hand.

"I hope that tasted like Windex," she snarks, narrowing her eyes and pursing her lips.

I laugh. Actually laugh. The feeling is so foreign it makes my chest hurt. "No. It tasted like you ate some pineapple today. But you also had some garlic. Not *too* bad." I run my tongue over my lips for extra affect. Her cheeks turn a bright shade of pink. "I'd eat it."

"Argh!" I watch her ass as she stomps away and up the steps. Once she nears the top and rounds the corner, she puts a little extra effort to make her perky ass swing back and forth. Right before I open the front door, her bedroom door slams.

Crossing boundaries is my go-to. But I'm reminded that I can't with her. Not anymore. I won't have her blood on my hands.

I shut the door behind me and my phone vibrates in my hand.

"I'm on my way, Santi. What's up?"

CHAPTER
TWENTY-ONE

DAISY

THE ROAR of Rocco's motorcycle grows farther away from the house as I stick up both middle fingers toward the noise.

I hook my thumbs on the sides of my soaked thong and shimmy the thin floss out of my ass, and they land next to my phone that's vibrating. I want nothing to do with anyone or anything right now. But what if it's an Egyptian prince calling to tell me I've inherited a fortune? Or maybe someone calling to extend my car's warranty.

Wrong on both counts. "Mom. What a surprise." I grunt, bending over to pick it up, but instead fall to the floor next to it. I assume she's calling to wish me an early happy birthday.

I swipe to answer and already regret it. "Hi, Mom."

"Hey, Daisy," she slurs. Tony's deep voice sounds in the background saying something I can't understand. "Everything okay?" she asks, slowly.

"Everything's fine. I actually got a job—" Against my better judgment and decision not to tell her, I open my mouth about a part of my life that brings me joy.

She laughs, cutting me off. "Tony! Another? Are you trying to get me drunk again? You bad boy."

Ew.

"It's the only way I can get what I want," he says too close to the phone for comfort.

Sharing a private part of my life with my mother is kind of a big deal since the only thing growing between us lately is distance. I try to tamp down the jealousy I have toward her new husband. Hell, she has no idea Jeremy and I aren't together. And if Jeremy's mom told her and she does know, she hasn't said a thing. But now I'm rethinking telling her anything.

"How're you doing with money? Doya nee-any?"

My eye roll is loud enough to summon a noise complaint from the neighbors.

"I'm fine—"

"See you in a week, baby." And she hangs up. My birthday is in three hours, and it sounds like she's going to be skipping that phone call altogether.

I throw my head down on my arm, but not before tossing the phone across the carpet. "Fuck men. All of them."

I need a girlfriend to hang out with, I think. God. Maybe I just need a good night's sleep.

Rolling over onto my back, I let the scratchiness of the carpet irritate my bare ass. Being half-naked isn't normally an issue, but when it's my bottom half without clothes, it only reminds me of how turned on I am.

"You know what? I'm not staying home tonight! Fuck him." I pop up, pull out a pair of leggings, and change into an old black tank.

I throw my hair into a long ponytail, run a red gloss over my lips, and give myself a confident smile. I'm a smart woman, but I never said my rash decisions were good ones.

The lonely life I live as a recluse is slowly starting to catch up to me. This house with nobody in it is supposed to be my safe haven. Like me, everything is bright and beachy on the outside, but when you sit back and think of the dark stories that happen between these walls. What really goes down with my mom and Tony when Rocco and I aren't home? Does he grab her the same way he grabbed me? Or does she refuse to question him about some of his actions? Is she just down for the ride? All questions that will go unanswered because the only thing we share lately is our DNA.

I zoom down the steps and grab my keys from the floor before I look around the foyer. Those few moments with Rocco feel like a lifetime ago. I should've known better than to get partially entangled with him, but we'll just chalk it up to hormones.

Glancing down at my phone, I notice a missed call from Jim. "Shit! I was supposed to work tonight." It's past eleven. He's closed by now. Another tough conversation I'm going to have to have.

I could have it now because sleeping in the back, but instead, I'm heading to the one place I should stay away from.

———

I POUND three times and the same guy as before lets me in, except this time I'm not with Brad. I trot down the dark hall, following the screams. People are chanting for the fighter Death.

As the dim neon lights appear, I see red. Everywhere. Blood. So much blood.

It's the guy I saw the other night.

The smell of sweat, blood, and dirty metal drifts through the air like it's coming out of the air vents. New splatters of burgundy coat the ropes surrounding the ring. Blood slowly drips down Death's body, covering the tattoos over his torso. Yet, his face paint is untouched. While the other smaller man has splotches of neon yellow, I'm assuming his blood turned the paint into a burnt sienna color.

"Are you here with someone?" I turn to the raspy voice, only to find a beautiful woman who's barely dressed. Dark hair curls down her tan back.

I lean closer to her. "Promise me, if you ever see me on the street crying over a man, you'll wipe my tears."

She gives me a sideways smirk with her red glossed lips. "What's that supposed to mean?"

"If I weren't stuck on someone I shouldn't be right now, or was a glutton for punishment trying to get dicked down, I'd take a chance on you."

Her laugh is loud and bold. "Name's Destiny." As screams and chants get louder, she wipes the side of my lip and brings it to her mouth. "Just so you know, babe, I don't clean up men's messes. I like to make my own." She winks. "So, if you're ever crying in the street over a man and I see you, I'll mess you up all on my own— with chocolate, whipped cream, and a whole lotta lust."

Destiny doesn't stick around to let me say anything. Instead, she walks off with her short denim shorts and legs for days, leaving me here in a pool full of sweaty dudes.

The sound of skin on skin doesn't tend to be my favorite noise considering where I am, but I follow the noise and see Death beating the other guy to a pulp. But I have to hand it to the poor soul—he's still standing, but barely. If I were him, I'd be playing dead in the corner after one punch to the nose.

"What are you doing here all alone?" A familiar voice startles me. I turn and there's Brad with his face painted in all white with a brown stripe down the middle. His face looks like a goddamn landing strip. "Hey there, darlin'."

Now part of me wants to walk away and play dumb. If I pretend it isn't him, maybe he'll leave me alone. The crowd is pushing themselves closer and closer to the ring like a mosh pit. If I have any chance of surviving this encounter, playing dumb isn't in the cards.

"Bowling wasn't exciting enough?" I gesture to the ring. "Needed to get your hands dirty, hmm?" His lip curls as he dips lower. The crowd screams and all focus is on the ring. He towers over me, taking each step slower, backing me up until I'm against the cold cinderblock. This man could slit my throat right here and not a damn person would notice. "You don't need to worry about my hands, pretty thing. They'll be well enough to pin you to your bed when I finally take what's mine."

I swallow but it feels like needles prickling the back of my throat and it's making it hard to speak. "I know one thing that certainly is not yours, and you will *not* be taking it," I rasp out, trying to square my body against his. It's what peacocks do. Puff up their feathers to appear bigger.

Is this when I should realize I've entered a losing battle? Comparing myself to a peacock. However, I have to hand it to the National Geographic channel for my useless knowledge about random animals.

"You're up, Beast." A deep voice rumbles from behind Brad. *Beast.*

The irony. Because his transformation is just as bad as the prince's.

I eye the keeper of the seductive, low voice. It sounds like velvet. Like being surrounded by silky sheets after you shave your legs. *It's Death.* Up close and personal. He's wearing a black robe with a hood shading his face—his skeleton paint still almost fully intact.

Brad—I'm sorry, Beast—turns to look at Death. I swear you'd think being the top two performers of this shit show, they would have some mutual respect for one another, but it seems as though both men are puffing out their own peacock tail feathers.

"Who's your friend?" Death's eyes find mine. Beautiful mocha eyes dive deep into my aura, sounding off every bell in my head. Except it's not the same siren head noise Brad comes with. This is less of a bell, almost an anthem—like the song that plays when the Joker asks Harley Quinn to live for him in The Suicide Squad movie.

Brad looks at me. "She's my girlfriend."

"Bah!" A weird noise flies out of my mouth. "Not his girlfriend. Not one bit. I'm Daisy."

Death glares back to Bra—Beast and speaks through gritted teeth, "You better get going before they forfeit your fight. I'll keep an eye on her for ya." The parasite moves away, but not before he steps over to a man in a suit. He points to me and the man nods.

Great. Now I'm being watched.

The hooded mystery man leans against the wall next to me. "If you wanted someone dangerous, you could have come to me."

I turn my whole body to face him. "Oh good, your ego is just as big as the last douchebag." A guttural laugh escapes him, and I swear I just came.

"You're not wrong." I can't help but smile at his nonchalance after he basically mauled a man to death only minutes ago. If it were me, I'd be heaving over a toilet or trying to slit my wrists to find my exit out of this caged world full of cruelty. Death turns his whole body, so we're face to face. Body heat to body heat. "Can I take you somewhere?"

Now it's my turn to laugh. "I'm neck deep in the smell of sweat and the smell of fresh blood…" I let my eyes rake down the sliver of torso exposed from his robe. "And from the looks of it, you are literally covered in it. You think I want to go somewhere with you?"

He looks down the dark hall that's a few feet away and back at me. His hand lifts my chin to look at him. "If the smell is the only issue, that can be rectified. If I leave for five minutes, will you still be here when I get back?" The crowd steals my attention as they start chanting Beast. Out walks Brad, giving people high fives like he is a starting quarterback.

"Yeah. I'll be here." Because if I leave now, that large-suited man, I'm sure, is trained to attack on command. Although, his belly is almost the size of a beachball, and his skinny suit pants accentuate his chicken legs. I could outrun him, but he'd probably shoot me or something.

Death doesn't say anything more before he dips into the black hole. I zone in on the fight. The crowd doesn't seem to worship Brad like they do Death. I wonder why? His stance is different, and while Death has a vicious fluidity about him, Brad's moves are jumpy and sharp. This poor man against him doesn't seem to stand a chance, though. He looks like he eats less than I do. Dark red flies through the air, landing on the front few rows of people and they cheer. What type of elitist sadism is this? I always imagined underground fighting as something with rules. Less rules than the fighting on TV, but rules, nonetheless.

"Ready?"

I turn to the milk chocolatey voice to find a clean Death with fresh face paint. "Couldn't dare show your face, hm?"

"It's for your own good." I look to Brad, trying to shake off a laugh.

"This sounds like the start of a bad romance novel," I say sarcastically, looking back at him. His dark hood from his hoodie is still shadowing his face, but his eyes. They feel familiar. They almost feel like home.

"Romance novels are subjective, are they not?" he asks, never taking his eyes off me.

"Depends on the author's voice." I stare. He stares. "We aren't talking about romance novels, are we?"

Death shakes his head slowly. The crowd roars as Brad kicks a guy when he's down. I glance at the guy in the suit whose eyes are still on me.

"Is he going to be a problem?" I look back to Death.

"Not if you follow my lead and move when I move." My stomach's doing somersaults, and my veins are zooming with adrenaline. "Okay. Let's go then." He nods and I look down at his extended, black-gloved hand.

In life, there are a series of decisions we make that determine our journey. But I feel like a person's destination is already mapped out. It's all about how we get there. Do I want my journey to be lonely? Or do I want it to be filled with questionable adventures with morally gray decisions along the way?

I'm being careless—I know this. I've been that way since I hopped on the back of Brad's motorcycle. But loneliness does that to a person. The whole thing with Rocco was a mistake. Maybe I need to look at him only as a stepbrother instead of someone who enjoys choking me or making me wet every time his jaw clenches.

At this point, what's the point of living? Why the hell not go with one, or potentially two, dangerous men who could easily crack open the rest of my cold, dead heart—or my soul? Have I done this to myself? Or have I simply walked away from those who are committed to misunderstanding me?

I place my hand in his and he pulls me behind him before he shouts, "Who we here for?"

Heads turn toward him and away from Beast, who's celebrating his obvious win. Everyone screams "Death" and runs up to him like he's some A-list movie star in public. They surround him, blocking Mr. Chubby Guard who has been eyeing me like a hawk, and we somehow manage to dip down the dark hallway. The guy who answered the door for me blocks the crowd from following, and I can't help but laugh as I run behind him. A loud creak of the door opening to the outside jolts my insides. The warm night air slaps me in the face while my boots crunch over the gravel in the parking lot.

Death pulls me to a Jeep Wrangler Sport, opens my door for me, and runs around to his side. Before I can comprehend that a man with the same trappings as the Grim Reaper is just as gentlemanly as Jeremy, we peal out of the parking lot, leaving nothing behind us but dust and burnt rubber.

"So, uh…where are you taking me?" I grab a small brown book from the center console, and he snatches it out of my hand. "Hey!"

"It's not your business," he snarls before chucking it in the back seat.

"You didn't answer me. Where are you taking me," I stare at the side of his face. From the time he got in the car to now, the hood from his sweatshirt is down and his dark hair is under a backward baseball cap.

Oh, hell.

"Nice car."

"Not mine," he quips.

When he doesn't say anything else, I add, "If you're going to kill me, can I at least choose how I go? I mean…" It's this moment I start rambling…and he lets me. "I guess I don't mind dying. I don't have much to live for." I turn my head to look out my side. Passing trees fly by. "My mom, I'm pretty sure we have never been further apart. She's intoxicated on her honeymoon with a man I *want* to like, but something about him rubs me the wrong way. And my stepbrother…" I look to Death and his hand is tense as it's wrapped around the steering wheel. The moonlight above is lighting the roofless cab.

I don't continue, but instead, I start picking the skin around my nail.

"What about him?"

"What about who?"

"You're stepbrother? You don't like him?" he asks, still not looking at me. The wind whips my hair around my face before I pull it up with the scrunchie around my wrist.

"I…Yeah, he's nice. I don't know. He's so hot and cold. It's like one time he's cold as ice, wants nothing to do with me, and the next he's got his hand wrapped around my neck and my panties are soaked."

Death coughs next to me, and I shake my head. "Shit. Sorry. I don't really have many people to talk to, and it just seems to be exorcising from me."

We pull into a small parking lot that's so well hidden between a bunch of trees. How have I lived here my whole life and have never known these places existed?

I make a mental note to try to remember how we got here so I can see it during the day.

"We're here." He throws the Jeep in park and opens his door, and I follow. Once my feet hit the ground, my shoes slide on the sand. I walk around to the back of the Jeep where he's standing with his hands clasped on top of his head.

I look out to the horizon where the full moon meets the sea. Waves are crashing and the wind is blowing the palm trees, washing over me with the most tranquil feeling I've had in a while. "What time is it?"

He must think I'm nuts. Instead of talking about the beauty that we're looking at, I'm asking the time. Like a girl who visits an underground fighting ring has a curfew or something.

The light from his phone illuminates his painted face. I wonder what he looks like without the paint. It's so thick. There are barely any facial features I can make out. Unfortunately.

"Twelve-eighteen." He slides the phone back into his pocket.

"It's my birthday," I whisper into the night sky.

CHAPTER
TWENTY-TWO

DAISY

SPILLING my guts isn't usually something I do considering when I was growing up, everything I told my mother was used against me. Transactional conversations. If I confided in her, it would be held over my head at a later date. Doesn't fucking matter. Eventually, I learned to keep my mouth shut. Yet for some reason, knowing how she is, I still crave a normal relationship with her… normal conversations.

I feel his eyes on me and all I really want to do is cry. I'm not sure why, but a single tear slides down my left cheek, the one farthest from him, and I swallow down a lump in my throat.

A loud creak comes from behind me, and I turn to see Death climbing into the back, laying out pillows and a blanket that he pulled the empty space where the back seats are supposed to be. His gloved hand is extended once again to take mine.

"Are you going to help me up? Or is this a Mufasa-Scar type of scene?" I let his hand sit in front of me, waiting for his answer.

"You think if you were to fall off the back to the ground, it would kill you?" The sides of his lips tilt like he's trying to fight a smile. I wonder what his smile looks like without all this paint.

"You never know. A three-foot fall could be my demise. Especially head first." I drive my hand perpendicular to the other. "More like a jackknife situation."

"Would you just get up here?" His voice is full of patience and humor.

Once I lose my internal battle to trust someone other than myself, I rest my hand in Rocco's and he pulls me up. "Do you often pick up random women and take them to watch the waves at night?"

"I usually sleep here. Outside in the back of the Jeep," he admits.

"Are you homeless?" Insert foot into mouth. Thank God he laughs. He. Laughs. And it's more soothing to my spirit than the sound of the ocean. The deep rumble of his chest and his smile that's illuminated by the moonlight draws me in, needing to know more about the man behind the paint.

"My home life is…complicated." Death exhales like he's been holding his breath. "It's my friend's…from the ring. He let's me borrow it when I need to get away and I don't want to go home. Don't want to be tracked." His voice trails off at the end.

There are so many more questions I want to ask. But I don't. It seems he needs this escape just as much as I do.

Despite myself, I ask, "Want to talk about it?" I cringe at how clinical I sound. Like an undercover therapist who needs her own therapy.

Ignoring my question, his lips pucker as he bites the inside of his cheek. "Happy birthday, by the way. Sorry if I took you away from your *boyfriend*." His head dips as he says the last part. His fingers fidget with a ball of paper.

"Ha. He is not my boyfriend. He is…certainly…something. But he's *not* my boyfriend. Definitely not my boyfriend."

"You said that."

I take a long look at him. I can't even make out the contours of his face because of his shading with the paint. He's had to have been painting his face for a while to master the skill of contouring that women sometimes go their whole lives without knowing. Even the shape of his lips is an optical illusion.

"Why did you repaint your face after your shower?" I ask, still unable to take my eyes away from his mouth.

"I would have had to convince you it was me without the paint, and we didn't have the time because you were being watched." I know I was being watched, but hearing him confirm it causes a shiver to run through my body. The hair on the back of my neck stands at the thought of where I'd be if I hadn't left with him.

Death nudges me with his shoulder. "Hey, I got you, D." The way that sentence rolls off his tongue, as sweet as sin and vaguely familiar, rattles every nerve in my body. I start fidgeting, rubbing the pad of my thumb against my pinky. "Tell me about your birthday," he says softly. "How old are you? What are you going to do to celebrate?"

I pinch my brows in thought. What the hell was my grand celebration for my twentieth chapter of life? Sit home and read? Perhaps watch *Sex/Life* on Netflix again? Who the hell knows? "My mom is out of town with her new husband, and my stepbrother seems to have a life of his own, so he's never home."

I look over at him again, waiting for him to speak.

"No friends?"

Normally this question would send me into a defensive frenzy. I'd pick a fight about how quality is better than quantity, and the fact that true friends who are more like soulmates are harder to find than a woman who is secretly spreading her legs for a sugar daddy. But I digress.

"For a while, my ex was my friend while he was my boyfriend. Then we broke up and you know, he said he needed space, so that's what he has." I slap my lap in defeat. "And I have—had a friend, Crew. We lost touch when I went away to college."

I loved him. But he was never interested in girls except for one, and I was not her. I'm boring myself with this small talk, and I can feel the need to run into the dark ocean and dare marine life to come and take me. "Can we change the subject?"

Death nods, sticking his bottom lip out. "So, you're a virgin?"

I snap my head to him so fast, it makes my neck crack, sending a jolt up my skull. "Wow, Death, you waste no time. Do you?" His dark eyes boar into me, never straying. "What would make you ask that? I'm pretty sure that's not your business."

A shrug of his shoulders is how he answers. No words. Who asks someone that randomly? But I give in. I open up. Something I don't do. I need to feel liberated. And if trusting this stranger with my secret frees me from something I've been carrying around with me like sack of potatoes, so be it.

With a deep exhale, it's as if I've released all verbal defenses. "Yes. I'm a virgin. I tried for years to have sex with my boyfriend, but he was always so awkward and just not into it." I turn my body toward Death, shaking the Jeep as I move. "I don't even think at the end that it was about being a horny teenager. It was more about the fervent craving to be desired. And the person I wanted to desire me was content on a PG-rated makeout session far away from the public eye."

"Sounds like a fuckboy. He had another girlfriend or something?" Death's eyes still haven't veered from mine—barely blinking. He's been focused on every word that was coming out of my mouth. The depth of his stare heats my belly, but the warmth doesn't fall between my legs. Instead, it seeps upward, making my heart beat faster…harder.

"No. Jeremy was a lot of things, but never a cheater." My eyes fall to my lap.

"So, your stepbrother. He cool?" Death swallows, causing his Adam's apple to move up and down. A movement that draws me in. Sirens go off in my head, alerting me that my body is moving closer to him without my brain partaking in any decision-making. I lean over and press my nose gently to his neck and he doesn't budge. His head lifts slightly as I start running my tongue over the bulge in the front of his throat, and it jumps under my touch. I breathe in a familiar scent of soap before I close my lips over his skin, and he releases a breath.

Bringing my hand over my mouth as I pull back slightly, I almost expect embarrassment to zing through me, but it's quite the opposite. An intense pull to him begins to consume me. Like I *need* to be closer to him. I fight it. I fight it *hard*.

The blanket folds under me as I retreat back to my spot, and I can feel the lick of the warm, humid air on my skin. The moon seems brighter and the waves a little louder. Is this what people mean when they say they can hear colors? All five senses seem to be heightened, and I'm too into the heady feeling devouring my mind to even look at Death's reaction to my licking him.

After letting my nerves simmer for what feels like hours—or maybe it was only minutes—I allow my gaze to find his. This time the corners of his lips are tilted upward, and his eyes are narrowed at me like he's been listening to my thoughts that are running rampant.

"What?" I ask, sounding annoyed. But that's the thing…I'm anything but annoyed. Intrigued? Yes. But not annoyed.

"I don't know. It feels like you kinda like me." A small crooked smile appears. Another feeling of familiarity washes over me.

I shake my head. "I just feel like I know you. Like you're not a complete stranger I ran off with, and somehow I feel safer with you than I did with…what's his face…"

He sits up so abruptly, I try to replay the last milliseconds to make sure I didn't say something that bruised his ego.

"I should get you home." His voice is stern and deep like he's reprimanding a child.

"Ah. I see. A little neck lick from a girl named after a dainty flower, and it sends you spiraling," I scold.

A part of my ego crumbles when he mumbles, "Yeah.

Remember that for next time."

Nope. Not today.

"That's the thing… There won't be a next time." I end up saying that to the back of his head as he jumps off the edge of the Jeep and onto the ground before extending his hand to help me down.

Hell no, sir. I can get down by myself. And I do. I jump down and land harder than expected, sending a double jolt of pain from my ankles to my knees. I guess that's what happens now that I'm officially twenty. I'm basically geriatric.

Like an independent woman who still needs a ride home, I climb into the passenger seat with a smile. Death slides in next to me, never sparing me a look. The engine is loud compared to the quiet night we were enjoying only minutes ago.

"Are you—"

"Just take me to my car, please." I offer him a kind grin and stare out the windshield like an emotionally stunted individual. I'm far from it, though. I'm more on the precipice of an existential crisis. A fifth-life crisis, if you will.

The ride back to the warehouse is quiet, and by the time we pull in, my car is the only one in the lot, and the single outside light is switched off.

We get out of the car and my entire body gets a chill. "This place gives me an eerie *Hostel* vibe."

"Nah. There's no smokestack where they incinerate the dead bodies here," he replies like he's watched that movie as much as I have. "And Jay Hernandez won't come to save you." He's definitely seen it as much as I have.

I walk to the back of the Jeep where he's standing. I may not be his biggest fan right now, but I'd rather be next to him if some rich elitist pops out of the bush in a rubber apron and a carving knife.

"Better get in before—"

I cut him off for the second time tonight.

"Please don't say 'elitist kidnaps you.'"

Talk about sharing the same brain wave.

The corner of his mouth turns up and I can't help but pick on him. "I'm surprised with the humidity that your contouring is holding up. Maybe you'll have to give me the name of the makeup brand you use."

Death closes the space between us and rubs my bottom lip with the pad of his thumb, sending a sudden, dull ache between my legs. Between this interaction and the one earlier with Rocco, I'm a live wire.

He pauses and I grow impatient. "Are you a dentist trying to see my bottom teeth? Or are you going to kiss me? Because I'm starting to think maybe you're the one who's going to kill me, starting with my tee—"

His lips push into mine as an invitation to kiss him back while simultaneously shutting the hell up. I wait for his tongue to seek permission, but it never comes.

So maybe it wasn't an invitation.

I'm left skin to skin—well, lip to lip—contemplating how necessary it is to deepen this kiss, but my eyes fall closed, and a tingle moves from my lips to the tips of my toes. A closed-lip kiss is something you have with your first boyfriend in middle school. But there is nothing middle school about this one as his hands move from my hips, up my rib cage, before his thumbs rest under my breasts. I arch into him and feel the bulge in his pants pushing against me, and I can't help but moan at the contact.

My lips grow cool at the loss of touch before I hear him say, "Goodnight, Daisy." I blink my eyes open, trying to focus, and he nods his head to my car that's parked next to his, and I scoff.

I have a smart-ass comment locked and loaded, but it never makes it past the filter that only works about five percent of the time.

"Goodnight, stranger." I don't call him Death. It reminds me of the end of something, and he feels nothing like an end. My body is humming, which can only mean one thing—this is definitely the start of something.

ROCCO

WHEN I WALKED out of the house last night, I didn't expect to hang out with Daisy as Death. Hell, I didn't expect to hang out with Daisy at all. The few run-ins I've had with her as Death and myself have been filled with some sort of off-kilter sexual tension. It wasn't filled with eye fucking, but more of those stolen glances I've grown to be addicted to when we're at home.

I was forced to sweat my dick off in that damn hoodie because I can't risk her seeing my tattoos up close—the woman stares at me anytime they are exposed at home. But the way Brad's guy was watching her, I had no choice other than to get her the hell out of there. He isn't the only one. My father has men there who watch me. The last thing we need is for him to find out Daisy is hanging out at the ring. They are dangerous and will stop at nothing to kill anything in my way of *his* punishment for me.

I splash water on my face, washing away what's left of the soap. After Daisy pulled away from the warehouse, I left the Jeep behind and grabbed my bike. I snuck in the back door like a champ. Although I've mastered the technique of being stealthy, sneaking by her tonight while she was on the living room couch made me feel like I was in *Mission Impossible*. The girl leaves every damn light on in the house. It's just a recent occurrence. Ever since Brad was here that one night, she's done that. So why the hell did she come to the ring knowing she could possibly run into him?

It's four in the morning and I'm ninety-nine percent sure I heard her slipping into her room about an hour ago. The girl barely sleeps and watches trashy TV like it's her job.

Before I go to bed, I sneak over to her room holding a birthday cupcake in a plastic container I picked up on my way home. I may be a dick, but the girl spilled her heart out to me—or Death—a few hours ago. She sounded pathetic, and it made something pull at my chest. I haven't celebrated a birthday since my mom died, but her mom isn't dead. But she's with my father, and that's as good as dead.

From the time it takes me to walk from my room to hers, my dick thinks it's about to get some. The three times I beat off since I've been home did nothing to ease the nagging desire I have for this woman.

Her door's ajar, allowing a sliver of light to slip through, slightly illuminating the hallway.

I look up to the heavens and I pray that she's just as feral for me as I am her. Maybe she's rubbing her pretty little pink pussy, outlining every fold with her slender fingers. Thinking about that first slide into her.

A guy can dream.

Instead, she's tits up in a see-through tank top that…wait… that's my tank top. The Anti-Social Skateboard Club logo is practically worn completely off. The shirt's not covering anything since her nipple ring is stopping it from covering her left nipple. Her blonde hair is fanned around her head while she lays like a body that's about to be outlined in chalk.

"You're a hot fucking mess. And who the hell can fall asleep with the lights on? Psychopath," I whisper, placing the cupcake on her nightstand with a note next to it. Her phone lights up, and as soon as I go to pick it up, a light snore comes from her open mouth.

Dear Jesus, she snores.

I glance at the phone once more to find a message from Brad. Without hesitation, I grab it and the message opens, showing me exactly what I need to see.

Of course, her phone doesn't have a lock on it.

> Brad: Why'd you leave with him?
>
> You aren't safe with Death.
>
> Come and watch me fight tonight. I'll show you how a real man fights.

Message after message comes through. This dude texts like a girl, one after another.

> Brad: I'm the right guy for you.
>
> You'll see...
>
> There's nothing he can do that I can't do better ;)

"He sure as hell isn't talking about me," I mumble a little too loudly as Daisy shifts. I freeze until her breathing evens. I want to text him back on her behalf and tell him to shove his egotistical texts up his ass. But part of me wants to see what his game is. Everyone in the world has an agenda. Everyone in *my* world anyway. And all I have to do is stay one step ahead.

CHAPTER
TWENTY-FOUR

DAISY

NOTHING THROWS a wrench in my morning sleep like waking up with the lights on. I must have forgotten to shut them off last night after that stimulating hangout with Death. *Fine.* A small part of me wanted to straddle him and have a hot makeout session in the back of the Jeep. Alas, I tucked my ever-loving urge of needing to desire and be desired away and made a grown-up choice, which led me here. Alone. *With the fucking lights on.*

Another wrench is when I wake up forgetting where I am or how the hell I got here. I wasn't drinking. If anything, I was drunk on whom I can only assume is a painted mask murderer named Death. Who, in turn, got his name by killing people. In the ring or out of it, killing is killing.

But something inside of me tingles at the memory of last night. The talk. The way his dark eyes met mine as the soft ocean breeze left kisses on my skin.

I shiver at the thought of him being the one who's leaving kisses on my skin. He's probably a man who takes it all. Like the guy who

would bend me over the seat of a motorcycle and fuck me senseless in a grocery store parking lot. Or would he?

Rocco seems like he'd be the one to do that. Death might be the kind of guy who gets all of this adrenaline out in the ring and wants to rock you to sleep during missionary.

"Enough of this. I'm turning myself on for no reason," I huff.

I shuffle around in my bed, tucking my rogue boob back into the tank top I jacked from Rocco, and completely dreading the idea of looking at my phone. I know Brad texted me. There is no way he wouldn't. He told me to stay put, and I did anything but. I'm still unsure why I was being guarded to begin with.

"Doesn't sit easy with me," I mumble to myself. "I need a friend. No. A dog."

I blink a few times, getting used to the light, and I spot a container.

"Is this…" It's a cupcake with a note taped on the side. "Happy Birthday. -D"

D. Death. That's the only "D" I can think of who would have the balls the size of Texas to commit a B and E just to leave a cupcake. I don't know much about that man, but from the gist of what he gave me last night, he doesn't fight for fun. More because he has to. Not sure how the hell he found out where I lived, so we can add 'stalker' to the list of possible crimes committed.

My stomach releases a growl like a lioness protecting her cub. I'm not sure I've eaten anything since lunch yesterday, and I'm about fifty shades past hangry.

This isn't just a store-bought cupcake. This is baker quality. The faint blue and lavender icing is perfectly spiraled to a point where a small purple daisy rests. I bite back a smile. I'm not sure when the last time I had a cupcake was. Actually, I'm not sure when I celebrated my birthday last.

My mom always called, and Jeremy would give me a coupon for free hugs. But when it came to a gift or any type of cake? I'd have to check the album on my phone. Knowing the string of events that's cursed my life , mostly dad's death, I think it goes back to freshman year of high school.

I grab my phone after I peel off the cupcake paper and scroll through my contacts. If Death was bold enough to break into my house and come into my room, which should terrify me but doesn't, then maybe he also put his number in my phone.

"Of course not."

Feeling a little defeated, I avoid looking at my phone and get dressed. It's time to head into work because I left them high and dry, and I need to make amends—and hopefully I still have a job to go to.

"I CAN'T KEEP you on the schedule if you don't show up for your shift, Daisy. It's not fair to Elle. Or me." Jim hobbles to the counter, leaving me behind him soaking in my guilt. Like I don't have enough of it. It's turning out to be my signature scent.

"Jim." I hurry over and gently grab his fragile arm. "This job is all I have. I messed up. I should have called. My mother is up her new husband's ass, her new husband is sketchy at best. His son... well, let's just say it's complicated. And I have no friends. I'm lonely and need something. Anything. And I'm not asking for pity, but simply pleading my case."

His dark eyes, wrinkled at the edges—well, wrinkled everywhere—find mine. "I lost track of what day it was. What time it was. I'm not doing too well, and just got distracted by life. I'm so sorry."

"I just expect the courtesy of a phone call if you can't cover a shift. I know we don't get too busy here, but Elle has a life, too."

"Oh, Jim!" I hug him tightly, feeling he may be my only lifeline for a pinch of happiness. "You won't regret it."

I relax my arms and step back, and like a father scolding his child, he says, "Prove it."

His light footsteps disappear into the backroom, and I make a beeline to Elle.

"Hey," she says quietly, not looking up from the cookies she's scooping onto the tray.

"Listen, Elle…I'm really sorry. I've been having somewhat of an existential crisis. And while it's not over, I'm trying to be less selfish and more present." It's not entirely true. The present is where my crisis lies, but she doesn't need to know about anything involving my personal life.

Her light eyes finally find mine, and she offers me a small, closed-lip smile. "It's okay. We all go through some hard times. I just hope you have a support system who can help you through."

Those words are supposed to make me feel good. But they don't. They want to push me into a deeper spiral. It's like I'm being pushed down a funnel into a black abyss and I'm clawing and scratching, trying to find anything to latch onto so I can stop the fall, but I come up short.

"What are you doing tonight?"

Elle's voice yanks me from my mind. "What'd you say?" I nervously start picking at my cuticle skin.

"My shift ends soon. You want to hang out after you're off?" she asks while putting the cookie tray into the refrigerator before laying the dirty dishes in the sink.

I wonder what hanging out with Elle looks like. Maybe sitting in her bedroom talking about boys and braiding each other's hair. Maybe watching movies and eating our weight in Ben & Jerry's. Part of me is curious about how she would respond to the warehouse.

"Actually, there's somewhere I need to go tonight, but raincheck?" I ask, hoping she'll ask again. Or that she'll accept my offer if I ask her the same.

She unties her apron and hangs it on the hook. "Of course, Daisy."

Hours pass slowly. I've only served a handful of customers, but this café is so peaceful. It lets my mind rest.

Once I lock up, I come to a dead stop on the sidewalk. A light breeze kicks up and I close my eyes. The only darker cloud looming over me than the loneliness I'm treading in is the heaviness in the pit of my stomach. Like it's the siren from *The Purge* warning me to run the other way. *Just go home.*

But when you have nothing to live for, why not dive in head first?

THE SMELL of sweat and metal, which at this point I believe is fresh blood, fills my nostrils and the bile rises to my throat. It's a smell I'll never grow accustomed to. As I step slowly through the dark hall toward the screams, a shiver runs through me. The energy in here is heavy, murky, even. Maybe it's the number of dead bodies they've scraped from the floor of the ring, or the amount of souls that have been sold to the Devil by participating in such hell.

When I reach the end, I don't step fully into the light.

"I'm here to thank Death for the cupcake. That's it," I mumble to myself.

"You're here to what?" *Awe, damnit. Shoot me.* "Where'd you disappear to last night?" Brad asks as he snakes his arm around my waist.

I push my hands against his chest, trying to put space between us, but my lack of muscles and caring about my body is preventing it. "Things were getting crazy, so I thought I'd dip." I offer a closed smile, hoping he'd buy it.

"Ah. Well, don't go anywhere tonight. We're introducing a new fighter." Brad nudges me into the neon lights of the open room, and my eyes lock on a set of brown eyes. My stomach does somersaults under his focused gaze. "He's supposably on the same level as me and Death."

I turn to his icy stare. "*Supposedly*," I correct him. Call it a pet peeve…or just basic English.

"What?" He cocks his brow. "That's what I said. Anyway…" His focus turns to the ring and mine follows—back to a skull-painted face still watching me while that guy who opened the door talks in his ear. "Death is finally going to get his ass handed to him."

Now that awakened something inside of me. "What do you mean?" Brad's head snaps to me. He heard it in my voice. Was it concern? I'm not sure, but it was far from the mundane tone he's gotten from me since we met. "I just…I thought the top fighters don't fight each other." Keep going, Daisy. Make it believable before this dude takes his aggression out on you. I wrap my hands around my stomach and hunch over. "I can't handle watching someone die. It's where my morals draw the line."

Dumbass buys it because he releases a guttural laugh before an unwelcome kiss falls on my neck. I no longer smell like ocean air and freshly baked cookies, but my new scent is that of a severe case of halitosis.

On the drive here, I had to dive deep as to why I was keeping Brad around, and I've concluded two reasons. One, that saying keep your friends close and your enemies closer. He isn't my enemy, but he is Death's, and after last night, I need to keep Brad on my good side. Two, I'm scared that if I ghost him, he'll stalk my ass, and that's not the type of story I want for myself—which leaves me with knowing it's impossible to ghost him if I keep coming back to see Death.

The hair on the back of my neck stands on end, and not from the leech nuzzled against me, but a gaze so hot, I feel it before I even look at him.

Death walks to the center of the ring, ready to meet a man who is equal in size, but he's still staring at me with his head shaking back and forth.

Trust me, dude, if I could shake this snake from my side, I

would. But he's unhinged, and I'd like to make it long enough to find out where my birthday cupcake was from. *I want another.*

The guy in the middle of the ring, who looks like they found a homeless person from one of the side streets in town and handed him a note card, starts screaming.

"Death versus The Reaper. Rules are stated there…" His dirty hand points to an old chalkboard stating the lack of "rules" and he continues, "First to unconsciousness."

"The Reaper. Ha! The redundancy…" I laugh out loud to whomever will listen.

Brad looks at me as if he's questioning what the word 'redundancy' means. "I'm just saying, Death is essentially the Grim Reaper, is it not? And now the same entity is fighting against itself?" The lost look in his eyes allows me to take this loss. It's really not worth it.

"Never mind." I shrug him off and focus on the masked men in the ring. Death's opponent gets an F for originality. His face is painted yellow, and from what I can see, the yellow is embedded in the wrinkles in his forehead and around his eyes. Maybe Death will have a chance since it seems that The Reaper is older. Death will have youth on his side. *I hope.*

An airhorn echoes around the cement walls causing a ringing in my ears, and the announcer disappears out of the ring faster than I can blink.

Death throws the first punch, but The Reaper doesn't flinch. *Shit.* Death throws another immediate hit on the side of The Reaper's head and he smiles. The screams from the crowd are loud and overstimulating as Death throws hit after hit at a man who seems to be unfazed.

Brad puts his hand over my shoulder, pulling me close. "This might be the one that finally takes him down a peg."

"No. I think The Reaper is playing a mind game," I shout back. "He wants to get in Death's head." *Is it working?* I don't know enough about the face-painted gentleman to know anything about his mental state. What I do know, from only one conversation, is that we're alike. A hard exterior and even harder interior. It may only soften for the right person, but even that major event is questionable.

The Reaper punches Death's chest, and Death falls back against the rope. And unlike real boxing, there's no tap out. The rules are to unconsciousness. There is no referee in the ring calling fouls. Death gets hit again in the chest. And again…and again.

I pull out of Brad's grip and fight through the crowd, trying to get as close to Death as possible. The smell of blood is pungent and making my stomach queasier with each step I take. I take elbows to the ribs and another to the spine.

When I make it to Death, The Reaper's fist connects with Death's face, and blood gushes to the floor.

"Death. Get up!" I scream loud enough for him to hear. I don't even know him, but I know I'm not supposed to lose him

The Reaper lifts his leg to roundhouse kick Death in the head, but Death sits up and grabs his leg using his body weight to flip him so he's face down. The Reaper's face is now lying in Death's blood.

"Nice try, fucker," I hear Death say before the rest is drowned out by a roaring crowd. These people aren't a ride-or-die crowd. They root for whoever's winning. If that's not mind fucking for the fighter, I don't know what is.

Death sits on The Reaper's hands that are pinned against his back and he delivers blow after blow to the back of his head until The Reaper's body goes limp under him.

I feel my face pale and I swallow back vomit. "Did he kill him?" I ask, not sure if it was out loud or to myself. A set of brown eyes lock on mine. In that moment, I feel my body overcome with goosebumps and my nipples harden, not because I was turned on, but the unmarred and unexplained pull my body has to a man I know nothing about.

And despite the hypnotism I've fallen under, *I run.*

ROCCO

FUCK.

Lifting a bottle of whiskey to my face has never hurt so fucking much. My hands, my shoulders, my chest, my fucking face. I got my ass handed to me tonight for the first time in five years. I've been undefeated for so long, I forgot what it was like to get kicked while I'm down.

I suck air through my teeth after I swallow down the burn of the brown liquid. Anything to take this pain away.

"Rocco?" *Her* voice calls through the door.

"Go away, Daisy." I don't want her to go. I want to unlock my door, invite her in, and tell her everything. Why I fight. Why I can't get out of it. Why *he* has me in a mental chokehold…but I can't. If she knows anything, she's as good as dead.

I hear the knob jiggle. "Would you just let me the hell in? We're both adults."

"Why, so you can try to ride my dick again?" I wince at my words, and the movement kills my face. The ice packs I brought upstairs are melted and are currently giving little to no relief.

She growls and punches the door, or maybe kicks it. "In your fucking dreams!"

"Every last one of them, woman," I mumble. I dream of her. I imagine she's next to me as I fall asleep. Her dark and disturbed vibe helps me feel less alone in this cold world. Is the whole world like this? Or have I been pegged specifically to live my life in my own personal hell?

I don't hear her walk away, but the slam of her door doesn't go unnoticed. The paintings on my wall shake.

"God, you're such a dick!" she screams through the wall before turning on Sleep Token. "Take Me Back to Eden" has been playing non-stop from her room.

> Rocco:Did you join a cult?
>
> Should I be worried?

Yes, their music is deep and on another level, but she also bought an obscenely large decal of the band's logo for the back window of her car. I can't wait 'til her mom comes home with a million questions. She doesn't seem to care much about her daughter's birthday, but I'm willing to bet money she'll want to lecture Daisy on how her music choices could impact the rest of her life.

> Rocco: At what point do I pose an intervention?

Three dots appear and she replies.

> Daisy:No, smartass. ST music calms me the fuck down.
>
> Daisy:Something that nobody else in this house can do.
>
> Daisy:...Especially you.

Her snarkiness makes me smile before I have to straighten my face. The pain floods back before I take another chug of whiskey.

I slowly situate myself on my side and turn off the lamp on my nightstand. I'm about to have a little fun with this girl next door.

Rocco: I'm not that bad.

If I remember correctly, there's a certain part of
you that's really taken with me.

Daisy: I have no control over her sometimes.

Daisy: She has a mind of her own.

Daisy: Why can't you open the door but you're
quick to be annoying over text?

Because I can't tell you who I really am.

Rocco: Don't change the subject, Daisy.

She leaves me on read for three minutes. I wait patiently as time passes when finally, my phone lights up.

Daisy: I don't have time for this.

I need my beauty sleep.

Rocco: Yeah? New boyfriend?

Daisy: If you're asking if he's better than you,
then yes.

Rocco: Better? We haven't done anything, Angel.

Daisy: Let's keep it that way.

A feeling in the pit of my stomach makes me hyperaware of the fact she's talking about Death. He can't get involved with her because he is me. And I have enough on my plate than to get distracted by blonde hair and a set of blue eyes.

My phone starts vibrating in my hand and dread fills me right before my nervous system kicks into fight-or-flight.

"Hello, *Dad*," is on the tip of my tongue, but I never get a chance to say anything.

"What the hell is going on with you, Mancini? You're distracted!" His voice rumbles through the phone and my jaw tics as I swallow down a new lump in my throat. "I heard it was a girl. Who is she?"

"There is no girl. I just had an off night." I was distracted by Brad hanging all over Daisy, but if I tell him that, he'll make a beeline home, and my punishment in private will be a lot worse than anything in that ring.

"We don't have 'off nights', son. You know what happens if you do." The silence between us for the next twenty seconds is deafening. "Don't make me come home early from my honeymoon because you're fucking around."

"Yes, sir." Those words taste sour in my mouth. Feigning respect for this sorry excuse of a man makes me physically ill. The front of my head starts throbbing more than it was before, and a pang in my chest feels oddly close to an oncoming panic attack. Before I can say anything else, the line cuts off. I look to see if Daisy has texted me again and I'm white knuckling the phone.

After a few breaths, my heart rate doesn't lower, and it feels like it's going to beat out of my chest. I roll out of bed, but not without a groan first. My vision becomes tunneled, and I break into a cold sweat and violent shivering. The hoodie I throw on is most likely dirty, but I need to get outside. It's the only way I'll feel like I can take a breath. That is, if I don't suffocate before I get there.

I stumble into my door and unlock it, and it's stuck. Dead weight.

"Move back from the door, Rocco," Daisy's voice sounds as muffled and murky as my mind feels. I take an uneven step backward and she pushes the door open. Her face is shadowed from the darkness of my room, but she's haloed from the hall light. Like a fucking angel. Like *my* angel.

A few minutes later, she has me propped up against the house on the back deck that's illuminated only by the moon. A cold pack of frozen veggies lands on my neck.

"Here. Drink this." Sitting next to me, she hands me a bottle.

I don't even look at what she's handing me, but I start sipping it until it turns into a full chug. The liquid stings my throat and I choke out the words, "I'm pretty sure this is expired."

"You're the only one who drinks orange juice in this house. I just assumed you'd be an adult and throw it away if it was."

I think I'm falling for this woman and her mouth. Her irises are mostly black from the darkness as she gazes into mine. "Are you hurt?" Her eyes move from my cut lip to my swollen cheek, to my bruised eye. A look of panic crosses her face as her mouth falls.

Her hand moves toward my face and I flinch. "Don't." I dodge her touch. "I got into a fight at a bar."

Daisy puckers her lips, and she give me an evil side-eye. "I thought you didn't drink. At least I thought that until you opened your bedroom door. Your room smells like a whiskey distillery."

There are a lot of habits that have started lately that I'm not proud of. But she doesn't need to know about the pills I've been taking to sleep. I stay quiet, trying to push away the ache in my chest.

"Are you going to tell me what happened to send you binge drinking? Or are we going to play this cat and mouse game for the rest of our lives?" Her eyebrow raises incredulously.

"I got a phone call. No biggie," I shrug and close my eyes before leaning my head against the railing.

My eyes are pinched shut, yet I feel her penetrating gaze locked onto my face.

She moves to my left so we're shoulder to shoulder and she lets out a breath. "Fine. You don't have to tell me. But I will say this—if you need someone dead, I know a guy."

I bark out a laugh. "Yeah, Daisy? You know a guy? Who is he?"

"I'd tell you, but then I'd have to tell him to kill you," she says calmly, and I chuckle. This woman next to me is turning out to be my favorite part of the day.

The cool breeze moves off the shoreline and hits our backs. I welcome the sensory change. It allows me to focus on something other than my thoughts, and I drift…into a deep sleep.

DAISY

SEAGULLS ARE SQUAWKING and my face is warm. It's more than warm. I feel like I'm pinned under a heat lamp, dying a slow death-by-sunburn. Squinting my eyes open, I see that it's not the light that's left on in my room this time, but the actual sun.

I'm outside? My left arm is completely numb, or possibly paralyzed for the foreseeable future, and it makes me wonder how long it's been trapped between me and these wooden planks. I try hard to roll to my right, except there's a wall stopping me...and the wall grunts and an arm tightens around me.

I pop my eyes open realizing it's Rocco behind me. Trying to pick up his arm so I can scoot away is a lost cause. "Your arm weighs, like a thousand pounds."

"Don't be dramatic. It's easily twenty pounds, though," he deadpans. His voice is deep, raspy, and tired.

He rolls onto his back, away from our spooning position, and the warmth between us disappears. The thing about winter in South Florida is the highs can go from forty-five degrees one day to eighty the next.

I sit up and rub my eyes, and he does the same as I take a peek of his face in the daylight. The bruises from last night are significantly worse. "Dear God, your face."

"I gotta go. Thanks for not trying to fuck me last night, *sis*. That would have been hella awkward." Rocco pops up like his ass is on fire and walks inside, leaving me more confused.

The constant push and pull from him is fucking with my mind. One minute we're about to fuck, the next he tells me to go away and locks his door, the next we're spooning like a couple in love on the deck of the house under the stars, and then he leaves. He's constantly running away.

That should be enough of a red flag to deter my draw to him, but like every red flag, I'll mentally bleach it and pretend it's all *fine*.

Nothing about this is fine.

————

THERE'S BEEN a nagging feeling inside of me all day. Customers came in, distracted me for seconds at a time, but when my brain wasn't ringing up orders, it bounced between Death and Rocco. Rocco's secret life, him getting into fights at the bar. It was probably over someone hitting on his girl of the night. Men get very possessive over their women. Or so I've read in books.

The more I think about never having a man in my life who would throw hands in my defense sends me into a lonely and depressed spiral of thoughts. And just when I think I can't get any lower, "Nazareth" by Sleep Token comes on, practically drowning me.

Somehow, I dig myself out of my funk and I find the mental strength to peel myself out of the chair and lock up the café. It's pitch-black outside, aside from the light that illuminates mere feet of the sidewalk in front of the building.

"You shouldn't be out here by yourself," a deep, gravelly voice comes from the shadows.

And like any masochist, I walk toward it. *Death.* The whites of his eyes and the white paint accented on his face are all that stands out from a man dressed in all black.

I wonder if his heart is as dead as mine feels. I don't think it is a question I can ask yet. Someone needs to know me for at least a year to understand whether I might or might not allow my intrusive thoughts to win.

He may kill people for a living, but he has a certain set of morals. But! I've been known to be really wrong about these things.

"I'm not really worried about the shadows." I try to find his eyes in the dark before I pull out my keys from my bag. "I'm more concerned about who stands in the light behind their own mask."

"Riddles. Not a fan," he says as he turns and walks away. I follow, but not because I want to. His eyes dart to me like I'm about to jump him.

I can't help but let a smile slip. "Relax, Rambo." I point to my car with my key. "That's me. Plus, I couldn't jump you if I tried." I stop in my tracks, stomp my black combat boots against the sidewalk, and his eyes follow. To jump or even run in these would be like trying to escape quicksand. His eyes rake up my torn fishnets, over my jean shorts that are barely visible because of the large Slipknot tee I stole from Crew back in high school.

He clears his throat and finally mumbles, "You going to the warehouse?"

I've been thinking about going all night. Literally hemhawing between wanting to see him and never wanting to witness anything like that again. "I think so," I answer.

"Oh! Before I forget, thank you for committing a felony to leave me a cupcake for my birthday." My lips tilt into a smile. This man has pulled two…wait, maybe three smiles from me in the past forty-eight hours. More than I've smiled in years.

The black paint crinkles on his forehead as he raises his eyebrows. "Felony? Really…"

"Yep. Felony. A good old B and E." I pull my lips into my teeth trying to feign seriousness.

"Fuck," he almost groans and it catches my attention. It was almost familiar. "I can't be caught committing a felony."

I start walking toward my car again. "Yeah? But you seem the type."

He almost violently shakes his head, keeping up with me. "Absolutely not. I draw the line at murder."

"Ha! You're…" I stop at the front of my car on the way to my door and he stops at the passenger side. "Something."

I unlock it and he opens the passenger side door like it's second nature. "Something. I've been called a lot of things. A lot of shitty things, but never *something*."

I slide into my seat and never ask him where he's going. His face has fresh paint on it and he isn't bleeding.

Turning to ask him why I'm giving him a ride, he turns to me first. "You're…" His eyes narrow on me as he tries to find a word.

"Psychotic? Crazy? I offer up words while I start the car, trying to keep myself distracted. I've been told I belong in a mental hospital. Or that I need medication for depression, or bipolarism. Which I have neither—so my therapist said. I mean, depression is debatable. But it shows up in everybody differently.

"No." Another head shake and he bites the inside of his cheek. "I know I don't know you that well, but you're a force. Like anything in your path will be taken down."

Well, fuck me. "And don't fucking forget it, Death." I nod and put the car in gear and drive to the warehouse. Despite me feeling a sexual pull to him the other night, I feel like he's more like a friend now. Like we're building some type of foundation. *A friend.*

Something in my chest flutters. Not sure if it was the seven vegan chocolate chips cookies I inhaled after I dipped them in almond milk or if it's my heart. My cold, dead aortic pump.

After a silent ride, we pull into the dark gravel lot and Death sits up and his eyes go wide.

"It's busy tonight," I say, not really knowing what I'm getting at. But he says nothing.

I park near a tree and we both slide out in silence. "Listen," his voice is low as he stops me at the back of the car. He splays his hand on my waist and pushes me against the trunk. My heart starts pumping full throttle.

"Look at me."

I do.

"Promise me something," Death breathes out, quiet enough I almost don't hear him.

"Anything." *Anything, Daisy? Really? You simp.*

He looks to the door with the light and back at me. "If anything happens, find Santi. The guy who opens the door."

"What?" I look past him at the door and back at him. "What do you mean? What would happen?"

His eyes fall to the ground beside us and his mouth opens slightly, like he's trying to catch his breath. I grab his face and turn his head to me, not caring about the paint.

"Death. What would happen?" I enunciate slowly, trying to get him to focus on me.

His brown eyes bounce between mine and fall to my lips. The winter breeze kicks up like it's about to rain. *It smells like rain.*

"Kiss me," he quietly demands. I don't allow myself to overthink what this means, so I lick my lips subconsciously, and my eyes fall to his tongue that is moving over his bottom lip.

I run my hands through his hair and push my lips to his. As soon as we touch, my body zings—my nerves are firing on all cylinders—and all I can think of is how this one kiss won't be enough. His hands move from my waist, under my shirt, and rests under my breasts. The feeling is foreign and something I've waited for for so long. My body arches into him of its own accord and I let out a light moan in his mouth. Our tongues dance, but our hands never move. Like they are content, not needing more. At least not right now.

He pulls back and I can't breathe. Now I need more. I want more.

The pad of his thumb rubs over his bottom lip and he looks at it. "I need to get in there."

I nod, trying to grasp what the hell's happening. I'm not one to go with the fucking flow, or am I? All I know is my panties are soaked, and I just had one of the most amazing first kisses of my life.

But even that monumental moment wouldn't prepare for what I'm about to walk into.

ROCCO

I POUND on the steel door, trying to get that damn kiss out of my head. I *need* to get that fucking kiss out of my head. It's nearly impossible with her scent still in the air around me. What the hell was I thinking? I needed a quick distraction before I lost my shit.

The door creaks open and Santi's concerned eyes meet mine. They jump to Daisy and back to me.

"What's going on?" I ask him, pulling Daisy in by her hand.

Santi closes the door and stops us. "*He* knows," he spits, his Spanish accent thick. His head gestures to the woman next to me. "You're…fighting Beast. And he's been dosing. He's not clean and he's going to kill you."

Daisy gasps behind me and I chuckle, trying to lighten the mood. She doesn't need to hear any of that. Beast has been taking illegal enhancement drugs for a while, and I'm guessing he's done a couple of lines of coke tonight, too. He won't feel anything. He's also sloppy when he's high. Unpredictable. "He can dose all he wants, I'm more aware. I have the advantage."

I push Daisy farther into the hallway, trying to nudge her away.

"Why don't you go in—" Santi grabs her arm to stop her. Daisy's eyes shoot to his hand on her and he let's go.

"I'm sorry, miss, but there are *eyes* everywhere," he says, looking at me. Santi knows my father. Tony knows there's a girl. He doesn't know who. He only knows I don't go with anyone past a fuck or a suck.

Fuck.

"Don't let her out of your sight," I tell him, moving past Daisy.

"Hey!" she shouts after me. I look back, and she is asking questions with her eyes. Her brows pinch and she shrugs. I take a sharp right and walk into the locker room. I have less than five minutes to get my head on straight.

The loudspeakers in the ring start playing "Bounce" by Timbaland and JT. Like we need to get hyped to kill each other or something.

I strip out of my hoodie, touch up my mask, and eye a silver bowl that sits on an old metal table—one that's so old that if you look at it wrong it could give you tetanus. My father encourages fights to go longer, so he supplies the fighters with cocaine. The longer the fight, the more money he rakes in on bets. "Only the best for my top men," he chides when he decides to bless us with his presence. I used to dabble, but once I started caring about getting the hell out of his grip, I stopped.

My phone rings in the pocket of my hoodie and I pull it out. "Goddamnit, Rocco!"

"Dad," I choke out and I swallow hard.

"You know better than to bring your floozy to my ring, son. Distractions will only kill you." His voice is eerily calm—like me dying is his end game.

My hands start to sweat and shake. "I don't know what you're talking about."

He must slam his fist into something, and I can hear him mumble in the background. "Fuck! You know better than to lie to me! I have eyes and ears everywhere."

He's right. What the hell was I thinking? I put her in danger by being near her. Whether I'm Death or Rocco, she's a dead woman walking, and it doesn't matter that she's his wife's daughter. She's collateral damage. And that fucking kiss. *Careless.*

"But you know me. I love games, my boy." He laughs maniacally and he sniffs what I can only imagine is the finest coke money can buy. "So let the games begin." The line goes dead, and I throw my phone against the wall with everything in me, shattering it to pieces.

The thump of my heart is pounding in my ears, and the obnoxious humming of the neon lights above causes a ringing in my head. I walk over to the silver bowl and lay out a line of blow. If I have any chance of winning tonight, I have to do one. That was the point of his call, wasn't it? Telling me I'm dead if I don't do it. His send off of him snorting a line was his kind of fucked-up riddle. A mind game that never ends.

I close a nostril and run the open one along the white powder, inhaling hard. Nothing about this is fun, but the upper hits almost immediately, and my energy skyrockets. Even though I don't think it's enough to go against Beast and his steroids mixed with high doses of powder, I need all the help I can get.

I've been here before when I first started. The only person who knew was *him.* I was sworn not to tell a soul.

Once I would come down off the high, I'd want more. Will I become addicted again? Or will I be dead?

The crowd's screams echo into the room, and I bounce back and forth on each foot.

"Let's fucking do this," I growl to myself before I step into the light.

———

THE ANNOUNCER SHOUTS through the speaker and the feedback from the mic is what gets everyone's attention. "Ladies and gents! Tonight, for the first time ever, Beast versus Death." The grungy man looks between us and the screams cause my ears to ring. "You know the rules. Fight 'til death!"

My eyes jump between Beast's as I try to focus while his are red rimmed and bulging. His face and body are already covered in sweat, which means the traction of my fist against his skin will be minimal.

No punches have been thrown yet. The noise of the horn hasn't sounded. And who the hell chose this music? The hype music isn't hyping me. All the noises. My mind is moving in short thoughts. It's overstimulating, but I need this fight to start while my high is fresh.

I glance past Beast and see my father's men moving toward one area. Each of them is laser-focused on Daisy.

Just as I start to get closer, the sound of the horn rings and Beast throws a fist, but I duck. I can't focus on Daisy and Beast at the same time. It's impossible.

"I just have to beat him, and then I can take her out of here," I think to myself. The horn sounds, and I waste no time making a move.

I connect a jab with his cheek, but just like I thought, it barely landed. If all of my hits slide off of him like this, I'm fucked.

An uppercut fist connects with his nose, and blood squirts all over my hand and down my arm. The cheers and chants have faded to background noise as I grab him and put him in a headlock.

He hasn't got a grip on me to get out of it, so I try to find one of his eyes with my thumb. If he loses an eye, so be it. This is what we do. Dear ol' Dad brings our opponents to the brink of death. Whether or not they get scraped off the floor is up to them. Are they willing to fight for their lives? Or are they over it? Do they feel as if dying is the only way out of the events that led them to the ring to begin with?

As my thumb pushes into his eye socket, he growls before he reaches up and yanks and twists my ear. Hard.

I feel the cocaine jetting through my veins, yet I can't feel anything at all. And neither can he. I bite down on the only part of him my teeth can reach. My mouth is full of his blonde mane as I chomp down on his scalp. He slides out of my chokehold and moves out from in front of me, and I'm left spitting the clump of his hair out of my mouth.

Blood runs down his yellow-painted face. He looks like the male version of the main character in the *Carrie* movie. Like pigs' blood was poured over him.

"Stop!" I hear a scream from my left and I turn. One of my father's men has Daisy by the arm, and another one is closing in. I turn to jump out of the ring, but a sharp blow knocks me in the side of my head, and I fall onto the rope. Stars are circling in my head as I fight to keep my balance over the ringing in my ears. My vision is blurred. Most likely from blood and sweat…at least, I hope.

As I start gaining focus, a set of teeth sink into my shoulder. "How do you fucking like it? I should kill you right now, asshole."

"Fucking do it." *Just end me because I'm too chicken shit to do it myself.*

"But I was told not to. So for now…" He doesn't finish his sentence, but he punches me in the head, the chest, the dick…and a kick to the ribs is what brings me to my knees.

I was told not to.

I was told not to.

I need to find her…I need to get her out of here.

I fall forward, and my swollen cheek lands in stale blood from the men before me this evening, and everything goes dark.

CHAPTER
TWENTY-EIGHT

DAISY

"YOU NEED to get out of here!" The door guy, Santi, comes from behind me. Death seems to have a decent and trusting relationship with him, so I have a gut feeling I can trust him. I hear a loud voice and chubster, who had a hold of me seconds ago, is now running toward the ring, screaming "Call the Godfather." That can't be right, because Vito Corleone is not here. Nor is he real. And I think Marlon Brando may even be dead.

Brad is standing in the middle of the ring with a smug look wiped over his bloody face as he looks down at the damage he's done to Death.

I turn back to Santi. "Is he—"

"You need to leave," he says sternly. "And if you are smart, you won't come back." His dark brown eyes are drooping on the sides, and his naturally tan skin almost looks pale. He's my height, yet his words are those of a guardian.

Santi leads me out of the crowd into the dark hallway toward the door. The screaming is drowning out my hurricane of thoughts.

"Okay. But I have no way of knowing if he—"

"You will know. Trust me. Now get." Santi nudges me farther out the door, shooing me with his hands, and I run to my car. Another night of no turning back. My heart wants to beat out of my chest. My brain wants to explode. And I want to scream, but the adrenaline coursing through my veins is preventing it all. I feel everything and nothing at the same time.

I start my car and peel out of the gravel lot, hurrying to get home. The strong scent of blood lingers in my nostrils. Never in my life have I wanted to squirt bleach up my nose until today.

"What the hell just happened?" I ask myself as I white knuckle the steering wheel, holding it at ten and two.

Not much rattles me. But as soon as I was grabbed by that man, Death went down—unconscious I heard somebody say—and I froze.

I'm trying to go the speed limit, but I want to get home. To safety. Off the road. And shower. I need a shower. I really need Rocco to be home. Palm trees whir by as I zone out on the reflectors on the road.

As I pull up into driveway, I search for Rocco's bike down the street, or his car in the driveway, and don't see either of them.

The walk from my car to the front door is a blur. I must have driven the whole car ride home in a partial coma. "How did I get here safely?"

I turn the key with a shaky hand and step in, locking the door behind me. I open and lock it one more time to make sure. My chest tightens like someone is sitting on it. Like I'm tied down and unable to inhale.

I fall down the back of the door and pinch my eyes closed, trying to even my breaths. The cold floor hits my legs, and I call out to Rocco, silently praying he's home. Or at least, I think I do.

"I've helped…you…through…two panic…attacks…already!" I clutch my chest as I struggle to inhale for four seconds, hold for four seconds, exhale for four seconds, and hold for another four.

After quite a few rounds of box breaths, I finally feel my heart rate starting to come down. I'm drenched in sweat, yet shivering.

The wood floor cools my back as I find myself lying in the middle of the foyer staring up at a chandelier with sea glass accents. *Has that always been here?*

Is this how Death felt while he was lying half dead in the ring? No. Of course not. How dare you compare this to his physical pain.

All I know is that I'm tired.

I'm *really* fucking tired.

––––––

AFTER I TOOK a nice snooze on the floor, I came to, breathing normally with an aching chest and unable to piece together the events of the night. A hot shower helped me fill in the missing parts, and I actively have to keep myself from having another panic attack.

I've been sitting on the couch for a good two hours wrapped up in my favorite microfiber blanket, checking my phone every minute —maybe like, thirty seconds. My hair has dried, unbrushed in kinky waves, and I give zero shits.

The obnoxious doorbell sounds and the remote goes flying, along with my soul.

Who the hell could that be? The blanket lands on the floor as I push myself off the sofa.

"If it's Brad, I'm going to clock him in the face and call the cops. That man deserves to be tied to a cinderblock and dropped in a swamp for the gators to eat."

Years later, it will probably be on the news that the ones that did eat him have some type of sexually transmitted disease.

I pull open the door, and a beautiful, massacred face stares back at me.

"Oh my God! You're alive." *Barely.* Death's eyes are almost swollen shut, and the blood is dried, coating his face and his neck.

I'm careful to help him inside, guiding him gently by the elbow. My hands are clammy, shaking against his black hoodie. I've never dealt with anything like this with Jeremy.

The only scary thing that we ever dealt with was our fathers' funerals. Oh, and that time he broke into a cold sweat when he walked in on me when I was naked.

Death leans against the wall next to the stairs and his head falls back, bouncing a couple times. I cup the back of his hooded head with my hand. "Jesus, no need to add insult to injury. The last thing you need is more brain damage."

He doesn't move or say anything. "I thought you were dead," I almost whisper.

"I wish," he grunts.

"Don't say that."

His hand finds my own that's hanging by my side, and his pinky locks with mine. "I can't die yet. I need to kiss you again."

A lump forms in my throat, and a million butterflies let loose in my belly. Nobody has ever said anything like that to me. It's the desire I've been yearning for. And as much as I want to poke him and ask what else he *needs* to do to me, I decide that his needs outweigh my own in this moment.

"Okay, Casanova. Let's get you cleaned up first. We'll use my shower."

His head subtly bobs up and down before he starts up the stairs, and I follow. Not that that's fucking safe. He is twice my size. If he falls back, I'm smashed and potentially paralyzed.

Death stops at the top of the stairs and lets me lead him to the bathroom.

I turn to situate the shower for him—grabbing a new bar of soap, setting up the shampoo, and getting a washcloth and a loofa. I don't know how hard one has to scrub to get layers of dried blood off. The steam from the burning hot shower from hell starts billowing around us.

"Now that you're in my house and about to be naked and

vulnerable, don't you think I should know your real name?" I teasingly cock my brow, but he isn't having it.

He grunts.

The sliver of brown showing through the swelling follows my every move. Because I'm jumpy and my adrenaline is pumping, I try to move slower and be more intentional.

"I…uh…can turn on music for you." I reach back to turn the dial on my Bluetooth radio and "Movement" by Hozier comes on. He stares at me, and I go to change it, but he pulls me back.

"I don't fucking care about the music, Daisy. It's a good song. Can you help me get this off?" His voice drips with frustration while his dirty hands pull at the fabric of his hoodie.

"Oh. Of course." Am I nervous? I'm not sure if it's because he was on the brink of death and somehow, I got involved in this underground fighting thing, or if it's because he was on the brink of death and *came to me*.

I'm not sure if it's the adrenaline moving through me, or maybe some type of a mother-bear instinct that's taken over, but I gently help remove the soiled fabric and toss it to the floor. His grunts and moans pain me in a way I can't put into words.

His head drops and he looks up at me as he chews on the side of his bottom lip. Death moves toward me so our faces are inches apart. I open my mouth to say something…anything… but I have nothing to say. Resting my hands on his chest, I feel his heart beating hard and fast—almost equivalent to mine.

Of their own accord, my fingers gently and slowly fall down his torso to the waistband of his gray sweats. *Pffft. Whore.*

"I'm not a whore."

His voice comes out gruff and low. "I wasn't even thinking that."

"Your face says otherwise."

I roll my eyes before I hook my thumbs on either side of his sweats, and a smirk spreads over his face, stretching apart his busted lip. Blood starts to seep from the cut, and he doesn't make a move to wipe it off. He may not even know it's there.

I swallow hard, unsure of what the hell is going through my head, but I lean in, and with hooded eyes, I focus on his lip. And in the turning point of any dark romance novel I've read, I let my intrusive thoughts win. I move the tip of my tongue over the drop of blood and pull it back. He releases a short, labored breath, and the sliver of brown falls to my mouth as I taste him.

We stand there with unspoken words and crackling tension marinating between us.

"I'm… Let's get these off."

My heartbeat is erratically pounding in my ears as I start to shimmy his pants down past his rock-solid ass. I've seen a dick or two, but being this up close and personal to one, let alone to a man I'm drawn to like a moth to a flame, I'm having a hard time deciphering whether I'm nervous or downright feral.

I don't look down, but instead I make some type of awkward-as-fuck eye contact. And they twitch, trying not to break it. The band gets caught on what I'm only assuming is his dick. He moves his hips in a fluid motion to try to…*unhook?*…himself. I wouldn't know because I caught it in my peripheral. Nope. Never looked down. Not that far, anyway.

Even though I'm looking at his eyes, my focus is on the ripples of his muscles splattered with crimson. *Pull yourself together.*

I let the pants drop once they get past his thick thighs, and he steps out. Dried blood is smeared down his legs, and I swallow down a lump in my throat.

So much blood. *So much blood.*

Flashbacks of pictures of my dad lying lifeless next to his best friend and partner, both in a pool of their blood overtake my vision. Friends since high school. They went through training together. They helped raise each other's kids with their wives by their side. And they died. The day I walked through the station, I found the photos laying splayed out on a table, like it was just a normal Tuesday. Just another day at the office for those guys, solving a double homicide of their own.

A light squeeze of my elbow snaps me back into a cloud of steam. "I can take it from here," Death says quietly before he turns and steps in the shower. And yes, his ass should be served on a platter in front of anyone who is willing to partake. It's that edible looking.

"Aggh!" comes from behind the curtain. "Uhh…"

I know what's coming next.

"Can you help me?" He sounds as if he's on the verge of tears as his voice cracks before he clears his throat.

"Um…sure." I start moving through the motions of getting undressed, but leave my bra and underwear on. Before I pull the curtain and step in to help him, I take a deep breath.

ROCCO

DAISY STEPS in and I make a point not to turn around. It's not because I'm hard, which I am. Because that's what coke does to me. But as ready as I am for a round of fucking, asshole Brad kicked me in the dick, and now my poor guy is hurting and resting between my legs.

I don't want Daisy to see my face. That will be when she finds out it's been me the whole time. How she hasn't known this entire time is beyond me. Or maybe paint job was just that good.

I've been taunting her, teasing her, and closed off while Death has been open and vulnerable. What if she doesn't't' want anything to do with me after this? Daisy seems to be the only part of my world that gives me a glimpse of hope. She shows me there is a life worth fighting for.

"Can you turn so I can see how bad your injuries are?" Her voice is smooth like hot chocolate on a cool fall day.

I turn my body as far as it will go before a shooting pain moves up my ribs. As I let out a pain-filled growl, she gasps because I'm caught.

My eyes are practically swollen shut, but she knows. She finally sees who I really am. Me for me. No mask. No paint.

"Rocco?!" Big blue eyes stare at me. "I…I…How…" Her gaze rakes over me quickly, in a panic. Unable to focus on any part of me for too long.

"Yeah." I swallow down what feels like a hundred rusty screws before I turn and open my mouth under the water. Hot water be damned, I'm thirsty.

"Look at me. What the–?" She moves frantically, running her hands over my arms, trying to cleanse me of the blood. "Jesus fucking Christ! Why didn't you just tell me it was you?"

Her reaction is saying one thing, but her pinched brows and tearing eyes are saying another. She runs her hands through her wild hair and pulls at the roots. "Oh my… Holy shit. It all makes sense. The disappearing and the bruises. Oh fuck!"

The hot water runs over me as Daisy works through her shit. As much as I want to comfort her, I'm in no headspace to. But that's what we do. In the short period of time we've known each other, we have also saved each other.

"We need to get you to a doctor, ASAP." She goes to step out and I grab her by her arm.

Her eyes fall to our feet, unless she's looking at my dick, but I don't think so. "I saw a doctor. Santi's wife's a doctor."

"Santi," she almost whispers. "The door guy."

Her eyes find mine and I lightly nod. "He saved me. Well, he told me to go when you were…"

"Yeah. Doc said I have a concussion and shouldn't sleep. He dropped me off here. If I go to a hospital—I can't go to a hospital. It's not an option. He'll—" Not that I had any intentions of telling her what's actually happening, but at the end of the day, I'm at the end of my rope. My life has reached a new low. I've kept quiet for years, but it's time to let someone in. Someone I trust.

"Why didn't you tell me it was you?" Once again, the pinch of her brows and the tears in her eyes leaves her conflicted. "In the back of the Jeep?" Her head shakes quickly.

"Because it's a lot *less* complicated if you don't know who I was —who I am," I admit. And damn, even an admission like that, it feels like a small weight has been lifted from my shoulders. "If you don't know Death is me and I am Death…"

"But you kissed me—as Death!" Her voice echoes off the shower walls. "What happens if I *kiss* you…as Rocco?" I finally allow myself to look at her slippery tits that are barely holding on from behind her black lace bra. And how her neon green belly button ring draws my attention away from the soft skin of her stomach. "And your voice. It wasn't your voice. I feel so stupid…" Her words trail off.

I pull her chin up so her eyes find mine. "It's acting. The voice…the paint. The kindness."

"Acting," she repeats.

Whatever perfume she is wearing starts mixing with the steam, and it's making me dizzy. Or maybe it's the fact that I know what all of this means. She's as good as dead. "It changes everything."

"Bitches Brew" by Crosses starts playing, and my heart rate matches the intensity of the lyrics. I swallow hard as Daisy pulls her hair tie out, letting her blond hair cascade down her back. It slowly starts to curl from the billowing steam.

The bar of soap in her hand rolls in her grip repeatedly like it's a shower-time nervous habit. "Let me get your back," she almost whispers. She pulls her lip between her teeth as her eyes bounce from one part of me to another. I know that look. The look of fighting desire.

Her glassy eyes find mine, moving from one to the other, falling to my lips and back. Hell, she might be looking at my mangled face, but nah. That's not it.

Those pierced nipples of hers are begging to be freed from their restraints—both pointing to me like I'm the only one who can finally liberate them—while her thighs are moving back and forth, searching for relief from an ache that's taken her over for weeks.

My hands move of their own accord to her hips, and nothing in me tries to stop it from happening. Goosebumps erupt under my touch and her eyes fall closed. Those pouty lips of hers open, and her hands land on my chest. They slide over my uneven skin, spreading the suds over the dried blood and bruises.

I lean down. "I'm not going to kiss you."

A quick nod, paired with a sweep of her tongue along her lips, tells me she doesn't believe me. *Good girl.*

Something about this woman makes me smile. Her ability to see through my bullshit.

I move in closer and feather my lips over hers. She never tries to kiss me, but her muscles tense, trying to fight the urge to.

With my luck, my father will walk in and shoot us both execution style.

No thought can kill a boner as fast as that one.

I pull back and turn, letting my head fall as her silky hands start rubbing over my back. She never complains or pouts. Instead, she's quiet, maybe in shock—or maybe she, too, is fighting the inevitable.

Water tinged with blood circles the drain. Is that all *my* blood? Possibly.

Why is all of this happening now? My father is right. I've gone soft. I got distracted.

But I want this with her. I want more than what that ring imprisons me in.

It's like the end of an era. I imagine the shower is my cleansing ritual. It washes my sins away. A new slate. A new day, so to speak.

Nah.

It's definitely the end of an era…but that era is the beginning of *his* downfall.

CHAPTER
THIRTY

DAISY

AFTER I HELP Rocco wash himself—minus his penis as he did that himself—I dried him off and went and changed out of my wet undergarments and into some night clothes. Normally I'd strut around in a cute outfit, but not tonight. The vibe is heavy, and so is my heart. Seeing him beaten to a pulp. I feel sick. And as much as my body wants—no, as much as my body is utterly consumed by the thought of me and him pressed against each other, my heart hurts for him. And for the first time in a long ass time, I'm scared.

"Stay," he rasps with his eyes fully closed. I'd love to tell him the swelling in his face is going down, but it's quite the opposite.

"You're starting to resemble a less bald Sloth from *The Goonies*…but with better teeth."

A laugh gurgles out of him before he starts coughing, but it slowly morphs into him hunched over and wrapping his arms around his torso. He looks so vulnerable. The little boy in him is trying to sneak out. Between his physical state and my confusion of what the hell is happening, I think it's safe to say a pending mental breakdown is looming over us. Not sure if it's going to be his or mine.

I eye the door, contemplating this part of my life that's led me to this point. Was it breaking up with Jeremy? Going out with douche canoe, Brad? How did I get tangled up in this world? I'm caught in a spider's web, and I'm not sure I'm trying to escape it. Or maybe I'm the one who weaved this tangled web. Like a black widow, or a brown recluse. Metaphorically, slowly killing anything positive that lands in front of me...and it's terrifying.

"Sure, I'll stay." Not one single cell of me thinks this is right. Not because it's Rocco, but alarm bells are sounding.

My feet are grounded like I've hit a wall. Something invisible is preventing me from getting to him, but I push through. I go against everything my body is telling me not to do, and I'm not sure whether it's my heart or my brain that I'm following, but it leads me straight toward the man who is pleading for my presence.

I lift his black bedspread and dark plaid Egyptian cotton sheets and slide in next to him. Not before I admire his body one last time. Although he's been beaten to a pulp, some type of chemical attraction thing is going on. But I tuck it deep down inside with what is left of my dignity.

The table lamp is still on illuminating the sacred walls of Rocco Mancini. Trying not to seem nosy, I strain my eyes from side to side trying to take it all in.

"It used to help me escape."

"What?"

"Drawing...and the painting. It used to help me get out of my head. Like how some people like reading and they live another life..."

A grunt the size of Texas slips out of him as he turns on his side to face me. I risk looking at him, and somehow my body doesn't get the memo that we're in moral mode. *Stay far enough away and stay clothed.*

"...I never painted what I was feeling. I used to close my eyes and imagine a place I wanted to go, or had been, and I painted it like I was sitting there." He pauses. "I don't do it anymore. No time."

"Can I ask you something?" I blurt.

"I knew this was coming."

"Never mind. I don't want to make you uncomfortable."

"Fucking look at me. Physically, I'm beat, and mentally, I'm spent. It doesn't get more uncomfortable than this, Angel." He closes his eyes. "Just ask the question."

That nickname slips out and it jolts straight to my lady parts.

"Why do you fight if you hate it so much?"

Rocco swallows hard before his pinky starts rubbing mine. "My mom. I killed her."

I freeze. Not that I was moving much to begin with, but it's my heart that stopped for a beat—or it felt like it. The possibility of me lying in bed with a homicidal maniac wasn't on my bingo card for this year, but I guess being sexually attracted to my stepbrother wasn't either.

"You killed your mom," I parrot like it was something that he needed to hear. "Care to elaborate? Unless this is a 'if I tell you, I have to kill you' type of deal. Then in that case, all I ask is that you give me a head start."

His inked hand wraps around mine, and my heart starts beating a little faster.

"I wanted to drive. Our song came on the radio. The one Mom and I would always dance to in the kitchen. I turned it up against her wishes and looked at her. She was smiling for the first time in years. Laughing. Singing. She was beautiful. Dark hair, and dark eyes, but completely radiant. Everyone used to tell me how much I looked like her. Anyway, I wasn't looking. I was happy I was making her happy, even if it was only for a minute.

"'You killed your chances at football! You killed my wife,' my father would shout before he'd burst into tears, but those tears eventually turned to anger. Not the type of anger that can be dissipated with time and a sincere apology." Rocco pauses and takes in a shaky breath.

"I knew when the look of revenge painted his red face, and his eyes turned glassy and wide, I was done for. His pupils would blow. But he never hurt me himself."

Not it's my turn to swallow hard. "What…" I clear my throat, trying to rid myself of the feeling like I just swallowed shards of glass. "What are you trying to say?" I grip his hand a little tighter and his brows knit together, pulling his silky hair down into his eyes.

"Fighting is my punishment for killing my mom," Rocco mumbles, his voice breaking at the end. "'You killed our dreams!' he screamed in my face. The nurses stood outside of the room in horror as my father got in my face. My body was in a fucking cast, and instead of being thankful I was alive…it's like he tried every way to figure out how he could slowly kill me."

Don't make this about me. Don't vomit at his words. Do not take this moment of vulnerability away from him because the thought of any parent torturing their child because of a spouse's accidental death would make you physically ill.

"His one and only love and my 'carelessness' took her away from him." Rocco rubs my knuckles with his thumb and a tear drops to the pillow. "My fath-*he* started me in his underground fighting ring empire about a month after my mom's funeral. Almost died a couple of times until Santi took me under his wing. Eventually I started winning. And here we are."

I open my mouth, but nothing comes out. All of a sudden, my sad, pathetic life feels a little less intense, and a whole lot more like I'm some entitled bitch who cried because her daddy died and her boyfriend wouldn't fuck her.

"Jesus Christ," I finally manage to get out. Tony is the Devil. His 'loving' vibe was a mask. Spiraling thoughts flood my brain. If I misbehave around him, will he start a ladies' fight ring and throw me in it? Or would he just kill me? Is my mother safe? Why has she only called twice? Is she on a bender? She's never touched a drug in her life, or so she's said. I believe her…and she wouldn't start now.

"Yeah. And if he sees you and I are close. You're…" His voice trails off before he lifts my hair off of my face.

As much as I already think I know the end of that sentence, I ask, "I'm what?"

"You're *dead*."

I swallow hard and muster up the best fake smile I can, because who better than to sweep shit under the rug than me? The master of disassociation. "That seems a little extreme. But if I've learned anything about you over the past few weeks, it's that you're the more dramatic one out of the two of us." I add a nose crinkle and a tiny bit of tongue to lighten the mood, except it doesn't. My heart is pounding out of my chest so hard I bet he can hear it. If he can, he's doing a hell of a job pretending he doesn't.

"I used to be addicted to cocaine…and pills. Uppers, mostly," Rocco blurts, and I pull the blanket up to my neck, all of a sudden shivering. Except I don't think I'm cold.

"Umm." I'm not sure what to do with this information. How do I react? The damage is done. Like a deer in the headlights, I lie there staring at him, except his eyes are shut like he's trying to not be seen.

His brows pinch. "I did a line tonight. Maybe two? I don't know it's fuzzy."

"Why are you telling me this?"

The gnawing on the inside of his cheek makes me nervous. I may be crazy, but one thing I've never done, or never want to do, is drugs. People who choose to do drugs turn me off.

"I don't know. Every time I touch that shit, I dread it. And yes, the feeling of it running through me lifts me, but I still feel the disappointment in myself. It can't be explained other than a feeling of dread."

I pull in a long breath before I speak.

"Then why did you do it?" Trying not to sound like a

judgmental bitch, I ask a question I don't know if I want the answer to.

"It makes me feel invincible enough to walk confidently out into the ring, but numb enough that if I get hit, I won't feel it. I was put up against Beast. Beast is my equal. One of us has to take the fall, and this time it had to be him." His hands rub over his face. "*He* keeps the locker room stocked with the 'good stuff'. In a genie lamp. Free cocaine for all the fighters. Maybe it's better that way. That way if you do die, you won't feel it." I reach my hand out to touch him, but pull back. Not sure why. Perhaps my body has entered a fight-or-flight state. I want to comfort him, but my body is begging me to comfort myself first.

My eyes fall closed as his warm hand falls flat against my cheek as his calloused thumb slides slowly over my smooth lips. Back and forth before my bottom lip is pulled open. His eyes are slits, but I can still sense his desire. It's been undeniable since we've met. And I'm done holding back.

I move out from under his touch and prop myself up onto my knees before I pull my tank over my head and toss it behind me, allowing my tits to bounce free.

Feeling his eyes on me nudges me to continue my little adventure. I crawl toward him, closing the space between us, and he rolls to his back. His sheets bunch under him, pulling me down on top of his bruised body and he lets out a grunt. I'm semi-hovering over his large frame, my nipples moving over the hills and valleys of his pecs.

Unlike last time when I was naked in his bed, the air has shifted.

"What are you doing?" he asks, his voice low and gravelly. His thumbs dig into my hips, and I feel him grow underneath me. A small smile threatens to escape me. Knowing we're both as broken as we are, we can still feel desire—that has to count for something.

I pull my bottom lip between my teeth before I find the words to answer. His busted lip is puffy and red and is begging to be kissed. "I'm crossing a line," I answer before leaning farther down and planting a soft kiss on the cut. His warm breath hits my face as he pulls my hips against him.

"Angel…"

I grind against him, only covered by his shorts and mine, and we both release noises one could only hear in the jungle.

"You can't do this. *We* can't do this…if he finds out." His mouth says one thing, but the way he's moving me back and forth is saying another.

I lean close to his face once more. "He won't find out," I whisper against the corner of his mouth. My bottom lip disappears between his teeth as he growls and releases it.

Before I can kiss him, I'm being lifted like a small bag of sand and placed on his face. His warm breath moves across my clit and a surge of—oh, I don't know, electric, or maybe a chemical reaction —flows through my body, causing shivers to run up and down my back.

He eyes my crotch that's hovering over his face. My shorts are thin and unable to hide my arousal. I feel like I should be embarrassed, but instead, I want him to know how badly I want this—want him.

"I knew you fucking wanted me. From the time you walked in the door, and in the hallway…at the wedding." I lower myself over his mouth, and slowly grind on his face. If I'm hurting him, he's doing a good job hiding it.

Rocco bares his teeth before biting down on my labia. "You wanted me first," he rebuts. A piss poor one at that.

"That's your comeback?" I look at him through hooded eyes as I trail my hands between my legs. His head moves slightly to catch my movement. My fingers curl around the inner fabric of my shorts and I slide them to the side.

Rocco takes a deep breath in through his nose and his eyes fall shut. "Fuck, you smell good."

I smirk, knowing he's giving in. "You seem to be unable to uphold your stony demeanor, Rocco."

His eyes fly open, and his hands go to my crotch before he tears my shorts up the middle. My mouth is left hanging open, and he smiles before his hands cup my ass cheeks and he brings me to his mouth as if my pussy is a bowl and he's eating his first meal. Like he's starving to *death*.

Blood floods my nerves in all the right places as he devours my clit. "You fucking taste good, too."

"You knew I would after you licked the table." He chuckles against me and my hips buck in reaction. "Pineapple and garlic, if I remember correctly."

"Mmmm…"

I start grinding against him, moaning at the intensity.

"It's more like sunshine and happiness."

My breaths start to shallow. This is my first time being eaten out. I'm not sure I'm doing anything right, but I've read enough romance novels to know I need to just enjoy it. I'm too selfish not to.

"Am I hurting you?" *Ahh, Daisy. Let's ruin this moment, shall we? Let's remind him of his injuries.*

His tongue dips to my entrance and I let out a moan. "Oh, shit." My fingers lock into his silky hair and I scrape my nails against his scalp. The moan that rumbles against me rattles me on the inside like I'm lying on the quaking San Andreas Fault.

Rocco Mancini's mouth has officially gone where no man's mouth has gone before. And I'll be hellbent not to finish this little adventure. As tight as his grip may be on my ass, his pinky fingers are extremely close to my asshole. But his tongue—it's otherworldly.

"Would you actually care if you were hurting me?" His tongue moves in and out of me before I push myself harder against him, dying for him to go deeper.

"Not at all," I pant and look down, our eyes locking.

With no warning, I'm flying through the air onto my back after he catapults me from him.

"What the hell?"

He kicks his shorts off in record time, and he falls forward, arms surrounding me as his body hovers over mine. His soft hair brushes over my forehead, and the cut is still bleeding. "Bad girls don't get to come, Angel."

"No shit. I'm twenty and I have only ever come with the work of my own hands…and Mr. Jones."

He cocks his brow like I just told him my one true love is the older man who lives across the street. "My vibrator. Relax, Rocky."

I dart my tongue out to his lip and drag it over the drop of blood again. He pulls back and his eyes fall to the tip of my tongue so he can see the blood. Slivers of his brown eyes zone in while his tongue moves over the spot I just licked.

I pull my tongue back in my mouth, and the taste of iron soaks into my taste buds.

His lips part and I cup his cheeks with my hands, taking in every inch of his face. "What do you need from me, Rocco?" I pinch my brows in curiosity.

A roll of his hips pushes his dick against my entrance. "I need you to tell me you love me."

CHAPTER
THIRTY-ONE

ROCCO

"TELL me you love me and that you need me as much as I need you…and this pull we have between us isn't in my head."

I'm falling and I don't mean in love. I mean, maybe love, but I feel like I'm drowning, and the only thing that can pull me to the surface is hearing those words fall from her lips. Her beautiful blue eyes look to the side, and her small hand rests on my chest directly over my heart.

No. It's definitely love.

That's it, I scared her away. Daisy is seconds away from pushing me off of her and walking out of my life. Until she looks at me. I close my eyes so I don't have to see the lie on her face *if* she decides to tell me what I just begged to hear.

"I love you," she whispers. Her hand moves up my chest to my jaw, and my skin fills with goosebumps. It's been a long fucking time since someone has touched me with something other than an agenda to kill me. "Look at me."

I swallow down the lump in my throat, terrified she'll laugh at me or scold me for being a pussy. But I open my eyes as far as they'll go, barely feeling the pain anymore. It's more a gnawing feeling of embarrassment. But not pain. Not while *she's* under me.

She smiles. "I love you," she says again, but this time with conviction. Her entrance pushes against the tip of my dick. We're lined up perfectly. With one thrust, I can steal the one thing she's yet to give up to anyone.

Without giving her a chance to speak, I ask, "You sure you want to do this?" She nods.

"It's going to hurt."

"I know." Her delicate fingers grip my hard-on and she starts stroking me. Her eyes fall closed and she whispers, "You feel different than I thought you would."

Pulling my lips between my teeth, I'm trying to decide if I'm stifling a laugh or stopping myself from coming by drawing some of my own blood. She's so crazy, yet so fucking innocent. She's never touched a dick before. Well, isn't that some shit. I knew Jeremy wasn't into it, but years of dating and she never had her hand in his pants? Mind blowing.

"What did you think it would feel like?" My arms are starting to shake. I may not feel the pain; however, I'm still a mess from the fight, but I can't bring myself to move from on top of her. My dick feels like it's going to explode as her finger traces the vein down the side.

She sticks out her lower lip before she hums. "I don't really know. Not this...soft?" Her blue eyes widen like she spooked herself. "Not that you're soft! I mean...you're really ready there, aren't ya? Nice and hard. It's just that...do you use lotion?"

"No. I don't lotion my dick." I finally found the one thing that makes her vulnerable. Sex. She has been through some shit, but never had the chance to be fucked. Let alone fucked well.

"Okay." She bats her lashes, something I've never seen before. "I'm ready, Rocco." Her bottom lip gets pulled between her teeth and I watch her. Really try to read her. She wants this.

"Okay," I repeat.

I push off of her and she crosses her legs together behind my back. "Where are you going."

"I just want to taste every part of you, Angel." I reach up and kiss the tip of her nose, her lips, her neck, between her breasts, before I trail my tongue down her stomach.

I want to rush every part of this. I want to taste her. I want to slide inside of her and feel her clamped around me.

When I position myself perfectly between her legs, she squirms and throws her legs over my shoulders. Using the tip of my tongue, I graze over her soft skin, moving down and stopping at the skin before I reach her clit.

My stomach is bottoming out with nerves, and my skin is hot to the touch. Like I'm running a marathon. My heart feels like it's beating out of my chest. I'm not sure I've ever let myself feel this much. It's foreign to me. Although it's far from it, this feels like the very first time I'm letting feelings into the mix. This is how it's supposed to feel.

I slowly lick the length of her soft, wet heat between her legs. *I'm a fucking goner.*

"Rocco," she raps, almost begging.

Hearing my name whimpered from her lips fuels my fire. I was the one making her feel this way. Literally not one other man has gone down on her, or touched her in a way that made her feel.

I pull on the hard nub of her clit, biting gently and releasing it. I push my forearms on her thighs and spread her farther. I need to taste every part of her.

I suck her slow and long, grabbing ahold of skin until she was thrashing under me like a shark out of water. I slide my tongue inside of her and drag it up to her clit. In and out, up and down. In and out, up and down. Her nails dig into my scalp, holding my head in place.

My dick is wound up. It's fully charged and ready to drive into her. But as much as my need to do that, to make her come undone, saying my name breathlessly—this is worth the wait.

I look up at her. Her face is flushed and her are eyes pinched shut. Her tongue darts out and licks her lips as she pants, like she is in the best kind of pain.

I reach up and palm a breast, putting that piercing to work. "Oh, fuck. That…" Her words trail off as her hips start slowly bucking against my face.

That's it, Angel. Take what you want from me. "You're so fucking beautiful. You should see yourself from down here."

I work her harder. Licking. Sucking. Licking. Sucking. Her body is moving like we're fucking, and I'm about to come from the vision of perfection in front of me.

She stops moving. Stops breathing. But I don't stop. I keep going. *She's coming.*

My name is moaned in a way I've never heard before. Her voice is deep, quiet…she's fully immersed in it right now. Her orgasm is barreling through her, and all I can think about is how I never want to stop.

I want to run away, get a shack on the beach and eat her out morning, noon, and night, feed her, and do it all over again for the rest of my life.

I feel her body relaxing as she comes down from her high.

"We aren't done, are we?" she asks, groggy and satiated.

"No, baby, we're just getting started."

The grunt that comes out of me when I leaned over to the nightstand was unattractive, but only hours ago, I thought I was dying. As I finger around in the drawer for a condom, I feel her eyes on me. Thin fingers glide gently down my arm over fresh cuts and bruises and scars that I should never have gotten in the first place.

Once I grab hold of the foil wrapper, I sit up with her legs wrapped around my waist. Making sure to take my time, I notice she watches my every move. Once I tear it open, I toss the wrapper to the ground and place the condom on the tip of my dick.

She's watching with such…gratification. Learning. I roll it

down and she licks her lips. As much as I'd love nothing more than to fuck her raw. Feel her tight pussy around me. How warm she is, it's better this way. I don't know if she's on the pill. I can't put her at risk. And that's all it would be.

The thought of having a child scares the shit out of me. I wonder what my father would do to him or her after seeing what he's done to me.

Soft hands cup my cheeks. "Are you there?" she asks with a slight smile of defiance. "Are you *scared*, Mancini?"

Daisy's eyes sparkle, and it's like I can see her aura grow devil horns. The air around her seems electrified. "Are you afraid after you pop my cherry, I'm going to corrupt you? Be your favorite addiction?" Her voice is lower and raspy, and it awakens some type of feral beast inside of me.

Yes. Too late.

"I'm not fucking scared of you, Daisy. Or how obsessed you'll be with *me* after we fuck." I lean down and run the tip of my tongue slowly up the front of her neck and she sucks in a short breath. "I'm terrified this is going to get us killed."

A roll of her hips tells me she isn't scared. Or she is and doesn't give an actual fuck. Part of me believes it's the latter. For the first time since the accident, I feel someone is on my side for once. "You shouldn't worry about how I'll feel. You should worry about how fast you caught feelings the day you walked in the door and saw me."

I don't deny it. In fact, I ignore it. She has one hundred percent hit the nail on the head.

I sit up and use my fingers to swirl around her arousal. Her hips buck. "We already did this."

Her fingers once again move over the scars and new cuts on my back, and she stops. She's going to ask questions about all of it. But I can't stop. Not right now. Not now that she's under me.

Instead, she pulls me into a hot, violent kiss. Her mouth is warm, and the sweetness of her taste is sending me into a spiral. She pulls my hair, and I pull back before she dips her head to my neck. She's wild, right now. *Feral.* And it's all for me.

Every time her tongue darts out to kiss my skin, my body screams '*Get inside of her now!*'

"Tell me what you want."

She pushes herself up despite me playing with her clit. "I want you to fuck me, Rocco."

Fuck yes. Her blues bounce between mine. And her tits are staring at me like they need to be fucked just as much as her mouth. "Unless you want me to fuck you…"

Some miraculous maneuver happens, and she's pushing me to my back so my head is at the foot of the bed. "You're wasting precious time here." She straddles me and hovers over my dick that's lined up directly with her entrance. I prop my head up with my hands because I'm not going to fucking miss this.

My brain is in overdrive as I take in her body over mine. Her stomach is taut yet soft. Tan, yet paler than her arms. She doesn't give a shit about an even tan, or if a cupcake would cancel out her workout. She lived life. And right now, in this moment, with her on top of me, she's choosing to live it with me.

Daisy's lips part as she slides herself down my dick. Slowly. One inch at a time. Or maybe it's a millimeter. "Take your time, Angel. I could watch you take my cock all damn day."

My smug expression must trigger something in her because the eyes that were closed seconds ago are zeroed in on mine. It's like we're frozen in time because she doesn't move, but that doesn't mean my cock isn't throbbing even more than it was before she was hovering over me.

But then it happens. She spreads her legs and takes the plunge. My hands fly to her hips. "Holy shit, I've never felt anything this tight before. Don't move!" I'm going to be a two-pump chump. "Wasn't ready for this."

"Does it feel like I'm moving? I'm trying to blink away the pain.

Holy shit. Ouch!" She winces, sucking air between her teeth. "Why are you so big?"

I bite back a smile and skate my hands up her ribs, soaking up a light coat of sweat beading on her skin. "I'm average, Angel."

"Average, my ass." She falls forward, and now it's my turn to wince. "Am I hurting you?" she asks, freezing in place.

Only my heart because the line we just crossed is going to be catastrophic.

"Nope. Take your—"

Just as I start to try to comfort her, she starts moving up and down. I'm not sure if she's watched a shit ton of porn, or what, but if the blood that's coating my dick wasn't a clear indication, I would have thought she lied about being a virgin. "You feel so fucking good."

My lip disappears between her teeth, and she smiles before letting it free. I jump on the opportunity, so I push my tongue into her mouth. She doesn't fight me, but moans into my mouth.

"Fuuuuck. Don't do that."

Her hips are at a steady rhythm as she grinds on me. "Do what? This?" Her fever-bright eyes align with mine as she continues to bounce on my dick. Her ass cheeks are moving up and down with their own agenda.

"Go ahead, I know you want to touch my ass. Don't be shy," she taunts.

Vanilla sex is not for me, but it's her first time. I'm not about to have her chained up watching my favorite grail knife move across her skin before I lick her blood that would drip from the marks I'd make.

A dull ache in my rib has ever so kindly reminded me that I have been brutally battered earlier this evening. But literally nothing will stop me from fucking her tonight.

"I want to go harder," she moans against my lips.

"Then go harder."

She smiles and her hips start to bounce harder…faster against me before my fingers find her clit. My senses are in overdrive. The light's on, her boobs are bouncing, the blood is now almost a light orange. "You're so fucking wet."

"All for you."

With one swift motion, I roll us over so on top of her as I pull out. "I'm the captain now, Angel," I quote the Tom Hanks movie *Captain Phillips*.

"You're so dumb," she laughs out and pushes her palm against my face playfully.

I help her wrap her legs around the backs of my thighs, holding me close. "Please…Rocco…" I nudge myself against her entrance.

"What? Tell me what you want." I want to slam into her repeatedly, take her for the ride of a lifetime, but I can't do all that just yet. She's going to be sore without me railing her like we've been doing this forever.

"Rocco…I…" She squirms under me, rolling her hips, trying to push into me.

"Goddamnit, Daisy! Tell me what you want from me!" I want to hear her say in complete desperation what she wants from me.

"Fuck me!" she cries out. "Fuck me hard!"

I rock into her, and we both let out a moan. "Are you sure you want it hard?"

"Yes," comes out more as a whisper as her eyes open and find mine.

I lean down and push my tongue in her mouth. She wraps her lips around it and sucks before I start pumping in and out. I start off slow, then get faster. Before long, I'm holding her hips so she stays in place as I'm pushing inside of her.

But that's when she lives up to the woman I've known for the past several weeks. She props herself up on her elbows and watches where we connect. Her head falls back as if the sight is pushing her over the edge.

She's a bundle of chaos in the best way.

I loosen my grip on her hips and palm her breasts before I lean down and kiss her once more. She's so fucking sexy.

There is a high chance I'm going to come soon, so I do what any gentleman would do in this situation, I reach down and find her clit with my middle finger. Her arms wrap around my neck, and her body starts tensing. I circle it using the mix of our arousal. It's rock hard and ready.

"Rocco. I…this is…it's so good," she whimpers, barely coherent.

"Because it's not our bodies anymore, baby…" I ready to finish the sentence, not caring if she thinks I'm some new-aged lunatic, but she does it instead.

"It's our souls."

She wails against me, throwing her head back. "Oh my—!"

I pound steadily in her, keeping the pace as I whisper in her ear. "I love you, Daisy. Now come for me."

Once again, her body freezes, our sweat runs together as her nails dig into my back. It should hurt, but she tightens around me, milking my orgasm from me. There was no stopping it.

Holy shit.

I've never felt anything like it. A mix of the elements…feeling both grounded and lifted while fire and pleasure flood my body.

She quakes under me, and it was the most amazing thing— feeling her crumble in my arms. Because of me.

I roll off of her while she catches her breath. Her body is relaxed, and her eyes closed. Once I dispose of the condom and clean myself up, I bring a small cloth to clean her up.

She doesn't fight it.

When I'm finally in the bed next to her and our breathing evens out, the girl of my dreams is in my arms, and she whispers, "Rocco."

"Hmm?"

"I love you, too."

CHAPTER
THIRTY-TWO

DAISY

THE DAY after one loses their virginity is like waking up in a brand-new world. Even the day I turned sixteen didn't feel this… transcending. The weight of Rocco's big fucking arm is pushing on my bladder, though, threatening to push the pee right out of me. Despite my need to get to the bathroom, I try to think of anything to suppress the urge. He has black-out curtains, and the dark color of his walls makes me feel like I'm in a safe womb of some sort.

The AC blows from the vent close by, but not directly on me. His blankets feel like what I only imagine a real fur coat made from chinchillas would feel like. I only know theirs is the softest in the world because it was a late-night google search. Almost as pathetic as searching if penguins have knees. I still don't know the answer to that one.

"Will you stop moving?" Rocco's voice is low and gravelly. I can only imagine what he looks like when he first wakes up. He's stupid amounts of handsome, and although I've been lucky to see him when he makes an appearance near the coffee pot some mornings, I have never seen him fresh out of the sheets. Today is my lucky day.

"I have to pee," I mumble, covering my mouth, trying to save him from my morning breath.

His big arm lifts like a drawbridge allowing a boat to pass under it, and I peel my skin from his. I'm not sure if we're stuck together by sweat or some other type of fluids. I'd say the latter, but there was spit and blood mixed in there, so I'm not sure if that concoction has a special name.

After I empty my bladder, I practically run back to bed, and he pulls me into him. "A cuddler. Who would have thought." His thumb moves back and forth over my nipple ring, and it zings straight to my pussy.

"I don't cuddle," his voice rumbles against my hair.

"You expect me to believe all those women you've had sex with, and you never cuddled?" His body goes tense behind me. "Thank you for being patient with me…" I awkwardly try and rectify how far I just shoved my foot in my mouth. "I've never had morning pillow talk before. So I'm not sure of the proper etiquette."

A puff of air pushes against my scalp. Was that a small laugh? "You are crazy. You're like a cat."

"A cat?!" I roll over quickly in his arms in the darkened room, but I can see more of his face. The swelling seems to have gone down, but you can still see discolored areas from the bruises. "Why a cat?"

He shifts slightly, wrapping me tightly in his arms again. "Because you could be sitting all calm, but then some intrusive thought pops in your head and you act on it. Like how cats chill on your lap and get up and walk away. But five minutes later, the cat's on a shelf next to your Aunt Bertha's ashes and it pushes the urn to the floor while looking directly at you?"

The giggle that slips out of me pushes my breath in his face, but he doesn't budge. Doesn't say a word.

"I'm not just any cat, Rocco," I say, stifling a yawn.

"Yeah?" The pad of his thumb is moving circles on my back now, and I'm three seconds away from falling back asleep.

Something shifts in the air. The conversation we had last night about Tony came flooding back, slapping me in the face. I have to figure out a way to help him get out of here. No matter the consequences. "I'm like a leopard. A recluse. Stealthy. Adaptable." I move my hand to his face and start rubbing my hands through his hair. "But as beautiful as us leopards can be, we wear masks. We camouflage. We move like an ambush hunter, quietly and quickly killing the prey."

His finger stills on my back, and he squeezes me and rests his cheek on my hand on the pillow. "I won't let him hurt you."

I whisper back, "I won't let him hurt you either. I promise. But I think you know what you have to do." He just nods his head as a tear slips down his cheek and lands on my finger before we fall back asleep. Rocco either feels relief, or he's given up completely.

———

"WHAT THE HELL is going on here?!" I pop up at the earthquake of a voice. The body next to me startles just as hard. I forget where the hell I was and who is next to me, let alone figure out who is yelling. Or maybe I'm having a bad dream.

"This is…this is not who we are, Rocco! Get the hell up." The blood drains from my face as I struggle to cover myself. Tony is back and *he knows*.

Rocco doesn't say anything but listens to his dad. My mom flicks on the ceiling light and now I'll be seeing spots in my vision for the foreseeable future.

Her yelling is nothing new. It's just something I'd forgotten about due to me being away at school. Simpler times. "Daisy! You…Rocco! How could you, Daisy?! That's your brother!"

"Step," Rocco and I say in unison while he's slipping on a pair of gray sweats.

"Oh please." My mom walks into the room once Tony grabs Rocco by the shoulder and leads him into the hallway. Emotional and mental manipulation is a hell of a drug. It makes even the strongest of men feel like they are weak and incapable of confronting their abusers. "You…acting like the trash you've set out to be. I was wondering when it would happen."

I rub my eyes, and she tosses a shirt—I hope—in my face. "I was wondering at what age you'd finally turn into a whore. Tony said you have all the signs."

The blood that once rushed below my waist has now made its way to my head…and my heart. "Signs for what, Mom." I slip on the dark t-shirt backward. Oops. There's no better way to pretend like you don't give a fuck than to put on a shirt backward and wear it proudly.

I roll out of bed and thank the universe that it's long enough to cover my naked ass. Must be Rocco's. But it doesn't smell like him.

Mom waves her hand in the air before she continues. "Signs that you'll be a slut."

"A slut?!" I look down at the shirt and see 'Tony' written in bold letters with a large number eight underneath. A number that is now ruined because of being associated with that dickwad. I violently throw my arms through the holes and rip the shirt over my head.

"What are you doing. Put that back on." My mother's eyes are wide, her face red. It's the first time I'm allowing myself to look at her since she barged in here. Her pupils are dilated, and a dress that once accentuated her best assets now hangs loose.

"I'd rather stomp down the streets of Palm Beach buck naked than wear Tony's shirt around. Nobody calls me a whore."

She looks to the blood-stained sheets and back at me. Her hands visibly shaking in front of her. "Mom. I'm not a slut. He's not my brother. He never will be."

Her thin hair moves from side to side with the disdain for her spawn who's standing naked in front of her. "Nipple rings," she huffs. "I guess Tony was right."

I follow her as she leaves Rocco's room with my arm over my boobs and my hand covering my vagina. Not an ideal way to argue.

"Mom! Talk to me!" The echo of my voice bounces off the hallway walls.

Slowly turning, she pauses, looking into my room. "I've given you everything. I only asked for one thing."

"You've asked me for nothing! You called twice and never bothered to wish me a happy birthday! You've been a complacent mom since Dad died, and I've had to pick up the pieces for both of us." My boobs fly free as my arms go into the air. "But then Tony comes along and saves the day, right? He's the best. He's the one who was holding your hair every time you cried too hard and vomited. He's the one who picked you up off the floor when you missed Dad."

She starts rubbing her nose. Something she's actually been doing a lot since I've looked at her. *She's fucking high.*

My stomach bottoms out and I feel like I'm going to be sick. My mom and I would argue, but she never called me a slut or a whore. She never visibly shook or was reactive to an argument in any way.

"You know what, Mom? Maybe we should revisit this later? After we both cool down." *Sober up.* Another emotional maturity point for me.

I sidestep into my room past my mom and she casts her blue eyes downward before walking away. Left alone with the lump in my throat and a deep burn from the excessive need to cry.

Slamming the door probably isn't the best way to get my point across, either, but I do it anyway. "Nobody slut-shames me and gets away with it." I brush my teeth, slide on a pair of leggings, and my new AirMax's, a sports bra, and a t-shirt and walk out.

I need to find Rocco.

ROCCO

HE PUSHES me into the pool house and his hand forcefully meets my bruised back. I stifle a scream from the pain. But as long as he's doing this to me and not Daisy, I can handle it. This is what I was built for.

The lock of the door echoes against the tile floor and bare walls. I don't bother turning around. I'm sure I'll only be met with a fist. Instead, he comes to me, blocking my view from the ocean I want to disappear into.

"Daisy, hmm? Those other women weren't enough?"

I swallow hard, not moving. Not giving him the satisfaction of his soulless eyes meeting mine. "It was nothing."

"It hardly looked like nothing." His voice is low, like the calm before the storm. "I have cameras all though this house. Your bedroom." He turns and his dress shoes click on the floor as he dramatically walks to the window.

"You found yourself a flexible one. Good for you," he says, smiling behind his finger. My fists clench by my sides and I can hear my heart beating in my ears. "How was she?"

He's taunting me.

"Her mother is pretty bendy, too. I had her in a pretzel while I fucked her within inches of her life." A chuckle slithers out of him. "She doesn't mind the drugs either. At first, she was scared, claimed she never even touched a cigarette, but once I did a line to show her it wasn't all that bad, she loosened up a bit."

More clicking of the shoes as he closes in on me.

"Listen, son, you know the drill." He steps in front of me and places his hands on my shoulders. I can feel my airway constricting.

There is one thing that doesn't get discussed enough when it comes to men's mental health. Or mental health, in general. If you're treated like a child in your most formative years, and you're never allowed to grow up...if you're raised by the epitome of the Dark Triad; a man who carries the traits of narcissism, psychopathy, and Machiavellianism, the only way to get through it is to ride the wave.

It seems every time I push back against him, I'm made to feel smaller.

"So, on my long flight back here, I was thinking of a suitable punishment for this behavior of yours."

"Do you not think my cracked ribs and swollen face isn't punishment enough?" I choke out.

And just when you think the impossible couldn't happen, his already black eyes darken. "Daisy will start dating someone else. We don't fuck family—"

"We've known each other for weeks! We aren't fam—"

A quick punch to my already purple cheek lights up my vision with stars. "As I was saying...Daisy will start dating someone else of my choosing. I love unrequited love. It brings a chill to my bones." He fake shivers and smiles like the Cheshire Cat. "Her new beau will fight you. And yes, he'll probably lose to you."

"What's the catch?" I ask, holding my cheek, trying to calm down the throbbing. I watch as he walks to the freezer and pulls out a bag of frozen peas before it flies through the air and I catch it.

"Face. Now." My senses are on high alert like I'm in the ring. I'm no longer on the precipice of a panic attack, but I'm in full fight-or-flight mode. "If her new man loses, Daisy dies."

"Dies? Why does anyone have to die? And what about her mother? Your wife?"

In seconds he's back in front of me, but I know better than to hit him. He'll pull a gun on me, or a knife. And right now, I have to think about saving the only person who has been my white light in years. She's giving me hope, and I need to give it right back.

"Someone always dies. It's the way of life. The *circle* of life, if you will."

"What if he wins?"

"Don't be ridiculous. He'll be trained to kill, just like you. Just like Beast." The side of his eyes crinkle and his nose twitches like I'm a little boy and he's telling me how cute I am. An innocent look along with words that drip with deadly venom.

More clicking shoes. That sound is driving me mad! "If Daisy's new man wins, you die. All is fair...don't you think?"

A lose-lose situation. "So, I have to die to let Daisy live?"

He rubs his hand along the stubble on his jaw. "It's only fair. That depends. You're selfish enough to take my wife from me with your carelessness, my *only* love..." Again, we are eye to eye. Man to murderer. "Are you selfless enough to kill yourself in order to save the woman you love?"

A nice slap on the shoulder and he walks out, leaving me with his parting words. My chest tightens and I take a few deeps breaths. Minutes go by before it feels like my heart isn't trying to escape my chest.

"Hey," Daisy whispers from the doorway.

I hurry over to her, pulling her in by her arm. "Did he see you?"

She shakes her head quickly and a concerned look washes across her face. "What did he say?"

"You go first. What did your mom say?" I rub my hands along her cheeks, giving myself peace of mind—seeing if she's hurt.

"Well, she called me a whore…" Daisy ticks off a finger. "Your dad called me a slut." Another finger. "Not to my face. Which makes no sense because I've had sex *literally* one time—"

"He's going to try to set you up with someone," I interrupt.

"He what?" She laughs and runs her fingers through her unbrushed, sexed-up hair. "I won't do it."

"You have to!"

Daisy puts space between us, taking a step back. "What the hell, Rocco? I'll just stay away from you."

I rub my hands through my own hair, getting frustrated. "Now is not the time to be a badass. Not until I figure out a way for us to make it out of here alive." That seems to get her attention.

"What do you mean?"

And that's when I spill it. Everything Tony Mancini just told me, about me dying and her living. And him setting her up. How everything is a game to him. Like after my mother died, I've been subjected to live with my very own personal tormentor. Living with constant mind games.

A short time later we're sitting in silence on the sofa that looks like it never gets used next to the beach that I never get to go to. My phone vibrates, and of course it can only be one person.

> Him:Fight tonight. Tell Daisy she will be picked up
> at the house at 8.
>
> Remember, cameras are everywhere.

Fuck.

"Come with me."

She doesn't hesitate when I grab her hand. She follows, not because she's after my body, or the money that's not even mine, but me.

Pushing through the back doors, our feet land in the sand and we run…I don't know how far. The sun is beating on both of us, and a light ocean breeze pushes against us as we escape as far as possible. We're both out of breath when we finally stop behind some rocks at the inlet.

"What's…with…the…relocation?" Her hands fly to her knees, trying to catch her breath. "You know I hate cardio. Fuck."

I can't help but laugh at her reaction. Yes, we're in a dire situation, but it feels good to smile. Even just for a second. Once she straightens, I pull her by her waist so she's against me. "You never told me you hated cardio."

"I hate cardio." Her eyes drop between us. "How are you hard after running?" A roll of her eyes earns my lips on hers. She never fights it but cups my cheeks instead. Her fingers move into my hair, and I hoist her up by her ass and her legs wrap around me.

"I don't want anyone but you," she says between kisses, and I swear my fucking heart is ready to burst. I'm not one to smile or be happy, but her saying that—

I push her into the rocks until we can't move back any farther. "Wait!" I release her and she drops to her knees and pulls my sweats down. Those pretty fucking lips part, but I grab her chin.

"Look at me, Angel." Blue eyes stare back at me. "Open your mouth and stick out your tongue."

She does and my cock jumps.

"Good girl." I move my tongue around my mouth and suck my cheeks between my teeth to gather my saliva. I look down at her and I just want to kiss-marry-fuck her.

The trust in this woman's eyes is unmatchable as I lean over and spit on her tongue. Once our saliva collides, she moans and rubs her thighs together. Her mouth closes before she drags her wet tongue from the bottom of my shaft to the top of my dick. And I swear to Christ, it takes everything in me not to come at the sight of her doing that with her big blue eyes with last night's makeup still smeared down her cheeks.

"Now I'm going to fuck your face," I rasp, before gripping her hair. I don't get a chance to push into her before she's doing it herself. "That's it, baby. Take it all." Red face and all, she gags and gets back to work. "Shit."

I pull my dick out of her mouth. "What are you doing?" Her voice is hoarse and her eyes glassy and cheeks pink…fuck if I don't want to come in her.

"I… Shit. I don't have a condom."

"Do it. If I'm going to die, I want to know I felt you. All of you."

Tears threaten to make an appearance, but Mancinis don't cry. We don't show emotion. We get shit done. So I kiss her like my life depends on it. A single sob escapes my throat as I push my tongue into her mouth.

"I mean, unless you…don't want to. I mean, what if I get pregnant or something. You'll probably leave me," she smirks against my mouth.

I would never…

"If you want the chance to be able to walk in front of our parents tomorrow, shut the fuck up, D."

"What's that supposed to mean?" She narrows her eyes at me and sucks her cheeks between her teeth. She knows what I mean, but she wants to hear me say it.

The pad of my thumb slides along her bottom lip. "I'm going to fuck you so hard, you're not going to be able to stand."

She rips her leggings off and tosses them into the sand, and once again I pick her up as she wraps her legs around my waist. I pull back from the kiss and stare at her. "Are you sure?" I ask, practically panting in her face.

A simple nod and a smile tell me what I need to know. I slide a couple inches in and pull out before pushing all the way in. The way my chest flutters when she moans, and her head falls back, I've never fucked without a condom before. This…holy shit. *This. Is. Everything.*

"Harder, Rocco. Harder." Nails scratch across my back as I plow into her, pulling a groan as I bite the soft skin of her neck. Our mouths collide like our air is the only thing keeping us afloat in the cynical life we're forced to live.

"Fuck, yes." Sounds of our skin slapping against each other echoes against the rocks. Tension takes over her body, her legs trembling in my grip. "Breathe for me, baby." Her breaths are shallow as she pants. "With every breath you take, Daisy, remember it's me you're breathing heavy for."

"Yes."

"Yes, what, baby?" I pound into her relentlessly as she reaches down and starts playing with her clit.

"Yes, I breathe for you…" Her eyes move from my dick moving in and out of her, and they find mine. They're dark and sparkling as she grins. "But you…you breathe for me, too."

Our lips crash once more as she writhes against the rock behind her, trying to take me deeper. Far cry from the virgin she was last night. She gave me that piece of her. Something nobody else in this lifetime will be able to have. "I'm com—ahhh!"

"That's right, beautiful. Take what you need from me. Take everything I am." A few pumps later, I drop her to her feet, pull out, and catch my cum in my hand. I'm assuming pulling out is more effective than not pulling out at all.

She watches in fascination as streams of semen pour out of me. "Thank you."

I pause my stroking and stare up at her. "Thank you?"

A small smile spreads on her lips. "For pulling out. Not sure how effective that will be, but anything's better than a straight shot to the uterus."

My hair falls into my face and I look down and laugh. "Always so forward, Angel."

After cleaning up in the ocean and dressing, we start heading back to the house. The sun is high in the sky, but a storm is moving in from the east.

"What does this mean for us?" Daisy stops walking and I turn.

Clutching her hands in mine, I kiss her one more time before we reach the house. I can't risk being seen with her again. It's not good for either one of us. "This means I think you like dirty talk in bed."

Puckered lips and bright blue eyes point toward me. "I'm sure I don't know what you mean."

Sand covers my feet as she kicks it on me, trying to slow me down. But I grab her waist and pull her into me, needing just one more hit. One more fix.

"It means we need to lay low if we want to survive."

CHAPTER
THIRTY-FOUR

DAISY

WHEN I STEP into the kitchen, my stomach drops, and I feel the blood drain from my face. Tony stands before me with his hand on the shoulder of a man that I haven't seen in years, as if they go way back. Crew Gallagher disappears for years, and now he's in cahoots with my new stepdad? Can't be!

Sketchy as fuck.

"Daisy. Meet Crew. He agreed to take you out tonight." Tony's evil eyes meet mine, and I try to swallow past my dry mouth. Buzzing resounds in my head…or maybe it's the refrigerator. Either way, I can't hear anything but the buzz.

As Crew extends his hand, he subtly widens his eyes, and gives me two quick shakes of his head. If I would have blinked, I would have missed them. *The fuck.* Once I place my hand in his, he smiles. "Pleasure," a familiar voice says. *I guess we're pretending like we don't know each other.* I nod in return, unsure of what to make of any of this. Both men stare at me like I just got done being fucked against a rock.

Rocco steps in the back door and reaches for the coffee pot without paying anyone any mind. Coffee is his comfort drink.

"Didn't know we were having a party," he mumbles, pulling my 'Cunt' mug out of the cupboard.

Joining the buzzing in my head is the sound of coffee being poured and the excessive pounding of my heart against my ribcage. One look at Rocco and I feel like I'm as horny as I was when Jeremy wouldn't touch me. His dark hair, unruly from our fucking, and sand covering his pants and feet. I'm not usually into men who wear sandals, but even his feet are sexy.

Let's just say, if he stuck a toe in my mouth, I'd probably suck it.

"I…" Using the palm of my hand to rub my chin, I hide my nervous laughter. Something that makes even the saddest of funerals uncomfortable. "…It seems Tony has set me up with… Crew?" I gesture at my old friend, faking not knowing his name. All three men nod once at the same time, like it was something out of a horror movie.

Crew has something up his sleeve since he is acting like he doesn't know me. I haven't changed *that* much since high school. But neither has he. His brown hair is now buzzed close to his head, and he has countless more tattoos than he did when we were eighteen. Familiar green eyes stare back at me, and I tilt my lips up quickly, offering a weird smile.

"A date, huh?" Rocco says before he obnoxiously slurps his black coffee, drawing attention from his father. His brown eyes dance between me and Crew, and the smirk he was just wearing is turning more and more into a scowl. "Right. Well…I guess I'll go get ready." I push through all of the testosterone and remember the ultimate reason this is all happening. *To save my life.* But it feels far from that.

"You do that," Tony calls after me.

Now would be the perfect time to have a girlfriend. Someone I could tell about my deepest, darkest secrets, like how my new stepfather is worse than I'd initially thought. How my stepbrother took my virginity, and if he asked me to run away with him, I'm ninety-nine percent sure I would. Or how I'm also willing to bet all of my savings—all thirty-thousand of it—that my mother has been high for the better half of her new marriage. But I don't. No estrogen is close by. Nobody to bounce my insane life off of while she raids my closet and tells me to dive in head first with Rocco because he's a god, then probing me to tell her how big his dick is and confirm how well he uses it.

My feet stop short of a set of white double doors. In a haze, I didn't climb the steps to my *wing,* but my mom's. "Mom?" I knock lightly. After a few seconds of complete silence, I chance the doorknob, only to find it locked. "Of course," I whisper to myself, both sad and relieved. Sad that she is my only hope for any insight on the dick-fest downstairs, and relieved that there will be no chance she will call me more names like she did an hour ago.

———

TWO HOURS LATER, I'm showered, dressed, and have covered up the questionable marks I had on my neck from Rocco. My air-dried hair has curled into something that resembles the female main character from the 1980s. I didn't choose the curly-haired life, but it sure chose me.

A light knock comes from the door. My stomach knots. No matter who's on the other side, it will set my skin ablaze for one or two reasons—anger or desire. Unless it's Crew, it would be more along the lines of embarrassment. *"Welcome to my shit show of a family, where my stepfather is trying to kill us all and I fucked my stepsibling."*

"Come in." My voice is that of a vocal fry--low, creaky, and pure laziness. That's what happens when I want to elude my true feelings. I pick at the skin around my nail, anxious, yet still trying to disassociate from everything. I need a break. I'm tired.

The door swings open and Rocco stands there somehow more sexy than he was two hours ago. "Don't go. We'll figure out a different way." The pad of his thumb swipes over his still-swollen bottom lip. His eyes are no longer slivers, but his face is fifty shades of bruised. If he isn't going to remember why we are doing this, then I have to.

I grab his hand and pull him into my room. But not before checking the hall to see if anyone followed him. Closing the door behind us, I lock it for good measure.

His hand snakes around my waist and he turns me around to face him. "Please. Don't go."

The sadness in his voice fuses with desperation and I touch his cheek. "Crew doesn't want me. I promise you. He's an old friend from school. But you know we have to do this." His heart starts beating faster against my chest before I rest my hand on it. "*Breathe.*"

"You know him?"

"Yeah. When I saw him in the kitchen and your dad's hand on his shoulder, I was taken aback." I pinch the bridge of my nose, trying to hold my shit together. "And he's pretending like we don't know each other? I'm not sure what to make of any of this. I just need to find out who's side he's on."

He nods and releases me. I want to push him onto my bed and snuggle up against him—tell him everything is going to be okay. I can't. It might not be okay. It might be far fucking from it.

"I need to go before your dad—" I catch myself. He doesn't call him Dad. I'm not sure I've heard Rocco call him anything except for "he" or "him."

"Before he comes. I know." His hands move through his silky strands and his eyes stare into mine, pulling my soul from my body. I'm his. I think I have been since he walked in the door the first day I met him.

We exchange one more glance before I go to push past him, but he stops me by gripping the bottom of my face, stealing my breath.

"You're mine, Angel. Do you understand?" His head tilts forward, blazing me with his brown eyes. The broodiness of his voice and the darkness of his words coat my aura. The air in the room shifts like we're in a snow globe and someone gave it a good shake.

Like a reel in my head, his face—his eyes—the way he looks at me plays from the day we met. In his black beanie, backwards hats, bandanas, and hoods, and thick paint, and bruised…and now. He's not smiling or snarling. The tension between us, innocently standing in the middle of my room, is increasing with a frightening intensity.

Tony's voice roars from downstairs. "Daisy!"

"I have to go," I whisper and place a chaste kiss on his cheek. Peeking out the door to see if we're in the clear, I breathe a sigh of relief. I spare one more glance at the man I'm risking it all for and close him in my room. Maybe he can hide out there. Maybe my room can be his safe space. But is any space under Tony's eye safe?

CHAPTER
THIRTY-FIVE

DAISY

CREW DOESN'T SAY a word until we get to his vintage red Camaro Z28. A car I've not ridden in, but I've heard through the grapevine—Jeremy—that his passenger seat is usually occupied by beautiful women. Not that I was ever jealous. Our ship sailed after —you guessed it—Melissa Winters snatched him up before she left in sixth grade. Tanner Lee wasn't enough for her, she had to take Crew, too. I loved Crew, but as soon as I spilled those beans, he was a goner.

It's another windy evening and darker than usual outside, and it's one hundred percent matching the vibe of life right now. Unlike Brad, the warning alarms in my head aren't going off. Nothing is telling me to run the other way. That has to count for something.

Like a gentleman, Crew opens the door, lets me slide in, and closes it behind me.

I reach over and unlock his door with nerves rumbling in the pit of my stomach. His car smells like one of those small tree air fresheners.

"It's Black Ice," he says as the engine revs to life. I'm offered a friendly smile as if no time has passed. "You were sniffing like a hound dog."

As we pull out, his emerald eyes bounce from the road ahead to his rearview mirrors. I, too, look back at the house and Tony is on the porch, hands crossed and a wide stance. But nothing will prepare me for the silhouette in my window. Rocco stands with his arm bracing himself against the frame.

As his image gets smaller, I forget what Crew said, and all I can think to say is, "Ah. Yeah."

Trees whiz by and I decide to break the awkward silence that's looming between us. "I'm sorry. This is just...weird." I nervously laugh.

His brows furrow. "Listen, D. I don't know what's going on. And frankly, I'm not sure I really want to know. Tony is not a good guy. I can't let on you know me. He's up to something."

Crew looks to me quickly and back to the road. "Do you know..." He lowers his voice like someone else is around. "Do you know what he's capable of?"

"Rocco told me." Just being questioned about Tony arouses fear. "Um..." I swallow hard and look at Crew, trying to figure out if I can trust him or not. "Rocco and I...um..."

"You fucked."

"Oh. Well...yes. Yes, we did," I say confidently. I'm not ashamed. Not at all. "How did you know? Did Tony tell you?"

Crew's laughter fills the car, and my shoulders fall in relief. "When Rocco walked into the kitchen and heard we were going out, he looked like he wanted to beat me to a pulp right then and there."

I giggle, but he's not wrong.

"So Tony found out about you two?" We turn into the parking lot of a restaurant I've never been to before.

"Tony walked in when we were in bed asleep. But it's a lot deeper than wanting to kill Rocco because he took my V-card."

Crew throws the car in park and turns his entire upper body to me, pinning me with wide eyes and a whistle.

"Shit, D. He took your virginity? And *kill*? Like, literally?"

I nod.

"Let's eat. And we can talk more. Yeah?"

———

I END up telling Crew everything, and it feels really fucking good. "Sorry for all of the word vomit, but now since my mom is Tony's new coke fiend, I have nobody."

He sits across from me, flicking the two sugar packets he's been holding between his fingers for the past ten minutes. I'm not sure if he's going to use them or if this is a newly developed nervous tic.

Our food is long gone and we just got our second round of whiskey shots. Crew knowing the owner has its perks. I'm guilty and twenty-one by association, I'm assuming. But Crew knows everyone.

"So take me to the warehouse," Crew blurts out of nowhere.

My head bounces back and forth. "Nope. No. Fucking. Way." I shoot my Jack Daniels and slam the empty glass on the table like they do in movies.

His shoulders move up and down like he doesn't have a care in the world. Well, he doesn't because it's not him whose head is on the chopping block. "Why not? What's there to lose?"

"Oh, I don't know. My life?"

A crisp one-hundred-dollar bill falls to the table, but it's not from Crew. We both look to the culprit at the same time, and my insides twist like someone is trying to ring them out.

"What do we have here?" *Fucking Brad.* "A date? Well, it's on me!" He swivels his head to Crew and opens his fat trap once more. "Careful with this one. She'll tease the shit out of you and disappear into thin air."

Crew sticks out his bottom lip trying to frown but smiles instead. "A tease, huh? Not Daisy here. You must be mistaken."

"Hell nah, man. She'll ghost ya. You're probably *fucking* Death. Oh wait…I heard—"

I push myself out from the booth and stand tall, reaching Brad's chest. "Maybe you should care about your oral hygiene as much as you do about my business."

Brad's dark eyes narrow at me and his fists clench by his side. All this time I thought it was pure rage running through him, but he's probably just craving his next hit of cocaine. He may already be high. Who the hell knows?

"Stop talking about my teeth!"

"Maybe if you'd brush them, I would!"

I prance around the douchebag, grab Crew's hand, and pull him out of the booth just as the waitress comes by. "Oh! Right on time." I hurriedly pick up the hundred-dollar bill Brad had laid down and handed it to her. "This guy right here paid for our first date." A little nose scrunch and an innocent smile had the poor girl swooning.

"How romantic!" Her hand moves over her blue button-down shirt as if her heart's ablaze.

"I wasn't *really* going to—" Brad tries to interject but I interrupt.

"Ready to go, baby?" A little nose nuzzle into Crew's neck has Brad swearing under his breath until he says something that triggers me.

My body goes rigid, and I turn to him. "What did you just say?"

He smiles like he knows he's got me where he wants me. *Smug prick.* "Nothin'."

"What did you call me?" Crew pulls me back by the hand, but I refuse to budge. My feet are planted, and I have no plans to leave until he says it.

Brad steps to me so we're toe-to-toe. "I said you're a whore."

The funny thing is, I don't remember winding my fist back. And I certainly don't remember clocking him with an uppercut to the chin. What I do remember is when everyone in the restaurant made some type of noise when his mouth started bleeding and then my world turned black.

"Jesus Christ, D." Water splashes my face while I'm lying flat on my back on the hood of the Camaro. "You sure know how to pick 'em, huh?"

I laugh and take the bottled water from his hand before I chug it. My knuckles are bruised already and hurt. His thumb rubs over them and he shakes his head. "You should see the other guy," I joke.

"I want to go to the ring." *Yeah. I heard you the first time.* He stands in front of me, pulling his arms across his chest.

"Why? You don't know how to fight."

A deep breath escapes as he stares into the dark sky. "I don't know. I feel like I need to help you get out of this situation. And do you really think every man that steps in there knows how to fight? It's an illegal entity. I'm scrappy. I was raised by the streets."

The loudest, most obnoxious noise flies out of my mouth. "You were not raised by the streets. Your father owns a golf course and your mother plays recreational tennis for a living at the clubhouse."

He smiles. "You've been stalking me, Reynolds?"

I shrug and raise my eyebrows, "People talk."

"People talk," he chuckles under his breath. "But seriously D, you need someone else in your corner, and I think it needs to be me."

Tears threaten to fall, and he must take notice before he pulls me into a hug that I really fucking need from a friend.

I wipe the tears that escaped and ask, "You'll be putting a bull's eye on your back."

"Don't worry about me." He helps me off the hood and tucks me safely into the passenger seat. Seconds later we're driving to the place I swore I'd never go back to.

ROCCO

TONIGHT'S FIGHT was an easy win. But seeing her there with someone else wasn't as easy. I know Daisy said he was an old friend, and that wasn't my concern. What if Crew is working with my dad? What if he's building an empire full of allies so it makes me and Daisy escaping impossible?

I flick the switch of my custom-made knife. The sound of the sharp, butterfly-shaped metal moving against the liner is a calming noise while "Vore" by Sleep Token plays on repeat to drown out all the voices in my head. When I first started fighting, I would lie in bed and flip the knife open and closed, imagining what it would be like to drive it into *his* temple. But I'd probably be more into using a butter knife. I want that shit to hurt. Or I imagined impaling his heart. How much blood would come out of a heart made of stone? And maybe if I twisted it after I stabbed him, it would cause even a fraction of the pain I've felt every day of my life.

Running my finger over the razor up to the tip, I imagine what it would be like to take my own life. End it all. Save Daisy. Let her live and have a normal life. Find a guy who isn't first-degree of fucked up.

"Hey," her voice is soft in the doorway. The door clicks behind her, and she locks it. We both know we're being watched under a microscope. But we'll only talk. That's it. No kissing. No fucking. No tasting her one more time…

I spin the knife in my hand before the tip pushes into my palm and Daisy winces. "Stop!" She whisper-shouts, running over to me and falling to her knees in front of me.

"How was your date?" How pathetic must I look to her, right now? Sitting here with a small table lamp on, barely lighting this massive room. My hair is messy from running my hands through it. I decided to pick up my charcoal set again. I needed an outlet—a healthy one. My sweats have a black stains on them from a drawing I made for her. It's laying on her bed, but judging from her not mentioning it, it seems like she got home and came right to my room. I won't lie and say that doesn't warm my insides.

"It wasn't a date." Her voice is barely a whisper. If I wasn't directly in front of her, I wouldn't be able to hear her. "He wants to help us."

"He knows nothing about what he'd be up against. I don't need more innocent blood on my hands, Angel." Another spin of the knife before I stop it with my thumb, drawing blood.

Daisy raises herself enough that her face is even with mine. Her touch on my cheeks is soft and caring. I almost buy it. I'm in a bad space mentally. Thinking that everyone has it out for me, including her.

"Be with me. One more time," she begs, and I dare to look into her baby blues.

"I can't. Every time I touch you or kiss you, or get close to you in the same room, I know that it's killing you. It may not be right away, but it's inevitable. And it fucking hurts." I tap my chest with the blade, wishing I had the balls to push it in and twist it.

Her pouty lips crash onto mine and I push back, away from

her, and hold the knife to her chest, hoping she'll leave on her own. Fear never crosses her face. Her lips part and one eyebrow raises, daring me to cut her. "Do you think the pain will stop if we fall deeper together?"

I stand and look down at her on her knees. "You want to suffer with me? Is that what you're saying?" A small nod confirms her intention.

"Get undressed and lie on my bed. Head right here." I tap the bottom end of the mattress, toss the knife on the plush fabric of my quilt, kick off my pants, and peel off my shirt. I don't care if he's watching on his stupid hidden cameras, and I'm assuming she doesn't either.

Daisy moves intricately out of her clothes, never taking her eyes off of me. Her tanned body moves across my bed as she lies on her back with her head hanging upside down off the side to look at me.

"Fuck, you look so good like that." Her tits are pointing to the ceiling, her nipples decorated with silver rings, and her skin— smooth and creamy. Blue eyes watch as I stroke myself in front of her.

"So do you," she says, ready with a shaky breath.

"Open up."

Daisy's lips part and I slide inside and lean forward with my hands landing close to her knees. I drag my palms up her thighs as I pump inside her mouth. Her fingers trail down my abs and follow the trail of hair leading to my dick.

My fingers dance on the soft skin around her pussy, teasing her. I feel her hands hold my ass. "Fuck my face, Rocco," she mumbles around me. I push into her hard and she gags around me. "Not touching her is impossible," I think when I slide two fingers into her and her body goes tight.

"You can't come yet. We haven't even gotten to the fun part," I say as I lean forward and roll my tongue over her clit. "Jesus, you're fucking soaked." I slurp her cum like I've been stranded in the desert, thirsty for water.

For not having much experience, she's pretty accomplished with a dick in her mouth. Daisy not only uses her tongue and lips, but the light graze of her teeth as I move in and out of her that is a pleasurable pain I'm falling for with each thrust.

I stiffen my tongue and move around her now swollen clit when I feel her fingers move closer and closer to the crack of my ass. "Try it and I'll make sure you come until you die," I say against her.

A finger slowly and lightly glides between my cheeks. *I don't hate it.*

Only then does she press on my asshole. The exit. Only an exit. My tongue moves feverishly against her, and she pushes her finger harder against me. *Again, I don't hate it.* In fact, I feel myself pulsating in her mouth, almost too close to cuming. *No. No. No. Too soon.*

I stand straight and pull my dick out of her mouth. When my gaze lands on her swollen lips, they're tilted in a devilish smile. "So you want to edge us both?"

"Something like that."

I'm in a haze. I can't concentrate until I feel something cold tap my hand. Still upside down, Daisy isn't smiling anymore but handing me my knife. Her nail scratches over the skin of her chest.

I kneel down so we're face to face like the scene from *Spider-Man.* Something I've always wanted to play out since I was a boy. She doesn't wait though. She pulls my head and pushes her tongue into my mouth. A dirty kiss that shoots straight to my dick. The idea of her tasting herself on my lips is enough for me to come against the side of the bed like a horny teenager.

We may have started out on the rocks. A relationship of both misunderstandings and saving the other by telling each other to constantly "breathe." But no matter how much we bickered, she never made me feel like I wasn't enough.

"Fuck, Rocco. Please do something!" she begs, moving so her head's on the mattress.

I take the knife from her hand, and in the pit of my stomach lies a temptation so great that no force can keep me away. My eyes fall to the perfect skin above her breast while my hand holding the knife has a mind of its own. Following the same path she made, with a steady hand I dig the tip in a little deeper, but not deep enough to cut. Not yet at least.

Her hands move between her legs and mine follows. With the touch of a feather, I move my fingers over her wet fingers and let them move together. My dick is throbbing and painful. What kind of sick fuck am I that cutting her is turning me on more than just the idea of fucking her? That has to have some deep psychological reason, right?

Her cheeks flush and the blade scrapes into her at the same time as she moans. "Yeah? You like this, Angel?"

"Mmhmm. I love knowing you could hurt me…but you won't," she rasps. "Here." Her finger taps her hips. "Try here," she says with a shaky breath.

Dragging the knife over her supple breast and down her flat stomach, her muscles tense under the metal. Her hand moves to my dick, and she starts stroking. "You're so hard. Harder than before," she drawls, hooding her eyes and meeting mine. "I love you," she whispers to me. Never had to ask her to say it. Didn't beg. She did that of her own accord. She loves me and here I am tugging a knife across her fucking heart.

"This isn't love. You're letting me do this to you and it's turning me on this fucking much."

Her hand grabs mine that's holding the handle in a death grip. "Do it." A small nod accompanies her direction. "Just this once. Because I want it, too. I'm empty inside and it's been so long since I've felt anything."

I swallow hard, contemplating what she's telling me to do.

The knife gets tossed on the mattress and I lie next to her. Of course, the idea of fucking her is in the forefront of my mind, but we have so many words left unsaid. And what if my next fight is my last fight?

A smirk lights up her face and she turns toward me, lying on her side. The warmth of her breath heats my neck. "What is it?" Tiny kisses cause a shiver to run through me like I've never been touched by a woman before.

I twist a strand of her blonde hair around my finger, debating whether I should keep my mouth shut or keep going. Her blue eyes bore into me.

Daisy pulls away from my neck and lays her head on the pillow next to mine. "Dark love."

My fingers trail down her arm and they leave goosebumps in their wake. "I love dark love. The longing, the raging desire. How consuming it is. Like it's stealing your last breath, and you don't give a shit."

She blinks at a snail's pace, like she's trying to weigh her words before she speaks. "That's what you think this is? Dark love?"

I huff out a laugh even though nothing's funny. There is nothing light or fluffy about what we feel for each other. Nothing normal. We don't go on dates. No carnivals or fairs. Just two broken people who are trying to put each other back together again.

"All I know is I have to die for you so you can live." A stray tear falls down her cheek and I wipe it away.

The tender touch of her slender fingers relaxes every bone in my body and my eyes close. "Oh, baby. Dying for someone isn't dark love." Her hand grabs mine and she squeezes it. "Dark love is holding your hand through the storm."

I open my eyes and find her already looking at me.

"We're doing this. Together. This is *our* storm now."

"That's enough!" *His* voice booms from the doorway, and Daisy whips the cover over herself. I hop off the bed in with a jolt of adrenaline, ready to fight. I cover my junk with my hand and look to the floor, trying to find my shorts. "Have you no respect for yourself, Daisy? When Mancinis make promises, we keep them."

I see Daisy fighting an internal battle. And she lost. "I'm not a Mancini, Tony. My last name is Reynolds. My father was a Reynolds. So am I. And he would never—"

"Daisy, don't." Her eyes snap to me as I pull my sweats on. "Please." He can't know she knows. He'll kill her anyway. Whether I live or die, she knows too much about his "business" and what he's done to me.

I don't bother looking at him. His face is red, and the vein in his forehead is protruding and threatening to cause a stroke. Hell, I pray to God it does.

CHAPTER
THIRTY-SEVEN

DAISY

THE CAMERAS. I totally forgot about them. Being spied on in my own home is new to me. And it's about to fucking end. "Get dressed and meet me downstairs." His finger wiggles between us. "Both of you."

"I want to talk to my mom." My nostrils flare and I clench my jaw trying to stay as cold as the man in front of me. A small smile creeps across his face. "I'm sure you do. But she's not home. She needed to *get away* for a while." Never in my life have words sounded so articulated to cover up such an utter horse shit of an excuse. My eyes fall to my fingers as my nails dig into my bloody cuticles.

The door slams and it's happening. I whip the covers off of me, not caring that I'm completely naked. Rocco is in front of me in record time with his sweatpants hanging low on his hips. I'd love to stare, but he knows the signs. He knows what's happening.

My nails are digging into my chest, trying to calm my heart. "I can't…breathe." As my lungs constrict and my vision tunnels, the prominent need to fight for my life isn't there.

I'm done.

Rocco wheels his desk chair over to me and has me sit and lean forward. "Head between your legs. *Breathe, Angel.*" A soft blanket lays on my back and his fingers rub my scalp in slow, calming circles. Triggering the para-sympathetic nervous system to calm me down is a stroke of genius, and not everybody knows how to do it the right way.

He kneels in front of me and the smell of him, always traipsing into my nose like fresh leather and coconut, floods my senses. My body—my soul—accepts him. *All* of him. I go to reach out to him —to clutch his arms, his shirt that I forgot he isn't wearing. I feel like I'm drowning, reaching for anything to hold me up, but nobody is there to save me—until his fingers intertwine with mine.

"Breathe," he whispers to me. Or it could be to the both of us. "Breathe."

As if timed perfectly, Tony's voice echoes through the house, calling both of our names like we are children ready to be punished for stabbing the babysitter. Although Rocco and I are both adults, my entire body is shaking, and his pupils are dilated. Adrenaline is pumping through both of us, except I'm not privy to what Tony is capable of. Rocco's been through it…he knows.

"Listen to me." His fingers tighten around mine and I'm pulled into his body. Our foreheads meet each other's. "This is it. I know him." The depth and seriousness of Rocco's voice is in contrast compared to when we first met. It was low, but there was a playful energy. It's long gone. "Putting Crew in the mix didn't work, so he's planning something." I fight against the tears blurring my vision as my eyes dart back and forth between his. My rib cage feels like it's going to crack open from my heart that's trying to escape. "Just do what he says. Play his game. If you fight back, it will only get worse." Rocco brings his lips to my forehead, and I pinch my eyes shut as a sob escapes at the same time tears stream down my cheeks. "I won't let him hurt you." He nods and Tony's voice is now closer…*and even louder.*

I'VE BEEN PACING my bedroom with the door locked for the last three hours. Not like it matters if it's locked. Tony would kick it down in a fit of rage if he had to.

The opening and closing of Rocco's knife and replaying what we shared in his bed has been keeping me distracted. No. I'm lying. I'm concocting a plan in my head on how to get the hell out of here before both of us die, and holding the knife feels like I'm being grounded in a world that's going to be upheaved at any moment.

After we went downstairs, Tony's eyebrows were so low, I'm surprised he could see. He handed Rocco a slip of folded paper and hightailed it out of the house, peeling out in his stupid BMW. Rocco wasn't any better. He looked at me and started chewing on the inside of his lip with glassy eyes. One nod and he was out the door. No words exchanged. *Nada.*

Hours have passed. I've been watching the clock like a child anxious for the school bell to ring at the end of a long day. I've tried calling Crew. Nothing. I haven't even thought about the job I most likely lost. Employee of the year, folks. Part of me wants to call Jeremy just to have someone around.

Finding my mother is like trying to find a needle in a haystack. I've tried her cell, and it's turned off. I called hospitals, police stations, local hotels, and *morgues.* I fear she might be dead, but I don't get that feeling. You know, the gut feeling that runs through you when the person who birthed you is in danger. Not that we ever really had that connection, but a girl can dare to dream.

"I was looking for you." The hair on the back of my neck stands up and my eyes dart to the door at the sound of Tony's voice. Trying to swallow is almost impossible. My mouth is painfully dry.

I grab the bottle of water I keep on my nightstand and chug it before I sit on my bed, hoping he will see me as less of a threat.

Tony offers me a cynical smile and his head tilts in what looks like pity. His loafers pad across my carpet, indenting the beige threads in the worst way. This is a shoe-free zone.

After a few slow paces back and forth like a lion ready to attack, he stops short of right in front of me. A yawn sneaks up on me and I can't hold it in. *I'm so tired.*

"Do you not want to know how the fight went between my son and your friend?" he asks with wide eyes like he's genuinely concerned about my inquisitions. My body sways from side to side and I steady myself with my arms. *He didn't. Did he?*

"My…my friend?" I push out, struggling to speak clearly.

"Crew. Rocco won. You don't have to worry. Your friend's dead body was removed and I couldn't wait to leave and tell you that your *brother* won."

Tears fall down my cheeks before I realize I'm crying. The hammering in my chest triggers short, tight breaths and my vision tunnels. "I look at it this way…" Tony rubs his clean-shaven chin as his brown eyes bore into me like he's ready to kill me. "You were going to end up killing yourself anyway. You get mixed up with my son while you're already one foot in the grave from your random bouts of depression." He shakes a small bottle of pills before pushing it into the breast pocket of his suit. Why is he always in a fucking suit? My muscles tense and a chill runs through me. "I was hoping you would drink that water so I didn't have to hold you down and pour these down your throat. Although, the thought of pushing something else down your throat…" He doesn't finish, but his eyes droop before he smirks. *Oh God. Please don't rape me.*

Herein lies the issue of being on a healing journey. Every day I could wake up thankful to be alive and knowing I have a purpose for being here. But then someone like Tony comes around and makes me question it all. He makes me feel like I'm a feral cat waiting outside of a restaurant for scraps of food about to be thrown in the dumpster.

Tony's hand pushes to my forehead, then moves to my wrist, two fingers on my pulse point. Keeping time on his watch, he slowly nods. "It's just a shame you couldn't keep your nose out of our business. You do tend to be like your mother in that aspect."

Mom.

"Don't move, will you? I have to take you somewhere for a little bit while I try to find your brother. Always a problem when I have to do all the heavy lifting by myself." He leaves the room and I spot Rocco's knife on my desk. Without second guessing, I grab it, lean to my side, and cover my mouth with my arm. The blade slides into my skin on the back of my leg, so Tony doesn't see the blood right away. I saw in a movie once where the main character cut herself to leave a trail of blood so she was found. It's my only chance.

Tony walks back in, oblivious to my leg, lifts me bridal style, and carries me out of my room. My eyes close, but the stinging scent of his cologne makes me want to vomit. He smells like those men who cover themselves with big gold jewelry. If those men had a signature scent, that's who Tony smells like.

Sweat runs down my forehead and back, yet I'm shivering. *Cold sweats and a pit in my stomach. I'm going to pass out. All the signs.*

Please don't hurt me. I'm not sure if I verbally speak it, or I'm screaming in my head. Begging for someone to hear me. For someone to finally come to rescue me. I can't see anything. My vision is non-existent, but I think my eyes are open.

Thick, coarse rope binds my wrists, and I feel my head fall—my chin hitting my chest.

"I put some medicine in your water so you can rest." Silence falls around me until he leans in and whispers in my ear, "Such a pretty girl with such promise." The cold metal of his ring touches my face before his lips press against mine.

God, please take me.

I'm ready.

The heels of his loafers scuff against the door before he says his final goodbye. "He refuses to lose, you know. He's been training too hard to win. He knew if he didn't win, I would take you away from him like he took his mom away from me. And it seems to me his life was more important than yours. I'm only helping you."

I don't say anything. Not that I can. I'm in and out of consciousness—trying to hold on.

"Anyway, sleep well, Daisy."

This is it…

I feel the darkness blanket me, and for once I feel warm and at peace.

At least I'll see my dad again.

ROCCO

SLEEPING on the beach was always my favorite thing to do after my mom died. My dad would force me into the arms of women much older than me and expect me not to come home until the next morning. "You have something that works—use it!

Some nights I would leave their houses after 'using it' and go straight to the beach, making sure to always have a blanket in the trunk of my car. But usually, I was driving my bike and I would just fall into the sand. The waves always brought a calmness to my mind full of chaos.

My phone rings showing an unknown number, startling me out of my thoughts. After tonight, I'm not sure how much more of this I can take. I push the side button to silence the noise. I wish I could swipe a button and silence the noise in my head as easily.

He fucking threw me in the ring with Crew. Don't care for the guy, but it's Daisy's friend. Once I saw who my opponent was, I knew I was damned if I do, damned if I don't. He's never trained like I have. I asked him when they were announcing our names. He stood no chance against me.

Never in my years of fighting have I cried, except for tonight. Each punch I threw at him, another tear fell. Not like anyone knew —it blended with my sweat. But it's not like anyone cared, either. The fucking psychos who watch me bring other men to death's doorstep have serious psychological issues.

I never turned around when they cleared his body from the floor. Nope. Instead, I went to the locker room, threw up my weight in nerves, showered, and got the hell out of there.

Another unknown phone call lights up my screen. I swipe to answer, and before I can say anything, all hell breaks loose.

"Jesus, Rocco! Where the hell have you been?" Santi shouts. "Crew called me because he couldn't get ahold of you. You need to get home! Now!"

Wait… calling from Crew's phone? *Home?* "Home? Like *my* home?"

"Get the fuck home, she's going to die, and we can't figure out how to get to her." The line goes dead and goosebumps erupt on my skin right before I feel a kick of adrenaline shoot through me like a rocket shooting to space.

Thank fuck I have my bike. It's easier to weave in and out of Saturday's late-night traffic. It must be wild to have a normal life. Get to go out clubbing with friends until all hours of the morning.

Minutes later, I'm hitting the kill switch and running into my house. "Santi, what the fuck is going on." I push past him with no clue as to what I'm looking for. There's a heaviness that hasn't been here before. I mean, it's always felt tense in here, but it feels like I'm stuck in mental sludge.

Santi runs up our set of steps two at a time before I see a beaten-up Crew, who until now I thought was dead, trying to pound a wall with a sledgehammer. The wallpaper is ragged and peeling from the hits, but the metal behind it is pristine.

What the fuck?

"Dude. She's in here. The trail of blood leads to this wall, but there's no door."

The random window that's above the front door. This whole time I thought it was a stupid faux window that rich people have to make their shit seem bigger than it is.

"Is it a safe room? This hammer isn't making a dent," Crew asks as he slams it into the black floral wallpaper repeatedly.

"Santi…call 911." I take the hammer from Crew and try it myself. My muscles are on fire, yet I'm numb. What a strange limbo. "There's a window on the outside of the house," I thundered, dropping the hammer.

"You have a ladder?" Crew's green eyes are wide with fear, and I nod.

"Did you hear her? Are you sure she's in there?" I start to pace and run my hands through my hair. Where is *he*? I'd never put it past him to harm someone, but Daisy is his new wife's daughter. Someone he's supposed to protect. Not that he's protecting his new wife, either. I knew she was high the whole honeymoon. He got her addicted to his drugs. His famous new mix of pink cocaine that's concocted of MDMA and liquid cocaine.

Crew runs his hands over his buzzed head. "I came to tell her I had a plan to get you guys out of here, so I came up to her room, trying to find her. Something didn't feel right, you know? And there was a trail of blood from her bed leading here, and I swear I heard a noise behind the wall, like metal tapping?"

I push past Santi and fly down the stairs and into the garage. Seconds later, I'm climbing a ladder like the flowerbed is on fire.

"Shit. Hurricane-proof fucking windows." My elbow won't break this. Crew throws up the hammer and I start pounding repeatedly. The glass spiders. This is all taking precious time I could be using to give her air, or life.

After I crack the bottom of the glass across the bottom, I drop the hammer to the pavement below. Hopefully Crew was able to dodge it.

I roll up the cracked glass. Hurricane windows never shatter. Thank God I watched a police investigation in our old neighborhood—a few doors down. I was sick and home from school and overheard the cop explain how robbers break through impact windows. *Clever fuckers.*

One foot into the room and then the other. "Daisy!" I cry out as sweat drips into my eyes. Her blonde hair is covering her face, and her head is limp while a string of drool leaks from her mouth to her chest. Drool is a good sign. If this happened a while ago, the drool would be dried. If she was dead, her body wouldn't be able to form saliva. *I think.*

There's a lot of blood under the chair. The only light in the room is coming from a red dot in the corner and the moon shining in the window I just destroyed.

Pushing my fingers to her neck, I breathe a slight sigh of relief. "Your pulse is weak, but you're still here with me, Angel."

I quickly untie the rope around her wrists and Crew's voice sounds at the window. "Holy shit."

He steps in and helps me lay Daisy's *almost* lifeless body on the wooden floor before starting chest compressions while I flick off the camera *he* installed.

"Fuck you, old man! I'm going to kill you!" I boomed, hoping *he* was watching. I grind my molars before falling to my knees, watching Crew give her mouth to mouth.

"Where the hell are the cops?" Crew asks as his compressions are starting to slow. He was working on post-fight adrenaline, and now he's crashing. I've seen it. Hell, I've been there.

"Move." I take over, and Daisy's moving like a rag doll with my movements.

Thirty compressions. Two breaths. Thirty compressions. Two breaths.

"Cops are on your dad's payroll, aren't they?" Crew asks quietly, as if he's giving up and I nod knowing exactly what that means.

His eyes widen and he crawls behind me as fast his beaten body can carry him. *The door.* With a simple turn of the handle, the big metal door opens to Santi pacing in the hallway.

"They aren't coming, are they?" I look up from Daisy and silently plead to Santi when our eyes meet.

He shakes his head, and I let out a sob. My tears and sweat are falling all over her skin. If only this were a Disney movie, and my tears had the magic to bring her back to me.

"Daisy, come on, baby. Stay with me." Just take me. It was supposed to be me. She's been innocent in all of this.

"Yes!" Santi pushes his phone to his ear. "We'll be right there."

He flips his old Nokia phone closed like the better half of millennials had the privilege of doing until the early 2000s. "My wife is a doctor," he cries out. "We need to get to my house."

The compressions end immediately when I lift Daisy bridal style and her head flops onto my chest. "Stay with me. I'm getting you help. Just hold on," I mutter against her matted blonde hair. I pass by Santi helping Crew up from the floor, and time turns into a haze.

The clock's ticking.

And the clock is just like every opponent...I have to beat it.

CHAPTER
THIRTY-NINE

DAISY

IF I COULD JUST STOP the pounding in my head. I try opening my eyes, but I can't. Everything's dark. Eerily quiet. The weight of my body is too extreme to move my hands. I feel like I'm being held down by a dozen Oompa Loompas.

I don't recognize this smell. It reeks of essential oils and cinnamon toast. Quite the pairing. And this isn't my bed. I can feel my body wanting to panic. My muscles try to tense, and my lungs want to constrict, but they can't. The need to hold my breath never comes. I'm almost too relaxed, but not too relaxed to recognize the insane need to chug a gallon of water.

"She's waking up," an unfamiliar voice says, and I turn my head to the sound, yet still can't open my eyes. "Daisy, I'm Doctor Miranda. Can you hear me?"

There is a slight tug on my arm. Still no panic. Where am I?

I don't hear the normal sounds of a hospital, the beeping, or the excessive smell of bleach that always whispers of someone's demise. You can cleanse the building from germs all you want, but you can't cleanse it of illness or death. Despite not knowing where I am, I don't feel the heaviness of a medical facility.

"What…" I choke out, but my throat feels like I swallowed a pack of rusty nails one by one. I seem to be having a fight with my own eyelids. *Traitors.*

Doctor. Why do I need a doctor?

"I have you on Xanax and IV fluid. So be careful not to move your arm too much. It was hard finding a vein. You were extremely dehydrated." Heels click on the floor and my eyes fly open. *His heels clicked on the floor where he put me.* They dart from side to side trying to find Tony. He drugged me.

I try sitting up and the heels click back to me in a hurry, and I pinch my eyes shut. If I play dead, maybe he'll leave me alone.

"Honey, you're safe." *A female voice.* A delicate touch lands on my hand and another one rubs my head, trying to comfort me. Dark brown eyes find mine when I open them, and she offers me a small smile, pitying me. "I called your boyfriend. He should be here in a couple of minutes. Can I get you anything?" *My boyfriend.*

"Water," I rasp with a hoarse voice. I try to say 'please' but nothing comes out.

"Of course." She smiles again, leaves the room, and I take a second to look around. I'm in a bedroom, but not one I've been in before. Not that I've seen many. The walls are yellow with family photos hanging and a Colombian flag adorning the wall behind a flat-screen.

My eyes close of their own accord as pieces of this night…or day…come back to me. What time is it? How long have I been out?

"She's awake, but take it easy with her. She's still a bit groggy from the meds, and may have trouble remembering the events of that night," Doctor Miranda's voice carries through what I assume is the hallway.

That's when it happens, my body recognizes his presence before I see him. "Daisy." I open my eyes and they lock with the brown eyes I pictured while I was falling unconscious. In only a few strides, he's next to the bed. Rocco brings my hand up to his mouth and kisses it hard. "I'm so fucking sorry. I'm so, so sorry." Tears fall from his eyes. A vulnerable side I've never seen before. "I missed you. I thought he killed you."

I smile. "Missed me? How long…" my words trail off in fear that it's been years. That maybe he's married with kids now, and my mom is six feet under somewhere. Most likely under Tony's house so nobody can find her body. Or maybe she's long gone, in Tahiti somewhere living her best life, finally rid of me.

He rubs my cheek, and I lean into his touch. We haven't had a very *gentle* relationship, but I welcome this feeling. "It's been, what…?" he questions, looking toward the door.

"Three days," another familiar voice says from behind Rocco's big build.

"Three days," he parrots. I try to peek around him at the voice, but he continues. "What can I get you, Daze? What do you need?"

I need about twelve more Xanax, a tattoo, a three-year vacation, and most of all, I need to get the fuck out of the state of Florida. "I just need some peace."

I take him in. His stubble is overgrown and the circles under his eyes are pronounced. Rocco drags his hand through his hair and a tear threatens to escape his tough exterior. "I can't be your peace right now." I want to tell him I don't need him to be my peace. I was it for the both of us. I want to save him—hell, save myself. Take us away from here. Find my mom. Save her if I can. "I can't sit back and let him get away with what he did to you. But I am sure as hell going to be your storm. I'll carry this fight for the both of us right now. I'll fight for you—for us—and take out anything or anyone in my path who tries to hurt you. He's got to pay for what he's done to both of us…and Crew and I have a way."

My heart gallops in my chest at the same time as a swarm of snakes are moving in my belly. His words…they're more than words. They're a whole damn love confession without even using the four-letter word. I fight a smile but fail miserably.

"I think you love me."

He shakes his head and his dark strands fall over his forehead. "Obviously."

"Look at me, Rocco." And he does. His tears of fear and sadness are biting back a grin. "I love you, too."

"Okay, love birds, I have to check Miss Daisy out now that she's finally awake," Doctor Miranda sings as she gracefully glides into the room, passing Crew who is standing stiff with his hands in his pockets.

"Crew! You're alive!" My voice rasps and he laughs.

"Yeah. I'm alive, kiddo." That's all he says, and that alone speaks volumes. He tried to warn me. Not that I had any clue how to dodge a criminal. We didn't learn that in my *almost* two years in college.

Crew's face is swollen and bruised, and his arm that's wrapped around his rib cage hasn't moved. *He looks how I feel.*

Dr. Miranda blocks my view. "Can they stay?" I gesture toward the guys with my eyes.

"They can stay," she says, smirking before pushing a stethoscope to my chest. I wait until she's finished listening to say anything. Crew's green eyes look hollow, and it's obvious he's been beat up.

The Doctor backs away before wrapping a blood pressure cuff around my arm. "Crew…are you okay?"

His jaw clenches.

"You should tell her. She's healthy, but she needs to know what happened that night," Santi's voice carries through the doorway. My eyes bounce from Santi's to Crew's to Rocco's.

"Will somebody just say something? I already have a headache, this isn't helping," I bite, finally being handed a bottle of water. While I chug my weight in water, all three men pull up a chair.

There is a significant amount of chairs in this room for being so small. I only have one chair in my bedroom and it's pretty spacious.

"The night I left after we…" Rocco's eyes fall to my chest and my fingers follow, trailing over a thin scab. *Oh, yeah.* "And I left…I had a fight." He looks at Crew and so do I.

Crew rubs his hands over the stubble on his chin. He looks as rough as Rocco. "Tony put me up against Rocco. He knew I would 'lose'. We thought if Tony thought Rocco was going to win, and kill me, that he would kill you."

"I already know all of this." That was Tony's original plan. If Rocco lives, then Tony kills me. He put Rocco up against someone who had no experience in the intensity of underground fighting. My only thought is Tony wanting to take me away from Rocco the way he thinks Rocco took his wife.

Rocco's thumb draws circles on my hand and his knee is bouncing nonstop, shaking the bed. "Anyway, it was Santi's idea for Crew to play dead in the ring. They didn't want to tell me in case *he* confronted me. I can't tell a lie to save my life."

"What a terrible trait to have as a cliché 'bad boy'," I joke, and he gives me a smile that never reaches his eyes.

"Crew and I seem to think if we can catch him trying to hurt me on video, we can send it to the FBI because the local cops aren't doing shit about him," Rocco assures us.

"Rocco…" I try sitting up a little straighter and fail miserably. He stands and I shake my head. "Sit back down for a minute, please. Your fath—Tony is a powerful man somehow, and if you record him trying to hurt you, he will use that power and turn it around on you, making you look like *you're* the issue." I fear we are going to have to take matters into our own hands.

"True," Santi chimes in. "He may turn it around and call it entrapment, or sue you for wiretapping or recording without his permission."

"Knock-knock."

I'm about as surprised as I was after I learned honey that is three-thousand years old that was found in Egyptian tombs is edible. My mother is here.

"Why don't you gentlemen give me a minute to talk to my daughter?"

Her voice is stronger than when we last screamed at each other in my bedroom—when she called me a whore. Rocco kisses my hand one more time, and Crew grabs my shoulder. "Good to have you back, kid. We'll figure this out."

"Thank you for coming around again." In my near-death experience, I realized I don't really want to die. It's just a comfortable way to not deal with the shit life throws at you.

The bed dips where my mom sits next to me, and I try to scoot over. "Don't. I'm fine." She looks tired. Her once full hair is wiry and weaved into a side braid. "I hope you don't mind me being here. Rocco gave me the address." She lets out a breath like she's trying to calm herself. "I wanted to say how sorry I am."

This isn't one of those moments where the mother will apologize and the daughter will do the same. I'm the first to take responsibility for my actions, but in the bigger picture, I'm not sure I did anything wrong.

Her hands rests on mine and she starts tracing my fingers with hers. Something she used to do when I was little. A gesture that always relaxed me—made me feel safe despite not knowing her emotional capacity was that of a wasp.

"I'm filing for divorce," her voice is low, almost a whisper. I'm not shocked. "He never gave me the impression he was…evil." A tears stream down her cheeks and she lets them. Wearing her emotions on her sleeve was never her strong suit, but maybe people can change. "Tony had me on a lot of drugs." She pulls in a labored breath like she's trying to stifle a sob. "He mixed most of them with my drinks—whatever it was. After that, we argued. He insisted he just wanted me to have a good time and relax, but I told him I can do that without drugs. Hell, I've gone this long without them, I think I'm okay. Once I caught him, he didn't try to hide it anymore. Him drugging me became more forceful. I was so scared."

This is where Mom and I differ. If I were her, telling my

daughter this story, I'd be swearing and sobbing, or probably both. I'm not one to cry at much, but if someone was forcing me to do something against my will to harm my body, I'd lose my ever-loving-fucking mind!

I sit there frozen. I've been blaming her for being high when Tony was the one who was doing it to her. I imagine him holding her head down and forcing her to snort a line. Or maybe he had a gun to her head and held the rolled dollar bill. Either way, the lump in my throat is about the size of Texas—and we all know everything is bigger in Texas. Or so I've heard.

"So you've been where? I mean, Mom…my life has been falling apart, and yes, it's been my fault completely, but it would have been nice to have you around to talk." A burn takes over my throat as I fight my own battle on being vulnerable with the woman I've never been able to completely open up to. "I needed you. Your advice." A single tear falls down my left cheek. "I don't have any friends—"

She throws her body on mine and sobs. "Sweetie, I'm so sorry. I've been so absent and caught up in everything—the wedding, Tony—I never caught on to his…" Her hand waves in the air, unsure of what to call Tony whatever he is exactly.

Our embrace is one for the books. I don't remember a hug this long since I was too young to realize the reality of what our relationship really was. Basic and superficial.

"Mom," I mumble into her shoulder.

"Hmm?" She squeezes me a little tighter, but I'm not mad about it.

Here it goes. "I went to therapy…in California." She releases me from my hug and her hands fall to mine.

My mother's eyes wander over my face and her head tilts. "Good," she says through a small smile. I feel myself staring like she has three heads, and my lips turn into a frown. "I want you to heal," she continues. "You deserve to heal. After your father died, I dropped the ball." The drop of her head sends a pang of guilt through my chest. "I was so deep into my own grieving, I never asked how I could help you. I figured you had Jeremy. You were always running off with him anyway doing God knows what." Her playful side-eye is a massive change from the soulless look she gave me when she slut-shamed me.

"We all grieve differently." I pull my hand from hers and wipe a rogue tear. "I won't hold it against you as long as you never call me names again. That's not what we Reynolds do."

When I was a kid, one day my dad took me to get ice cream close to a local park. There was a little girl, curly pigtails and crooked teeth. She was standing smack beside me waiting for her mom to get her ice cream. I asked her why her teeth are crooked and commented on her hair. I never meant it maliciously, but my dad pulled me aside with my ice cream in hand. He knelt down at eye level. "You don't comment on things people can't change within thirty seconds." I remember being so confused. "If they have something in their teeth, tell them. If their zipper is down, tell them. You don't comment on someone's appearance if it's a part of them. You don't know how they feel about it themselves." My eyes drifted to the little girl who was still watching me, then down to my now dripping ice cream. "We're Reynolds. It's not what Reynolds do. We're kind. We don't attack appearances or character." He nuzzled my head with his clean hand and handed me my ice cream. "Now why don't you go over there and tell her something kind." I did. I told her I liked her dress. It was hot pink with black and white skulls. It was pretty cool. We ended up playing in the park together for hours that day and I never saw her again.

My father was a great man. A great protector, and had the patience of a saint with me. I miss him so fucking much, and all I can do is heal and let him live through me.

She sobs once more and grabs a tissue from the nightstand. "You aren't a slut. Or a whore. Not sure if there is a difference, but you are amazing. And I knew when you'd meet Rocco that you might fall for him. That you'd fall for each other." A moment of silence passes through us. "He'd be so proud of the woman you're becoming—your dad."

"I have so much to do. I need a real job. I probably got fired from the library café since I have been a 'no-show' more than I've actually worked."

"Daisy. You'll find your way. You're young. You're smart. You've been through some shit. These unfortunate experiences make you stronger." My mom taps my hand a couple of times and leans in to kiss my cheek. "I have to go meet my lawyer." Her mouth falls into a straight line and her brows pinch together. "I will not let him get away with doing this to you. The only reason I haven't killed him is because I'm on a doctor-prescribed dose of medical marijuana and I feel oddly calm. I refused the Xanax."

"Mom does the weed now," I joke, and she smiles.

"Perhaps you kids have been on to something this whole time." I watch as she walks out of the room, and the relief that washes over me is that of a tidal wave. I also have an inherent need to get the hell out of this random bed and help Rocco take back both his life, and mine.

CHAPTER
FORTY

ROCCO

THIS IS IT. I had Santi text the sperm donor and tell him to meet me at the ring. This may not be the best way to handle the situation, but at this point, my moral compass is broken, and I need to end this once and for all. Once you touch the ones I love, it's game over. I haven't seen or spoken to him since the Daisy incident. Thinking about how terrified she must have been, my hands start to shake and my shoulders tense. I've fallen so madly in love with the woman next to me and the thought of losing her because of his fucked up reasoning— 'you took mine, so I'll take yours'—it makes my blood boil.

"Hey, you ready?" Daisy asks as we stand on the sand looking out at the sea. Our shoulders are barely touching, but that featherlight touch is all I need to bring me back to the present.

"As ready as I'll ever be." *Lies.* I want to give him no reason to try to kill me or Daisy off again.

Four days have gone by, and this is the first time I've seen her since Santi's. She looks beautiful. No makeup, messy hair, one of my shirts, and her peeking out underneath.

263

Pulling in a deep breath, I try to center myself. I told Daisy I'd take care of *him* myself. It's been seven days since my dad tried to kill her. He hasn't said anything to me about her. Nothing about me flipping off the camera. Nothing about Daisy not being in the room he left her in. The house has been eerily quiet.

Maribel was able to rent a small apartment in Delray Beach, so she and Daisy have been hiding out. He probably knows where they are because he knows everything. But this was his agenda, right? To get Daisy out of my life enough that I just reach the point of taking my own life. Or maybe his agenda was to remove Daisy and keep me as his money maker for the rest of my life.

"I bought you something at the Swap Shop." She pulls black fabric out of her back pocket and ties it around my face like a mask. "It's still a skull, because let's face it, you look hot rocking one. But it's not paint. And we aren't calling you 'Death' anymore. We'll call you Karma. And this will be the last fight you have to win. But it's the most important one."

I look down at her, searching her baby blues. "Since when did you become empathetic and wise?"

"I've always been wise, jackass. You were just too busy trying to get in my pants," she scoffs, nudging my arm. Being sure not to get to close since we're being watched, she takes a small step back. I want to reach out and pull her into me. Taste her. Let her consume my soul a little more.

"Stop undressing me with your eyes and listen, Mancini," she scolds.

I've been caught.

"You won't be alone. Okay?"

But I will be. It will be me and him with his verbal mind games and mental warfare that has led me to be a shell of a human. I'm ready. I'm ready to finally be able to breathe. Not have to worry about fighting. Or him watching over my shoulder, forcing sex on me with random women while a figurative gun is being held to my head.

"It's time for me to go." We stare into each other's eyes like this is our final goodbye. I die, so she can live. Wasn't that the game he was playing? I reach out to her, but she backs away, shaking her head. A light breeze kicks up as tall waves crash onto the shore. It's right now when I become aware of my surroundings. Adrenaline has kicked in.

"Remember, *karma,* you aren't alone." I nod once and turn to walk away.

"Wait!" I don't bother looking at her.

"Why do you love me, Rocco?" her voice breaks.

"Because you helped me see the light at the end of the tunnel." I don't hesitate. "You helped me realize that there is more to live for. That dying isn't the only way out, but the only way out is through." I speak into the wind, hoping it will carry the words to her with grace and all the love in my heart.

"Why do you love me, Daisy?" I don't call her Angel. That's for when we are free and living our lives together somewhere; far away from here. Even if it's in the next lifetime.

She sniffs like she's crying, but I stay frozen, clenching my fists by my side. Battling the need to hold her and tell her it will be okay. But I don't make empty promises. I have no idea if it will all be okay. "You helped fix something in me that you didn't break. And even though I'm putting my own pieces back together, you never thought less of me. You treated me as an equal. Well, except for when we first met. I wanted to smash your pretty face in with a long piece of driftwood." I laugh. It could be the end of the world and Daisy would have something feisty to say about it. "I'm healing and you helped me get here."

That's all. That's all I needed. I continue walking. She doesn't stop me. No secret touches. No seductive glances. Just fucking words in our hearts left unspoken in fear of the inevitable.

———

DESPITE THE BIRDS chirping and the sky being so blue, my view would make the entire island of the Maldives jealous. But where I'm entering, there is nothing but the fires of hell and the Devil himself waiting for me.

The loud, rusted metal door slams closed behind me as I make my way through the darkened hall. My Nikes crunch through the dirt that's ever present in this prison. The stale smell of blood, sweat, and tears coat these walls. My insides start crawling. He's already here. His car is parked in the back. Thinking he's so slick. But he's bound to slip up.

"I was wondering if you were going to be on time." He checks his watch like the condescending dickface he is. As he stands in the ring like he's admiring the view, I pull my knife from my sleeve, and the sound of metal echoes off the walls. His eyes fall to the sharp steel. "At least you can do something right." The asshole laughs and my body tenses. I feel my jaw clench and I grip the knife a little harder. "Always be prepared," I say under my breath.

The heels of his shoes shuffle toward the edge as he grabs two bottles of water and tosses me one. Always the bare minimum thing he did for the fighters. He gives them free eight ounces of water should hydrate us enough to continue, right? But always delivers top of the line cocaine. Solid father figure.

I climb into the ring, which is just one movement for me.

He takes a big swig from the bottle and tosses it over his shoulder before pulling his gun from his breast pocket. What a stupid fucking place to keep a loaded weapon. Too bad it didn't go off and shoot him in the chest.

The barrel of the gun is pointed in my direction, but he's holding it close to his waist like a man out of a bad gangster movie.

"Since your little girlfriend lived, you know what that means." His shoes move along the dried blood that's caked on the floor. "Tell you what, I'll let you take one swing at me before I shoot you. Help you go out with a literal bang."

My thumb rubs along the handle of my knife. I'm fast, and if he were fighting fair, I'd have a good chance to beat him. But I'm not faster than a bullet. As the saying goes, I bought a knife to a gun fight and have no idea what move to make next.

He knows my adrenaline has kicked in. My eyes bounce subtly back and forth, trying to figure out my next move.

"Last dying wish, Rocco Mancini."

"This won't bring Mom back."

"Don't fucking talk about your mother! You don't have the right!" His spit lands on my face. "Now hit me, you fucking bastard, before I put a bullet through your head."

My father. The man who would take me to baseball games growing up, or would read to be at bedtime, hates me enough to kill me. That empty feeling will forever live in me. But I refuse to let it define who I am anymore.

"Swing at me you, little shit." One punch. That's all it would take. It's been done. But I finally chance a look at his eyes and his pupils are the size of pin drops despite it being barely lit in here. He's helped himself to his special cocaine.

One punch.

A fist to his chest to try to stop his heart. *Cardiac arrest.*

To the temple. *Brain bleed.*

Or uppercut to the nose. *Frontal lobe brain bleed, possible broken neck.*

Hit to kill.

"Fine, you pussy. Would it help if I told you that before our little Daisy was tied up in that chair, she was immobile. I slid those little shorts down those tan, toned thighs of hers…"

No. There's no way. Did Dr. Miranda run rape tests? I never asked. Fuck. No.

"I went in bare." He steps toward me, pushing the barrel of the 9mm into my chest. "Did you dare to fuck her bare?" His eyes close briefly before they lock with mine. "She gets so wet. Those tiny moans." He leans closer. "Between you and me, I honestly think she wanted it."

"You're fucking dead."

Another laugh, but he stops and moves the barrel to my forehead and leans in. "No, you are."

"If you fucking touched her…"

"I didn't, but I jacked off thinking about it after I left her in that room." His browns raise and he smirks like he's proud of himself.

"Now that I've had that little bit of fun, anything else you want to get off your chest?"

I can't punch him now. He's too close. "I want my punch."

"Too…" The gun drags across my forehead, and he stumbles to the side. "Too late," he states, righting himself in front of me.

The fuck.

"You…did you…?" His head swivels to the table of water and back at me. "There's no way." Another fumbled step and the hand holding the gun falls from the side. Just when I wind up to punch him, a familiar voice comes from the hallway.

"I did." Fucking Daisy. She steps out wearing a skull mask like the one I'm wearing. "It's just you seemed so depressed." Her head tilts, eerily calm and possibly psychotic. Three more people step behind her wearing the same mask. Crew, Santi, and…is that fucking Brad?

Jesus Christ.

"So depressed," she says again, this time shaking her head like she pities him while he struggles to stand straight. He falls to his knees, gun still in his hand and finger on the trigger. "You were going to kill yourself, anyway, weren't you?"

"You didn't. You wouldn't. You don't have a selfless bone in your body, you whore. You're dead!" He raises his gun at her and I roundhouse kick him in the back of his head, and he falls face first on the floor. His own blood pouring out over all of his victims who were just trying to make money for their families. Except for Brad. Which I still don't understand why he's here.

I kick the gun out of the ring and jump over the rope to Daisy.

"Are you okay?" She grabs my face and inspects the only parts of me exposed. I pull her into a tight hug, and she whispers in my ear. "I told you…you wouldn't be alone, and I'd never let him hurt you again."

I give a nod to Crew and Brad (fuckface). Fortunately, they don't make it any more than it has to be.

"I'll help you with the body," Santi's voice is muffled behind his mask. I pound his fist. "I'll help." I turn to Daisy and place my covered mouth to hers. As much as I love to fucking see her representing me as a fighter, I'd rather see all of her face than to be reminded of this hell. "I'll see you at home."

"The fuck you will!" My father lunges over the rope through the air right at Daisy, I step to the side to protect her when three gun shots stun the shit out of all of us.

Who's been hit? My ears are ringing. I look back at Daisy and she shakes her head. "Not me." I check myself, then look down at my bleeding father. Exit wounds in the shape of a small triangle show on his back. Blood pours from one specifically.

I look around, unsure where the shots came from. "Across the ring. Holy shit," Brad mumbles. My eyes follow his gaze.

It's a woman with her face painted, which matched the guy I fought just a week or two ago. "He killed my husband," she says as she wipes the gun with a rag. He promised it was for a lot of money. That he was safe. He never came home.

"I…I didn't kill him, though," I choke out.

"I know you didn't," she still shouts from across the ring. "Javier made it home in one piece. Bruised and broken, but it one piece. But he threatened to go to the FBI about this operation. Tony made a visit to our house when I was getting ready to take our baby boy to his six-month checkup. I came home and my husband was hanging from our garage ceiling." Her voice breaks, but there is nothing but fire in her eyes as she turns to leave. "I trust none of you saw me here." The new widow cocks her eyebrow before tossing the gun into the trash can and leaving the same way she snuck in.

"Welp. If he wasn't dead from your kick, he definitely is now," Brad jokes, leaning against the wall tapping away on his phone… With. The. Volume. On. Max.

Fucking Brad.

Fucking hell.

CHAPTER
FORTY-ONE

DAISY

"I'M surprised you only have a backpack. Are you sure you don't need the rest of your emo wardrobe?" Rocco jokes as he loads my bag into the seat of his bike.

"Ha. Ha. Maybe I'll just stay behind with my mom." I wiggle my eyebrows, and for a split second he believes it. His eyes widen, and his mouth turns down.

The front door of the soon-to-be old house slams closed.

"You will do no such thing, Daisy May!" My mother shouts as she walks down the front steps for the last time.

Goddamnit. We were so close.

Rocco's head falls and his shoulders shake. He's laughing. At me. "Daisy May. How did I not know that was your middle name?"

I narrow my eyes at my mother who is beaming like she did pre-Tony exposing himself as the lowlife that he was. Then I shift them to my boyfriend. "What did you think my middle name was? Duck?"

He shrugs. "I don't know. I kinda like Duck. Hey, I have to run inside really quick. You should talk to your mom before she leaves."

Normally, I'd internally roll my eyes—forget that, my eye roll would be loud as fuck—but since the whole Tony thing happened, my mom and I have been closer than ever. Not saying we're besties, but we had to start somewhere.

"Remember, Mom, let me meet the man you're going to marry next time. It's important we vet him." She walks over and wraps her arms around me. "Ugh. Too tight. Remember, you don't have to beat the moving truck."

She finally pulls back and tilts her head; her eyes are filled with tears. "There isn't going to be another man. I had the happily ever after with your dad. I don't want anyone else. I think I was just lonely, and Tony filled the void at that moment."

"I get that. You deserve to be happy…to have someone."

"I have me. And I'm going to join a reading group. And maybe start hiking. Find a friend better than Leanne. I need a friend who won't want to fuck my stepson."

"I'm not your stepson, Maribel. Sorry to disappoint," Rocco chimes in while hugging my mom. We decided it's best for everyone if we moved forward. Now that my mother is opposed to having an extra child, but she was only married to Tony for about a minute. My mother has decided to get an annulment since Tony's not around to sign papers.

If anyone asked, we decided to tell people Tony fled the country. He's probably in Morrocco living like a king. Shockingly, it's been about three months, and not one person has come looking for him. The cops on his payroll haven't asked questions. He literally fell off the face of the earth and not a soul is missing him. The only people who know where his body is is Rocco, Santi, Crew, and Brad. *And maybe me.*

After Javier's wife shot him, the guys took Tony's body and 'disposed of it properly'…whatever that means. They dropped him into the Everglades via airboat in the middle of the night. Or so I was told. I also heard from Crew that he was gator food seconds after he hit the water.

Crew stepped away from fighting and he plans on teaching women and children self-defense tactics.

I never told Rocco why Brad was there to help, and he never talked about it. When I asked Brad to meet us at the ring, he was gung-ho. Yes, he's still a douchebag, but he never actually liked Tony. He just felt like he finally belonged somewhere. Tony made him feel important. It turned out that even Brad could sense something was off with the asshole.

Rumor has it the warehouse was sold at auction, and the inside is being renovated and being turned into a no-kill dog rescue. I personally would have demolished it, but not my monkey, not my circus.

I had to quit my job at the café. It was no shock to Jim. He was kind about it and made a point of telling me if I don't quit, then he's going to have to fire me. And that I was one of his favorite mysteries, but the "most godawful employee he's ever had."

So much has happened in the past months, some of it feels like a dream. Life was so different not even a year ago. I was battling my invasive thoughts, unwilling to change my ways. I was with a man who wasn't right for me and lost myself trying to be what he wanted. Jeremy and I haven't spoken, but have only waved in passing since he lives down the street.

Rumor has it, he started dating Melissa Winters. He felt it was best if we ended our friendship and insisted it had nothing to do with her. Fucking Melissa Winters. Old habits die hard, I guess.

As for me and Rocco, we're together. Officially. We both decided to start therapy. Separately, of course, where we can each work through our own trauma. We both have jobs waiting for us on the west coast. After a few zoom interviews, Rocco landed an art teacher gig at an elementary school, and I got a full time job at a surf shop. It's not much, but it's a start and we're happy.

We watch as my mom pulls away in her packed-to-the-brim SUV. Rocco snakes his arm around my waist and looks down at me.

"This is good," he says in a hushed tone.

"This is really good." I smile in return and his dimple shows. I have seen his dimple more in the past months than I did when Tony was alive.

Our lips meet and the kiss is a promise. An ending. A beginning. A dream.

"I wouldn't want to do this with anyone other than you." We turn to look at the house that held some of our best memories, and certainly most of the worst. With the sold sign hanging outside, I'm able to breathe a sigh of relief. And as our new apartment awaits in Laguna Beach, we both are excited to start anew together.

"Let's get going, Daisy May." We hop on the bike, and I hit his bicep. He leans back and lays his head on my shoulder where I use my nails to scratch his scalp like he likes before he puts his helmet on. "Always better together, Angel."

"Always."

ACKNOWLEDGMENTS

Daisy and Rocco's story was so unique to me. I stepped out of my comfort zone and wrote something taboo. It needed to get out. Enough that I haven't even finished the Dream Trilogy yet. But these two spoke to me. Dealing with invasive thoughts, narcissists, gaslighting, emotional neglect, abuse… it was all there. And now it's for you to read. They may not be completely healed yet, but they're headed in the right direction.

I'll start off by thanking Tiffani Jo. You powered through in a time crunch and executed beautifully. You're a diamond in the rough and your comments are always a great motivator.

Naemi Tiana and Shanen Ricci, thank you for taking the time to give me fellow author feedback. You both are amazing humans.

Carian Cole, without you, my sanity would have been rocked. I appreciate you more than you know.

To Devin for the sweet looking swag and listening to me excessively ramble about the cover. BUT THE COVER!!! I mean, have you seen it?! Of course you have, you made it and it's perfect. I can't explain how grateful I am to have you in my life.

Elain York for your awesome editing as usual and long conversations that stray far from the book world. I can't explain how happy I am to have found you.

To my two girlies, you helped me take pictures of the cover for marketing and I hope someday you will be able to follow your dreams. Dive in with no fear and take the steps to make them come true.

And to my readers! Thank you for allowing me to become a

part of your lives. Daisy had a big piece of me in her, but so did Rocco.

I'd be extremely appreciative if you could a minute to leave a review and tell me what you thought about Crushing Daisy.

See you soon!
Kellie Storm